THE SHACKLED BALLOON

Lara Bronson

Tacit Press, LLC
2022

Copyright © 2022 Tacit Press, LLC All rights reserved

The characters and events portrayed in this book are fictitious. Any similarity to real persons, living or dead, is coincidental and not intended by the author.

No part of this book may be reproduced, or stored in a retrieval system, or transmitted in any form or by any means, electronic, mechanical, photocopying, recording, or otherwise, without express written permission of the publisher.

ISBN-13: 979-8-9853864-1-7

Printed in the United States of America

To mothers

The sacrifice of mothers inscribes into us all,
No matter how little, no matter how small.
How many or few can really atone,
For maternal martyrdoms from sunset till dawn?

CHAPTER 1

IT happened again. This time, it wasn't a shock anymore—just pain. Pain so old, I forgot how to live without it. Sometimes sharp, sometimes prickling, but most of the time simply there, coexisting with my mundane reality. And it would've been fine if it weren't for the twinges of guilt haunting me like a sinner's ghost in a church.

"It doesn't matter how I feel," I whispered. "You aren't here anymore. You were a part of me, and now you are not. You were close to me, and now you are too far. You died and left me alone. Alone to lick my wounded sorrows. Alone to yearn for your miniature hug and delicate scent of dawning. Don't worry, my precious, I died with you today as well. It's not my first, but every time, I am never the same. You, my little angel, were my everything: my light, my hope… a dream. The dream was a prelude to your coming of life, the reason why I opened my eyes in the morning. Now, I will have to open my eyes to an abysmal black hole in my heart. Do not worry, my little petal, it's not your fault. It was I who killed you. I poisoned you with my blood and asphyxiated you in my womb. It was I who didn't live up to your expectations. I disappointed you and your siblings, all of heavenly matter now. You will join them soon, and my canvas of little angels will become even bigger. Your beating heart might be stopped, but you will forever beat in mine. While I live on, battling the pain of a meaningless life, you will be there to remind me of the reasons why I do it."

As the tiles under my body finally warmed up, a flicker from the lights above brought me back between the walls of my tiny bathroom. I guess I've been lying on them for quite some time. What should I do? Should I cry for help? Gavin was watching his favorite car show. Should I call him? Or wait till the show was over? He already had his evening predetermined, so I'll let him watch. I raised myself on my elbows and looked at the crime scene. My white dress performed the job of a towel, transforming into the color of shame, and as the weight grew heavier, it slowly halted any movement I might consider. A trickle of blood lingered along my inner thigh. Then another. It felt like life was draining from me, and it was, just not mine. After a few moments, the flow stopped its abundance. The river of regret started to calm down. Now it was indeed over.

"Are you okay?" a voice spoke, and for a moment, I thought it was my baby, but when I raised my eyes, it was only Gavin.

"What happened? Why are you lying on the floor?" he asked, well aware of what had occurred.

He took my palms in his and raised me from my new homely spot.

"I lost the baby."

The reverberations of these words hit my ears harder than I imagined. The tears I held in for quite some time spurted uncontrollably, cutting off my ability to speak. I embraced my husband like a life-saving buoy and began my mournful wail.

"Let's take off the dress and wash you," he said in a calming voice while caressing my hair with his free hand.

I didn't budge. He tried to free himself from my deadly grip, but I wouldn't move. He looked at me with a hint of surprise as I was flooding his shirt with tears. A big sigh followed, along with the rattle of the shower curtains swooshing next to me. As I was scooped up like a hurt kitten, we both discovered ourselves in the bathtub. With a swift move, he turned on the right and then the left handles. The spout began spewing large amounts of water as if eager to take away my baby. A battle I already lost. The cold liquid first touched my heels, then my toes, and as it grew warmer, the color of hibiscus and pomegranate flowers got swept by a mild vortex diluting them into hues of apple blossoms. He leaned to grab the shower diverter, his face in doubt whenever it was a good idea. In the end, he changed his mind. He chose to seat me close to the spout and let the waterfall wash me and my sorrows away. The ache in my arms released his body, which made him sigh again in trepidation, but the water's warmth made it somewhat better. Just a little bit. I could smell the steam rise from everywhere, enveloping me in a cloud of wet heat. He tried to remove the straps of my dress lightly, careful not to touch me, as if I was a broken doll. He didn't want to ruin me even further. I understood his intention, so I decided to help. I lowered the dress to my waist, leaning to the side to let it slip down my hips. From there, he took care of the rest. The sole witness of the crime scene disappeared behind our bathroom door. I embraced my knees to hold on to the dissipating heat. My toes were drowning in the still murky water though a reoccurring current would flow by my side and dissolve what was left of the life I once bore. Good thing I didn't tell my mother.

He returned with a fresh towel and a bathrobe.

"I turned on the kettle," he said, "I'll make you some tea. What do you prefer, chamomile as usual?"

I didn't answer. I simply grabbed my pink luffa, poured on it my favorite rose-infused shower gel, and began rubbing my skin in exasperation. When Gavin saw me attack myself, he ripped the luffa out of my hand and said, "let me do it."

I let him. He was gentle.

CHAPTER 2

"I'M already in my thirties, doctor. Will it make my issue worse?" I asked while leaning across the desk.

"Most likely not," said the doctor without removing his gaze from the analysis charts. He was a man in his fifties, clean-shaven, hairy hands, surrounded by an aura of a harsh cologne.

"There must be a reason why I miscarry all the time."

Gavin, silent and dejected, listened to my interrogation while seated on a chair in the back.

"Usually, it's because of a chromosomal abnormality," said the doctor, eyes still glued to the papers.

"I've heard this information for the past five times. Maybe there is a better answer out there, doctor?"

"That's what we're trying to find out." His gaze finally turned towards me and pointed at the papers.

Silence befell. I glanced at Gavin, who was still in a dejected position. I, on the other hand, was furious. There had to be a reason why it kept happening. I couldn't be the only one with such issues. My eyes wandered across the room, searching for answers. A perfect but plastic uterus was displayed on the table. A few charts with the necessary vaccines and a giant sign with pictures of a fetus' weekly growth were on the walls. I searched for the eighth week. My baby was supposed to be the size of a raspberry. Most of the time, it never got past the week of raspberry. I returned my gaze to the doctor; he was still searching for an answer. And right when I attempted to say something, he spoke.

"I believe there are two potential reasons why you keep miscarrying, Mrs. Miller. First, there is a hormonal imbalance due to an undiagnosed polycystic ovary syndrome, and secondary, your husband's swimmers might not be at their prime. The count is not as low, but..." His voice trailed off with a matter-of-fact intonation.

My tired brain couldn't listen to the same preach over and over again. Every new doctor would find a different reason for my fallibility to conceive. Sometimes it was purely my fault; other times, Gavin's. Or like today, when the scale of social solidarity leaned towards both a female and male perspective, it created an equilibrium in our latent imperfections. I, of course, didn't care for the doctor's social afflictions. I could only breathe for my baby–the one I might never have.

"...But there are good options even in the most severe cases. There are IUI (intrauterine insemination) and IVF (in vitro fertilization). Both produce wonderful results..." His voice returned to my ears.

As expected, I already knew most of what he was saying. I've done my research thoroughly. The terms of my success were represented by pills, syringes, frozen embryos, and the possibility of multiple failed attempts at the price of thousands. The doctor continued, "...a lot of couples conceive after the first try of IVF, but I do not want to give you high expectations."

My husband cleared his voice from its idleness and said, "How much will this break the bank, doctor?"

"It's priced at one thousand for an IUI and twenty thousand for an IVF. Indubitably, IVF is better..." he continued while disregarding Gavin's reaction, who began lowering himself vertebrae by vertebrae back to his original deflated state.

My throat tightened, seeing him withering like a dehydrated fern. I turned towards the doctor, who was still talking. I interrupted saying, "thank you, doctor. We'll discuss our next steps and come back to you."

I grabbed my bag from the adjacent chair and motioned to Gavin my intention to leave. The doctor got up from his desk, shared a healthy handshake with Gavin and me, and advised us to speak with the receptionist about future appointments.

In the car, Gavin was quiet. I watched him in suppressed silence while thinking of a way to open a discussion.

"What do you think about all of this?" I cracked.

"I think this is a rip-off for desperate people who do not have anywhere else to go. That's what I think." His grip tightened on the wheel.

"We have the savings and the money from our vacation plans. It should be enough," I said sheepishly.

"It will be enough for a few IUI's and maybe one cycle of IVF. What if it doesn't work?"

"We have to believe it'll work. The doctor said–"

"I don't care what the doctor says. It is your body they will be experimenting with."

"I know, and I don't care. It's our only chance."

He didn't respond. Actually, he did not talk for the whole trip and evening, and I was reluctant to ask. I let the silence heal our sadness and bring back a tacit balance of contentment.

***

Driving was my way of meditating. My loyal companions were the steering wheel in front, the road ahead, and the perpetual murmur of the motor. My morning commute to Seattle gave me the chance to enjoy the simple pleasures in life. But after a period of indulging in my surroundings, a stream of memories would always flood my mind. At that time, it revolved around the darkest episodes of my hopelessness.

My first miscarriage happened a long time ago, maybe seven years. I don't remember the date, but I remember the sun's glimmering rays ricocheting from the brass wind chimes into my backyard. The wind fluttered the chimes' hollowed tubes hypnotizing the tiny leaves into a dance of warm colors. I sat on our deck with my ears caught in the intermittent clatter, wrapping a rectangular box. It was Gavin's birthday the next day. He was turning twenty-nine. I bought him a fountain pen I wasn't sure he would ever use, but I was confident he would hold dear since the main surprise was placed beside it.

When I gave him his gift, I couldn't stop fidgeting, so he already suspected something, but no betraying emotion could clue him into what happened next. As the dark brown ribbon unfurled and the navy lid dislodged, he beheld two objects. The first meant to induce euphoria, the second to write about it. I've never seen Gavin cry, but there he was, tears clouding his eyes:

"Is this true?" he asked in disbelief.

"You think I would ever lie about something like that?" A whisper escaped my mouth.

"I am so happy. Come here." He embraced me. "It's the best day of my life."

"The best days of your life are yet to come," I said.

But the best days never came. I miscarried the following week. I was afraid to tell Gavin; his reaction scared me, but, to my surprise, he responded with an unusually positive attitude.

"It's okay," he said, "we have time, don't we? In the end, it will be worth it." Which he followed with a kiss on the cheek.

Indeed, we did have time. I was twenty-five, recently employed as Mr. Rogers' PA at FeirTech. I convinced myself it was a chromosomal abnormality; any article would proclaim so. It happened in one out of four women. They should talk about it more. Nonetheless, I still felt in control, and the data supported it.

Then came the second pregnancy. This time, I shared the good news with my mother as well as the consequent obituary. She made a big fuss about how the baby needed a healthy body to attach to, and since I was not fatter than a twig, I would keep losing babies. She left as soon as she came leaving me with a headache and a box of nettle tea. Her distress and tyrannical coping mechanism embedded my soul with even harsher internal rhetoric. I regretted opening up to her, as she always had her own ways of dealing with sorrow.

I didn't share her ways, so when the third miscarriage hit me, she never knew. I kept my dark phantom of grief to myself even when it grew to an egregious size. Weird was how most of my miscarriages happened at the eighth-week mark as if a personal threshold of viability. Once, I miscarried earlier, but none made it past the eighth.

The fourth time I prepared myself. On the first day of my eighth week, I checked for stains almost every hour. I wore a pad every day, and just when I felt a sliver of relief, it commenced–the purge of death draining my hopes and dreams. Wandering through the streets of Kenmore with a pad between my legs, I noticed little girls bobbing their glittery unicorn backpacks as they rushed towards their parents' cars. They could've been my firstborn's classmates. I observed tiny tornadoes hastening near my skirt, toddler boys who could've played with my second born. A stroller would pass by with a plump baby babbling and gnawing on a pink ring toy. She could've been my third. My unrealized family pranced down the street with strangers as their mom and dad. I knew it was wrong to think so, but helpless were my thoughts or my will.

Worse was the experience of singularity in contrast to such sceneries as if I was the only woman to hold the sin of infertility. In my world, it was me, a barren land, against all potent females bearing a cornucopia of life. I knew I wasn't alone, but those other arid lands did not divulge their impotence, and I didn't dare to ask.

Dry soil rarely would interconnect their misery. More often than not, the notion was kept hidden in a buried chest of dirty secrets and shattered dreams. I was no different. I kept mine neatly folded in the most forgotten place of my soul and continued to roam the world in blissful denial.

"Nobody knows," I said to myself as I searched for a parking spot, "thus, for most of the world, it isn't real, and I'll make sure it stays so."

CHAPTER 3

MOST of the time, my workdays were of a routine semblance, though I had to leave early on numerous occasions for my doctor's visits. The benefit of working in downtown Seattle was the walking distance for many medical locations, which helped not raise any suspicions. Gavin also worked downtown as a data analyst for King County, where he flourished even with his modest salary. He had a few years to pay off his hefty student loans, and then he could enjoy and appreciate the fruits his hard work bore.

    I had other plans. I would stick to my job as a personal assistant until I finally got my baby and left. It wasn't a bad job. My boss was reasonable, and the company had reliable policies, but the tech world was synonymous to change, and each wave of innovation felt like a tsunami in my strive for stability. I preferred a slower-paced, less prone to errors kind of routine, a style Mr. Rogers appreciated and supported. At the same time, when it came to business matters, my loyalty proved very useful to him since the company's requirement for an endless cycle of fresh blood made me his rocky island in a myriad of sandhills.

    But there was another thing reinforcing my job's security. Mr. Rogers appreciated my talent for nonjudgmental listening since, most of the day, the main subject didn't concern the company at all. He loved talking about his new, young wife, Tiffany. He could speak (and I could listen) for hours about his wife's predilections: how his Tiffany preferred customized golf clubs, how she only rode stallions during horseback riding, and how she never got fed up with lobster. Being a confidant cost me nothing more than another cluster of useless information I had to process, reduce to the slightest bit necessary to remember and discard the rest. Long story short, I appreciated Mr. Rogers's trust and leniency to grant me more time to finish my work impeccably, while he enjoyed opening to an ear that never spilled through the mouth. We were a good team, so we decided to retire jointly, him at sixty-two and me hopefully at thirty-two with my maternity leave. He knew I wanted kids but never pushed the question further.

On the other hand, my co-workers were intercepting signals with my every move to not miss the moment of the big reveal. I would mostly speak to them over lunch, and though I wasn't keen on spending my free hour with them, I considered it a mandatory team bonding experience. Part of my team was Marie and Jasmine, and from the HR department was Cassandra and a friend of hers. I could never remember her name. The only thing I recalled was that she had three kids. Whereas for Marie, she had two kids, Cassandra had one, and Jasmine, none. It was easy to imagine who I was closest with, and though it started because of our motherless status, with time, Jasmine had nested a warm spot in my heart due to her peaceful nature and tender manner.

Most importantly, she knew by instinct how to cheer me up, which was the proper medicine for my monthly disappointments. I didn't know if she ever planned on getting pregnant. Then again, I would never ask. What worked for us was that we could bring up subjects of discussion other than the eternal question: "To use or not to use a pacifier?"

On Thursday, before my doctor's appointment regarding our next steps towards conceiving, I met them at lunch. As we sat at our usual table at the cafeteria, an allusion seemed to concoct in my co-worker's mind from the appraisal of my pensive demeanor, which, of course, propelled the launch of the big question:

"So, Laura, why the long face? Are you, by any chance, nauseous? Are you finally hiding a bun in the oven?" said Cassandra with a horse-like grin.

Everyone smirked in various degrees with their faces still plastered to their meals. What was this? Adulthood bullying inspired by the series: "Who got a boyfriend first" and the sequel "Who got married first?" I didn't want to answer such obnoxious inquiries, but if I wouldn't, it would make them even more suspicious.

"Not yet. I don't see the rush."

"You should put on some weight. You're too skinny. How are you going to carry a child with less than a hundred pounds?"

"How about you tell us how you conceived?" I redirected.

"What is there to tell? I conceived on our first try," said Cassandra.

My teeth clenched and began grinding their enamel.

"Then tell us how it is to have kids so we can prepare ourselves? Jasmine and I?"

It was the favorite question of all mothers everywhere; it was my weapon used for deflection and curious observation. Cassandra didn't even stand a chance. After years of listening to these subliminal ego boosts under the pretense of child-rearing, I came to notice several types of moms reappear. There was the mama bear who would never let you touch her baby unless over her dead body. The mama elephant who thought her kid was the best and did incredible things even if these things were to poop in a diaper. Then there was the mama wolf, who had an efficient and hands-on approach to teaching her offspring, and lastly, the mama sloth, who had an unobtrusive but warm attitude towards raising her child. No matter what zoomorphic creature they feigned, the "it's so hard to be a mom" always concluded the discussion.

Cassandra, the epitome of motherhood, represented the zoo. Every day she would change her mantra, and every day she would make us hear her arguments as to why that particular method reigned the daily chart. Today Cassandra was a complaining sloth. As she blabbered all about the books on relaxed motherhood, ancient practices, and supporting a child's growth through minimal intrusion, I couldn't help but notice something unusual. The three-kid mom from the HR department never complained about her offspring. It was the one-kid mom, or specifically Cassandra. The bigmouthed, constantly interrupting Cassandra, who loved to lavish us with a plethora of self-professed *"momsplanations."* I looked at Jasmine. She ate quietly, drained from all the fuss at the table. I reached for her back and gave her a pat. Startled, Jasmine turned towards me, then smiled with her radiant all-too-forgiving smile.

CHAPTER 4

AFTER work, I took my iced tea on the deck and sat on the rusty chair with its perpetually damp cushions to relish the view of my favorite place, the backyard garden. The sun's final rays shot through my self-made oasis of plants as if through a colander, magnifying their light and shadows.

I called it the Hanging Garden of Kenmore. Though a miniature version compared to its inspirational relic, I liked to think of it as a wonder of MY world. Indeed, the backyard of a humble two-bedroom home couldn't offer much room for the dense foliage of my imagination, but I managed. Inside our fence, I organized a system where I would experience blooming flowers each season. Spanning years of trial and error, it took me many attempts to reach an ideal symbiosis. In the end, I succeeded with minor tweaks here and there.

In the middle, I planted a small circle of spring beauties like crocus, peonies, tulips, and daffodils. Next to them, forming a larger sphere, were summer stunners in flower now, such as daylilies, miniature roses, hydrangeas, and sunflowers. The fall season blessed me with mums and pansies, whereas winter was the time for my jasmine tree, sedum, and firethorn to flourish. I recognized the arrival of a new season not by the numbers on the calendar but by the fragrance each group of plants adorned my garden with. Spring smelled of rejuvenation, summer of new adventures, fall of sunsets, and winter smelled of celebratory freshness.

For annuals, I planted geraniums, begonias, or marigolds in ceramic pots, usually attached to the roof's rims. Honeysuckle and wisteria were planted on opposite sides of the fence, slowly weaving into an aromatic live rug. And, of course, I never passed on an excellent perennial like coreopsis, lavender, dahlias, or hostas. I finished the ensemble with sage, ferns, feather grass, and red Japanese maple trees with bright mossy rocks underneath. I loved touching the moss; it felt like an earth monster's fur tickling my fingertips. The center of it all was a fountain made out of a dark marble slab with glistening water trickling on its walls. My garden hosted all kinds of creatures, from hummingbirds, butterflies, and bumblebees to squirrels and birds of any kind. The adjacent Douglas firs and pines blessed my garden with shade during the hotter days of summer, and on the other months, the drizzling weather persistently nourished my babies, creating a perfect environment for an evergreen haven.

Vivacious and earnest in soaking the sun's warmth, plants were my bliss. And if I shared some love with them, they would always reward me with the nectary and ambrosial fragrance of gods. It fascinated me to no end the process of discovering such various gems of nature, which most took for granted. I once found a book on herbal medicine in an old library and skimmed through its thousands of pages, realizing it was only the first volume. There were too many to even remember, an encyclopedia of nature's way to heal us. So, I promised to myself if I were to not pursue a career as a botanist (a decision insisted on by my mother), at least I would know all there was to learn to create my personal miracle: my Hanging Garden of Kenmore.

I learned with great fervor, and, truth be told, the instructions were simple. It needed the right time to plant them, the right amount of water, the right balance between fertilizer and soil, and of course, the right amount of love. As an amateur gardener, I made multiple mistakes with my plants, but they were very forgiving of my mishaps. When my errors were corrected, they would rise from their wilted state and greet me with their cheerful abounding.

Most flowers were given by Margaret from her nursery, others were gifted on any given celebration since it was my gift of choice, and the fountain was Gavin's idea. Thus, on drier evenings, when all the good parts about Seattle weather aligned, Gavin and I cherished the moment by admiring the miracle of nature in front of us with only the sound of streaming water and wind chimes to accompany us.

In my darker days of defeat, my vivid companions had risen to even greater importance. My hands could produce life. Me, a tiny goddess, could create her own greenhouse world, with all its residents adoring her power to give and maintain life. I was a mother to my flowers, and it was… easy. I didn't have to torment my body with pills, syringes, and palpitations, nor burden my mind with fret and hopelessness. I had control, and even when it would slip away under a misguided decision, I knew how to save it. I felt prosperous in my Hanging Garden like the fertile women I've seen on the streets or colleagues I've met at work. My lips would talk to my plants, my voice would sing to them, my fingers would caress them, and they would respond with more love. I was also a righteous goddess. They lived as long as possible with only slight touch-ups: removing a dried stick, pruning an overpopulated perennial, or simply gathering dried leaves. Necessities of life. I was doing specifically that when I heard Gavin's steps. He interlaced his arms around me.

"You blend well with the scenery, my dear."

"I know what would make the scenery even better."

He regarded me in surprise. After a pause, a gaze towards the sunset, and a resigned exhale, he said, "what do I have to do?"

I hugged my husband with the love of a thousand flowers, as I knew it wasn't easy for him to accept help. He reciprocated.

CHAPTER 5

WE met at a boat launch, Gavin and I through a couple who knew us from work (she was a secretary at my company, he was a colleague of Gavin's). They invited us to show off their brand-new boat and potentially drown us in lake Washington. Our friends' inexperience and horrendous ability to maneuver boats could've cost us at least an undesirable swim. Several times, it felt like we would hit nearby boats with only my shrill voice to deter us from devastation.

I suppose near-death experiences welds people since the moment we escaped the death trap, we went to drown our potential existential crisis into a glass of cabernet. The afternoon sped up like a ball of yarn rolling of a hill, permeating its path with our most lustrous life stories. As the light moved from the window to the flicker of a candle, I came to the realization: he was the one.

I've dated enough guys before; most were trifling experiences that I never cared to remember. The few that lasted transformed from princes into my childhood ogre: controlling, unabashed and narcissistic. They reminded me of the bullies in the sandbox who trampled my sandcastles to get their fill of power, and as I got older, the bullies attempted to crush my autonomy for the same reasoning. I couldn't feign the idea of letting some brute with heavy paws decide my life's path or worse, being kept on a short leash by a hairy arm. Better alone. "Better alone" was the mantra thudding through my veins every time I would meet such abominable characters. I would whisper to myself, over and over: "Better alone. Better alone. Better. Alone."

Gavin, on the other hand, was the kid who built his castles next to mine. He didn't need to subjugate my self-expression for his sense of self-fulfillment. He intuitively felt what I needed and how to love me without touching my wings. Each of us was doing our separate thing together.

At first glance, Gavin looked like an average guy, not taller than 5'10, with a slim build and dark hair, but a closer consideration would reveal intricacies of beauty specific for those able to appreciate it. His eyes of an aquiline shape and the color of roasted chestnuts could entrance me into hypnosis. When he spoke, the low tones of his voice seeped into my ears like dark honey. He wore glasses for his myopia which shaded in the sunlight. A choice he made for comfort, but it confined his ability to grasp the subtlety of the sun's scintillation. Nonetheless, I loved how I felt when I was with him, more beautiful, more cheerful, and happier as if his light could penetrate my glassy heart and reveal my essence through a kaleidoscopic prism of colors.

I, of course, wanted to maintain a slow pace in our relationship, to see where it would get us, but he, as if fearful I might fly away like a bird from a marital cage, didn't want to wait. And in all honesty, it might've been a good call. By the third day, I was his official girlfriend, and by the end of the week, he had already met my mother. To my indignation, they became friends quite fast. Sometimes, I felt like an intruder in their close friendship. He told her first he was going to propose two months later. As best buddies, they both chose the ring and even planned my proposal from start to finish. Even if I were to say no, which I didn't, I was sure they would still keep in contact. For many years, when I looked at my engagement ring, I could smell my mother's paws all over it. Despite that, I swallowed my pride and tried to not let the moment of our love's expression be ruined by a meddling hag.

I also met Gavin's dad when we traveled to his hometown in Alaska. His mom passed away of cervical cancer a year before we met, which explained why he quickly befriended my mom. His dad, Tom, still mourned like a swan's mate alone in the home they shared for a couple of decades. He greeted us with hospitality and relief for Gavin, who moved forward from the grief and found himself a significant other. And so, with all parties' accord, we let the fairytale take its course and, in a year, we were married and living together happily ever after.

It took time for me to get used to living with Gavin, though he was one of the cleanest people I've ever met. Nevertheless, anything he did, bothered me to a great extent. The way he ate, it felt like slow motion to me. Any sound he produced in the process of mastication made my skin shrivel. The lavish way he would wash the dishes with too much dish soap and not enough water made me crack my knuckles in an attempt to intervene. When he rubbed his eyes, he moved his eyelids so forcefully it would make a gross sound in the process and a gross reaction in me. When Gavin brushed his teeth, there was always the exquisite blob of toothpaste landing on his shirt and staying for the whole day as a badge of honor. Of course, I didn't tell him about it, and I hoped he never noticed. Plus, the fact that he never left his socks unattended on the floor and always put the toilet seat down made me somewhat complacent since, generally speaking, he was the perfect husband. If I ever complained, he adapted pretty well. If my request seemed reasonable to him, he would agree to it straight away. If there was something I could do better than him, he would point it out with a prideful smile, as if my achievements were also his. Gavin's ability to harmonize with my needs astounded and motivated me to skip on minor technicalities.

Then there was the sex. At the beginning of our relationship, I couldn't keep my hands off him and he of mine, any repulsion generated by his behavior, I would sublimate with sex. I could connect to the beauty of his soul through his physical side. For someone who couldn't focus on anything except to-do lists, lovemaking would throw me on a remote island of passion, a fusion of spirit and ecstasy. I've never tried LSD, but certain moments brought color to our merging souls in ways I've never seen before. Sometimes, it sent me falling from a tall cliff into grappling oblivion, other times, it ascended me into a stratosphere of blissful awareness. Waking up in his embrace represented the peak of our enraptured consummation till his foul breath would bring me back into the harsh reality.

Time passed, and I found myself enjoying the time spent with my lovable oaf. Though far from perfection, his care and attention to detail slowly seeped under my skin, staining me with the colors of mundane love. My fondness of our cohabitation morphed into togetherness where I wasn't only one individual but one of two, one side of a couple. Two streams melded into one larger, more potent river.

***

At lunch, the "mothers' club" ladies, with one *jasminian* intruder, were already at the table munching on their salads or carb-less meals. I sat next to the intruder, who welcomed me with a smile.

"How are you doing, ladies?" I asked.

"I had the worst fight with Russel yesterday," Cassandra rambled.

"What happened?"

"Oh, it's a kid issue. He wants me to stay with Abby home for the weekend while he goes fishing. Again. First of all, weekends are for us to be together as a family. Second, what am I going to do with the fish if he even catches one?"

"What's the issue, though?"

"You ladies who don't have kids don't understand. Men always get a free pass from fatherhood and always get to be the "fun" parent, while mothers are expected to be the perfect parent."

"What's the problem with exercising your motherly privilege more often than dads?" I asked.

"It's not always a privilege, my dear," Cassandra said while assessing her manicured nails, "most of the time, it's responsibility—never-ending, always nagging responsibility we mothers don't get enough rest from. And the moment we open our mouths to complain, we get arrows of judgment in our direction. The problem is that while dads get praise for babysitting, moms get an inquisition for their parenting. We are expected to work our butts off at our job, then go home and work our butts off cleaning the house and taking care of the children. When you have a kid, you'll see."

I glanced at the mother of three, and she signaled approval, the first one since Cassandra's rants began. Marie did likewise.

"Well, if you put it this way, I might as well not have children," I retorted.

Shadows of remorse appeared on Cassandra's face. Marie intervened, "she's not talking about the fulfilling part of having a child. It's the parental inequality many women experience."

"What about James from my department? Didn't he quit to stay at home with his kids?" I asked.

"It's the exception to the rule glorified on social media. Gender norms are still a guide to how fathers and mothers are perceived," said the three-kid mom.

Since when did the three-kid mom speak so eloquently about anything? She usually didn't talk. Was this a wound I was stepping on?

"And don't forget, Lana…"

Ah, that's her name.

"…when you confront them, they say WE wanted kids and not them. As if their whole purpose in reproduction is sperm donation," said Cassandra as she re-tied her dirty blonde curls with a fury.

"The last time my husband complimented me was when I gave birth to my firstborn, saying, 'How majestic is the female body in birthing life.' My daughter is six," Marie complained.

"And now I have to be a mother 24/7 while hubby goes and gets reconnected with nature," Cassandra added.

"Aren't your kids in school on weekdays? Don't you miss spending time with them on the weekend?" asked Jasmine unknowingly.

Three fuming pairs of eyes turned towards her. Jasmine contorted herself into a small ball with eyes pinned to the ground. I, on the other hand, was gloriously gloating, perhaps a bit too much.

"It's impossible to explain to people who don't have children," said Cassandra, furiously picking at her meal.

"I babysat my brother when he was little. My mom was a single mother. After my younger brother was born, Dad left, so Mom didn't have a husband she could complain about. It doesn't refute your statement about gender misbalance, though," said Jasmine.

"Babysitting a brother is not the same as having a child," said Cassandra clinging to the last pillar of her motherhood identity.

Observing the sour state this debate had turned into, I switched to a subject related to work so Cassandra's blabbering mouth wouldn't continue its quest for self-righteousness. As the discussion entwined around a particular event, I couldn't help but conclude that these ladies lived unhappy lives, in unhappy marriages, and with the only intent of not spending time with their kids. No one forced them to have kids unless they planned on finding a good reason for bitterness. Playing the victim in marriage was wrong, but doing so in front of your child was worse.

My Gavin was nothing like the men Cassandra described; he always wanted kids, just like me. If I were to work, he would definitely be a great stay-at-home dad. Even now, we split our household chores. What could change with the birth of a precious being? Won't honesty and clear expectations help with the additional tasks? I might be missing the experience part, but, for sure, I would be prepared when the time came. Laziness should not be an excuse. Children represent a complex system of care. Haven't they read a book on the subject? I already was on my third concerning pregnancy and the importance of a medical plan and all. I would imagine a baby would require much more.

I could not wait to have my baby and prove to these superficial moms the arrogance they spewed came only from their tangled personalities.

CHAPTER 6

THE second part of the day flew by in a heartbeat. Files, documents, and emails encompassed my whole consciousness; my subconscious, though, was beating the drums of anticipation. I called in for a doctor's appointment the morning after Gavin gave his approval. We had only twelve chances per year; there was no time to waste. I knew that day was supposed to be different; I had to make a choice in our journey's further steps. After sending a few final emails for the day, I packed my bag and marched out the door.

When I reached the reception at the fertility clinic, I was greeted by Ginny, the overly jolly receptionist, who was busy working on something on the computer, potentially Solitaire. In a high-pitched voice, she asked me to take a seat. Magazines were scattered across the coffee table. Who read them anymore? I grabbed one out of reflex and boredom, and of course, there were pictures of famous models and actresses announcing their pregnancy.

"Is this a joke? At a fertility clinic?" I whispered.

I threw the magazine back and began scrambling in my bag for my phone when the nurse called me in. At the doctor's, the same uterus greeted me. It looked more protruding today but still perfect. We've become friends throughout the years. Though my uterus didn't seem to reciprocate.

The doctor came in with speed, leaving a whiff of his strident cologne behind him. Oh, how I wished to be nauseous from such smells. He greeted me, took a seat, and said, "after our previous discussion, has anything changed in regard to your next steps?"

"I spoke with my husband, and we're thinking of proceeding with IUI."

"There is a risk of multiples in such cases. Would it work for you? Compared to an IVF, it's–"

"We know, doctor, the choice is made."

"Okay," he said, "since you are determined to proceed with IUI, I will enumerate the steps you will take to achieve your goal. We'll first prescribe you Clomid, which helps produce more estrogen in your body. Then, through an ultrasound, we will verify how many follicles your body has produced. On your peak ovulation day, we will perform the procedure. Do you have any questions?"

"Should there be any? It seems pretty straightforward to me."

"There shouldn't, but in case you do, give us a call."

"I appreciate your time, doctor." Politeness returned to me.

As I left, my thoughts piled into my mind. I guess I was a bit rude to the doctor. It wasn't his fault, but I was so furious to spend money on something others got for free and in abundance. Disgraceful mothers left their healthy babies so they could maintain their frantically selfish lives, while I had to rip my savings apart to create my miracle of life. It felt like extortion. Dejected, I hopped into the car and went straight home, where my garden, eager for my caring hand, awaited me.

At home, the garage door was blocked by an improperly parked Nissan Juke. I already knew what awaited me. With my Toyota parked on the curbside, I reached the door to my beige house and pushed the key to unlock it, but to no avail. The door was left unlocked. As it opened ajar, my mother's bedazzling garb sprung into my face.

"Hi, Laura Tatiana, I haven't heard from you in a while," she said as her thin brow arched inquisitively.

"Been working, Mom, like most adults," I said. My keys clattered into the mosaic bowl next to the entrance, followed by my exhausted crash onto the couch.

"And you can't find time to call your dearest *mamochka*? Am I a stranger to you? If I die, you will not even notice."

"It would be hard not to notice your death, Mother since you will probably haunt the daylights out of me."

"That's right. It's what a mother does, even for ungrateful daughters."

"Now I am ungrateful?"

"If you never care to call or visit." Her sparkly chiffon scarf took a spin around her neck (she had a chiffon scarf for summer and a wool one for winter).

"It's been a hard couple of weeks. I will try to call more often. Promise."

"Good. I expect you to make good on your promise," she said in a more relaxed tone. "So what's been going on? Is work tiring you, my dear?"

"It's nothing, Mom. Where's Gavin?"

"Well, he, like a good son, went to make some tea for his favorite mother-in-law."

I gazed at my embellished mother and realized how my attempt at a relaxing evening just flew on the wings of her ravenous bickering. I waited for Gavin to come back and diminish her argumentative state as she always did for her newly formed favorite child. He did not disappoint.

"Oh, thank you for the tea, *golubchik*." Her voice sparkled with joy.

"Laura, would you like some tea as well?" Gavin asked.

"Would there ever be a negative answer to this question?" I replied in a mellow tone.

With our tea mugs settled in our hands, Gavin took it upon himself to inquire, "so, tell us, Svetlana, how are you? How's work?"

"Oh, as usual, lots of work, and most of it is done because of me. All of them are lazy, bootlicking nincompoops. Like the other day, Marta from accounting came to me with this massive pile of documents, and I had to revise them all by the next day. As if I'm the only one who works there. I mean, I know I'm good at my job, but it doesn't mean I am someone else's doormat. If Marta did half of her job description, everyone, including myself, would have it so much easier. Also, there is clumsy Julia who…"

I peeked at Gavin as he gulped all this abundant and nonsensical information, and my love for him grew a little bit bigger, as well as my respect for his patience. Then, I looked at my mother, blabbering the same worn-out story with its single goal of self-aggrandization. I learned to shut my ears to such inefficient analyses since I memorized every inch of my mother's brain, and let's be honest, it reflected a boring path of disappointment.

Though she donned a Russian name, she had a quarter Russian in her. It's not to say she didn't behave like one. Her false semblance to Russian livelihood came from her mother, who was, respectively, half Russian. At least, grandma knew the language, whereas my mom knew *kak dela*, *do skoroy vstrechi*, and a couple of curse words. She could mumble some *chastushki*, learned purely by ear, and express her love for the great Russian poets though she never read any. Mother would deem herself a vodka connoisseur, which presented itself through the enumeration of multiple vodka brands, which she would always dilute with soda or orange juice.

Though her Russian patrimony was similar to her diluted cocktails, it did not stop her from exerting it on me. Her obsession over long-haired braided russet beauties singing next to a birch tree tainted my entire childhood. I had to wear long hair up until I got my driver's license since no matter the logical reasonings I brought as arguments, like bullying, neck pain, or even lice, none could deter her from approving a cut. I mustered some bravery to trim my ends from time to time, without her knowledge, of course, but not enough for the big cut.

Consequently, the day after my driving test, I took measures into my own hands. I went into the first salon I saw on the road, approached the first hairdresser who happened to be free, and asked for the shortest bob possible. An act she took as treason, but the feeling of weightlessness, the touch of breeze lingering along my neck, and the joy of defiance compensated it all.

She also learned from grandma (or so she said) how to never take the blame for anything and guilt-trip the life out of me. Of course, this wasn't a cultural thing, just human frailty, but every time I would corner her, she would say something about her prideful heritage and how Russians are not good at expressing emotions. Mother lived on cushions of Russian stereotypes, which she used whenever it befitted her.

The most ludicrous of all her Russian assimilations were superstitions of Slavic provenience. As a kid, I remember throwing salt behind my back when we returned home to grab something we had forgotten. I had to spit three times over my left shoulder whenever a cat (or worse, a black cat) would cross our path. If we had to leave for a longer trip, we had to rest in silence for a bit on our luggage to ensure a safe journey. I was never allowed to sit at the corner of a table in case I would never marry. The idea of opening an umbrella in the house, which would guarantee bad luck, seemed preposterous to my mom, and if, heavens forbid, I placed my bag on the floor, it was a guaranteed loss of money. I did have a purse as a kid made out of pink beads and red ribbon. It held a dollar, two dimes, and a penny. Never lost one of them, no matter how many times I hid it under my bed.

By the time I reached my teens, exasperation had reached its limits, but she was still relentless as the day grandma recounted those phantasmagorical fables and poisoned her fair judgment. I tried talking her out of it, providing facts and even video proof made by a Russian scientist, but it was all in vain like all her Russianist compulsions. In the end, I had to respect those farcical requirements and forced myself to take preventative measures every time we would go out. I was the one who reminded her of every little detail she needed before we left the house. I was the one who kept a tiny salt shaker in my pocket in case of unexpected occult occurrences. I was the one who avoided table corners. I was the one who placed any encountered bag or umbrella on the coat hanger. And I was the one who dropped the act the moment I moved out of her house.

"Laura, are you daydreaming again?" Her voice startled me.

"Yes, Mother, I remembered how you made me throw salt behind my back when you would forget something. It always happened when we were late."

"And every time we did it, everything turned out great, am I right?"

There was no good answer to this question, so I morphed it into a rhetorical one, sipped my tea, and let the demagogic discourse continue.

After a prolonged exposure of her job's internal affairs, it was done. She proceeded on sucking the last sip of her ginger tea, as well as all remnants of Gavin's energy. She then went to the mirror, put on her usual burgundy lipstick, waved a vague goodbye, and said as she went out the door, "Laura, there's *semechki* on the countertop. I bought them for you. *Paka*, Gavin. *Paka*, Laura Tatiana."

"Mother, please park properly next time," I said, but there was no response except for the door slam.

"Your mom is really nice. Such amount of exuberance is to be admired," said Gavin as he sat next to me, enveloping me in a hug.

"Let's not confuse her sweet exuberance of an older lady with the lunacy she was in her youth. I barely got out normal."

"I wouldn't reach so far as normal." He tried to camouflage a smile.

"How dare you?" I pinched his arm. "Do you want to see how normal I am?"

A tickling session had commenced.

CHAPTER 7

ONE must not get me wrong, I loved my mother, but she never was a good one. Or better said, she was too reliant to be capable of being a good mother. Most of my essential childhood experiences were skewed by my mother's decisions. When my father died, the only hell I knew was hers. Actually, all my troubles began after he died, since my mother never returned to her old self. He passed away when I was six. There were still some images of him lingering in my mind, but I never really knew him. And though many said he was a tremendous guy, I never actually got to experience it.

One image of my father, though, I cherished the most. It was in July; I remembered well since I could feel my forearms scorching in the sun's blaze. It was in Norman, Oklahoma. Our hometown. I remembered him barbecuing beef patties on a newly bought grill. A slender and golden figure in a buttoned shirt with suns spread on it and khaki shorts fitting him perfectly. The only incongruity was his receding hairline which resembled the fruitless corn crops at the edge of vast lands encompassing our vicinity. As I regarded his presence while he worked on portraying a fatherly role conquering the new contraption, he reminded me of the tanned preppy men in those technicolor drawings from the 1950 advertisements. I suspected some of those lines were traced by my fallible memory and theatrical imagination, but nonetheless, I chose to believe them as real.

As he was managing his grilling inexperience, a spark fell on my arm. It didn't seem different from the sun's heat, but his whole stance changed from a glowing Herculean frame to a fearful lion. He couldn't imagine himself capable of hurting his only daughter, so out of despair, he shoved my whole arm into the freezer. That moment became an image frozen in time. The smell of soap and smoke, his agitated but strong embrace, the shattering sound of multiple ice cubes on the floor, his mellow voice apologizing with fervor. To this day, it's a story my mom and I always reminiscence with fondness and the one memory from which I still have the scar as a tattooed memento.

He died in an accident. He didn't have his seatbelt on, so technically, it was his fault, though he was not the one who collided. The other guy did. He was drunk, and he died too. It happened sometimes, two separate fates, two stupid decisions, two cars collided, two people died. One of them happened to be my father.

I remembered crying the day we got the call. Not because I was sad he died, but because my mother was. Her agony was so profuse, I could hear her behind the bedroom wall. She howled like a sorrowful wolf. It was loud and protruding though not constant. Most of the time, she wept silently with tiny hicks, then, out of nowhere, the howl would reverberate the walls, probably, when she relived the realization of Dad's death, over and over again. It would trigger me to cry for her. I even attempted to join the bedroom mourn, but I was too afraid to knock on the door. It was her and me crying on opposite sides of a wall. It was the exact description of our future relationship, sharing the same feelings but never together.

I tried along the years to give reason and maybe close this chapter in our abandoned lives. She refused. My mother never allowed herself to love anyone as ferociously as she did my father, not even me. So, it always puzzled me, did she do right? Was it correct to gift one's soul in blissful ignorance for, in the end, to crumble under the thumb of a vertiginous love's dissipation? Was it frailty of heart? Or the intoxication of courage? It didn't matter. My mother's wistful vulnerability cost her more, for she paid a steep price for such an imbalance of fortitude. She took a risk upon herself, which didn't prove long-lasting. Though probably she didn't have a choice, for he had a light to which she couldn't resist. Even at six, I could discern in my mother an ability to synthesize into my father's presence, to melt into his hands and merge into his radiant colors. She reflected the light he dispensed, like the moon reflecting the sun's light, thus becoming the sky's brightest object. She bathed in his rays of incandescence with no fear, for love gave wings, but it didn't teach her how to fly. Thus, when his light dispersed, my mom became a dull cold mess of dust and rock, with dead craters instead of phosphorescent vessels. Did my father think he would live forever? Longer than my mom? To build her a glass castle and imbue her with his love's glisten, he must've believed in his immortality. Who knew? One thing was true, though: the day my dad died, his soul's dissolution imprinted on me the same way as my burnt scar left a mark on my arm. As a result of such a plight, the lesson struck close to my heart. I absorbed it with the force of inevitability and dread. I learned how to file my own taxes, how to set up a bank account, and how to fight for myself in a boundary-defying world. My body repelled vulnerability with an adamant repulsion. I knew not to let my guard down and resorted to pushing through at the expense of my own efforts. Till I met Gavin. My plan was never associated with a successful relationship, but his ways of taming my apprehensions calmed most of my fears. He perceived them at an intuitive level as I never expressed them openly. I suspected such were the ways in his family, and he might've been abiding by his dad's proclivities. I couldn't be sure. But compared to my parents, in our lives, the planets aligned for our unity and ignited all required elements of balance, creating a goldilocks zone of harmony. Every time after my mother's visits, lying in bed, eyes ready for their well-deserved sleep, it was pleasant to close them with Gavin's presence next to me. I had the best dreams.

***

After the doctor's visit, I assumed the process would be straightforward: I was to take pills for five days before ovulation, get an ultrasound to monitor the follicles, receive a trigger shot, then, on O-day, Gavin would go and indirectly share his genetic material with the lab personnel, and I would arrive a few hours later to receive it. Plain as could be, with only one unforeseen complication, my reaction to the hormonal medication.

Clomid, a famous medication to all infertile women searching for the Holy Grail of fecundation; I knew of it from my first miscarriage but always shoved it aside as nature should be invoked first in cases of reproduction. But as an unfavorable worshiper of the goddesses of fertility, I knew the medication was the only variable possible in my pregnancy journey's formula.

Intrauterine insemination or IUI seemed like the most uncomplicated procedure to achieve my dream. If anything, it was supposed to be harder on Gavin, who was forced to produce sperm in a secluded room with the help of a few dirty magazines. I, on the other hand, had to simply lay on the gynecological chair and receive the genetic material with the help of a thin and flexible tube. But nothing could predict my reaction to the drug. Massive migraines accompanied me on every move; my belly looked like I'd ingested an inflated pufferfish; I constantly felt as if needles were poking me from the inside, while on the outside, a painful numbness made me jolt at any touch. If I dared to drink tea or any hot beverage, my body temperature felt like volcano magma. After a week of such diverse symptoms, I felt like a tornado pillaged through me, depleting all my energy supply. I was a wreck. My body became emaciated and puny with only eyes for a face. I could only question how a baby would stick to a dried-up liana.

Two weeks seemed like internal and external infernos, but I pushed through since I knew it would be better after. On the day of my ovulation, I felt dizzy from my heightened hormonal state but excited. I went there as if I was their first patient ever. I asked a million questions and questioned every move the nurses made. I made sure to verify each step so I could be at rest with its successful outcome. The ladies were nice, probably because they experienced before the clucks of a wannabe hen.

I lay on the gynecological chair and waited for the doctor to do the procedure. It felt cool in the room. It could have been because they kept a specific temperature inside facilities or because I was exposed from my waist down, ready to be fertilized. The walls had a yellowish hue, and on them were pictures of flowers, mainly orchids. How befitting. There were no plastic uteruses or posters with gestational weeks of the baby, just my rancid reproductive system alongside images of magnificent flowers.

The doctor entered the room. She was a tall, stunning lady, wearing long multicolored glass earrings reminiscent of Venice's Murano chandeliers. It seemed overly extravagant to show off her illustriousness to women filled with despondency. Was her presence there to show me how much I lost in the genetic lottery? She smiled amicably, presented herself as Dr. Devi, and proceeded to prepare the tools for insemination. I stared at her gracious moves and keen reflexes, and she smiled back at me as if aware of my hawkish glare. She sat and then rolled with the help of her chair's caster wheels, and in one swift move, she was behind the cover. When she disappeared out of sight, I could reassess my situation and address my concern:

"Are you sure it's Gavin's sperm and not some other guy's?"

She exhaled such a delectable laugh it made me unsure of my question.

"I get asked every time I perform this procedure," she said with a subtle accent. Then her chair rolled back close to my face and showed the vial where Gavin's genetic components lay.

"See, there is his name, birth, and hour when he visited. We take this potential error very seriously. For it to happen, there must be another Gavin Miller with the same name, birth date, and he must be present at the same hour as your husband. Since this information reduces all risk of coincidence, you don't have to worry about it."

"Good. One less problem to think about."

She then rolled back into her previous position. As I wondered why the doctor preferred swooshing around the office instead of walking, she raised her forehead and asked, "ready?"

"Ready."

CHAPTER 8

AFTER Dr. Devi, the prominent display of genetic fortitude left the room, I was told to remain still and stay with my legs bent for ten to twenty minutes. I waited for twenty-five to make sure. I slid off the gynecological chair slowly to not disturb the potential germination of life. I already could imagine how my little baby would establish conjunction and multiply by two cells, then by four, then by eight. I walked every step deliberately towards the reception in an attempt to soften the sail of my baby's journey. When I reached the lady at the desk, I was still in reverie until I heard the price I had to pay—what a way to disturb one's daydreaming.

In a begrudged mood, I went to work and hoped to not meet anyone annoying for the rest of the day. Fate, as per usual, was not on my side. When I reached my house, I noticed my mother's Nissan parked in front of the garage. Even though it was parked correctly, I decided to leave my car on the curbside again. Maybe I could get another chance at teasing her for her bad parking. I got to my home's entrance, I exhaled, pushed my bloated body through the door, and stepped in. My mother's fake designer sandals were lying sloppily near the coat hanger where her bag resided during her visits. There she was, glorious in her hypocrisy.

"Laura, how are you?" Her voice sweeter than syrup.

"I'm good, Mom. What brings you in? Where's Gavin?" I sat beside her at the square maple wood table. She already was chugging wine.

"Is everything alright? You look fuller. Are you pregnant by any chance?" Her eyes enlarged with curiosity and angst.

"No, Mother, I don't have time for this. What is it that you want?" I rose from the table in an attempt to distance myself.

"He called."

"Who?"

"Robert."

"What did he want?" I pressed the kettle's button.

"He wanted to meet up."

"And?" My arms crossed tight at my chest.

"I was wondering if you would be okay with it?" She leaned over with pleading eyes.

"Listen, since you live alone, do what you want. I don't care. I simply don't want him near me. Ever."

"And how do you imagine that happening?"

"So, you want to make it serious again? After everything he's done?"

"He said he was very sorry and has suffered a great deal. Are you really not able to forgive him?"

"How can you?"

"He changed." She glanced at me with a painful gaze.

"Says he."

With my lips pursed and jaw tight, I placed a teabag in my Space Needle mug and dunked it a few times, all the while she appraised my disposition.

"Fine, mother. You can date him, sleep with him, I don't care. If I ever encounter him, I will keep my distance as if he were the plague and answer him with one-syllable words. Is it clear?"

"Yes, yes. Thank you, dear." She rushed to hug me and kiss my cheeks as your usual traditional Russian assimilator.

I conformed to her superfluous enthusiasm and seated her back to her place. She downed her wine in one go, which left a red Salvador Dali mustache on each side of her mouth. She then smiled at me, rushed to the hall mirror, wiped her mouth, puckered her lips, and drew on them a burgundy color. She then calmed a few flyaway strands of her blonde coiffure, turned towards me, and said, "I have a date with him tonight. I will tell you everything tomorrow. *Paka*, Laura Tatiana." She closed the door, still waving bye.

I didn't even have time to ask where Gavin was and why was she driving after drinking alcohol. Gavin texted he was at the grocery store buying more wine for Svetlana. I told him to come home as the calamity went away on its own. After, I took my tea into the bedroom, analyzing the deceitful tactic my mother displayed earlier, and with her, the image of the ogre flashed before my eyes, and I shuddered.

After my dad's funeral, we went to live with my mother's older sister. Mother didn't have a job or viable education. The little money we had we spent on the funeral and could cover the expenses for a month. So much for a responsible parent. Thus, commenced our journey of unstable living, hand-me-downs, and questionable food. She scattered me across the country like she did with the ashes of my father in the ocean. One day, we would be with Billy in Texas, another with Bobby in Maryland, and another with Bucky in Portland. My hatred for in-state traveling stemmed from the impoverished adventures I had been subjected to in my early years. From motels with eager cockroaches and earwigs to greet us to rentals with bloody mattresses in neighborhoods sounding like a shooting range. I've met people whose lives were worth little to them, and nothing could change their opinion. I've met people who traded their bodies for a glimpse of happiness in whatever form they took it. It made me want to know more about the lives they led or were led through. I suspected more lies than truth, but still, I was curious to learn more.

My mother, though, didn't want to deal with any of it. Her fear of my convergence to the troubled community made her mad and insecure. So, in an attempt to prevent my debasement, she switched the plan with the power of a concerned mother, and out the door, we went first thing in the morning of the next day. In the end, we settled in Seattle. She found a guy here: a tall, broad-shouldered guy with a pin for a spine and a stone for a heart. He was a navy guy out of the Naval Station somewhere in Bremerton. My mother saw the answer to all our problems in him, so she married him as soon as he proposed. I was devastated.

I knew we wouldn't get along, and, in time, I got my premonition confirmed.

CHAPTER 9

IN the beginning, he gave me time to adjust to life with a fatherly figure. I was grateful. But then he took it upon himself to educate me as if I was a delinquent or a potential one who had garnered information from all those corrupt places I had been exposed to before. It took time for me to realize it was my mother who had spewed some exaggerated narratives to the guy, in which I represented the primary threat against my own decision-making abilities. And one thing Mr. Navy Guy knew was how to tackle threats. I never expected it, and to this day, it pains me that my mother used me to secure herself a shoulder to cry on, a broad shoulder, that is.

Thus began a time in my life I would rather skip or rip it from my memories' scrapbook. I had been deemed a friendly kid throughout my early childhood, the kid who feared getting in trouble and never bothered adults with nonsensical attention-grabbing aberrations. Now I was cataloged as the broken, gone-astray kid in need of a thorough investigation, discipline, and punishment. I didn't anticipate such an attitude from the uniform guy or my two-faced mother, so I behaved as usual, like a normal twelve-year-old, a bit cocky, a bit sassy but integral to my juvenile innocence. I couldn't have predicted the "talk" planned to destroy my trust and reliance on adults.

He sat me on the leather sofa in his large living room with walls filled with antique swords and weaponry. My mother slithered next to him, like the traitor she was, on the opposite side. She knew not to make a fuss in case she might accidentally attract the spotlight on her hypocritical presence. I still didn't understand what was going on. His face shared a similitude to an Easter Island head; his fingers interwove, forming a giant fist as his whole demeanor maintained an inclined position ready for action. Whereas my mother's face was turned downward, likely measuring the length of her manicured toes to one another, her hands massaging her neck in an attempt to subdue her counterfeit guilt, a contrast to her whole body, which mainly looked unconcerned. He began with arguments against my precarious personality and how he planned to reconstruct me into a viable adult with a sure-fire future. My reaction was a speechless embarrassment, as I had never witnessed such presumption about myself. He then described my schedule and the benefits my life would reap from a written plan detailed to the minute. My present apprehension didn't matter; sometime in the future, I would appreciate it. I gave it a thought and then pleaded to their rational minds with solid arguments, but then I peeked at my mother's nervous lip-biting as if she was ready to be done with the whole thing. Then I realized it was all in vain, my future was decided long before I sat on that couch, and my only choice was acceptance. I, of course, didn't accept. Who in their right mind would sign away their freedom? But the moment the schedule was nailed to the wall, I had no choice but to respect everything on it with the precision of a ruler. I woke up at six-thirty a.m., made my bed, ate breakfast, and left for school on time. Being late was a grave mistake. In the evening, I was supposed to show all my grades and report on events or occurrences at school. Bedtime at nine p.m. "No playdates, no friends, no sleepovers. School isn't supposed to be about making friends and socializing. It's about growth, in spirit, and in character," he used to say.

My manners were to be impeccable, even if Svetlana didn't follow most. Mr. Double Standards was lax in that way towards his mistress, you know. While I had a future ahead of me, so I couldn't afford a dropped fork or talking with a full mouth. He would admonish any wrinkle on my bed in the morning, my lack of appetite at breakfast, and the insufficient number of perfect scores on my papers in the evening. I was to address him as "sir" in all circumstances. I was to stay in my room for most of the afternoon and study or practice the flute. If he didn't hear the flute for five minutes, his massive footsteps would resonate the staircase with impending doom. My mother saw everything, and she didn't care. She had found her haven. Nothing else mattered, not even her daughter. She mastered the blind eye so well; it became second nature.

After half a year of rigorous cohabitation, my grades went up, I looked decent most of the time, and I even learned to force myself to eat. The neighbors regarded us as a beautiful family risen from adversity. I had forged my most deceiving smile during those times, but on the inside, I felt like a battered apple. A cage of moral integrity was built around me, and my wings were fused to it.

My mother did not visit me on my locked-in afternoons as if she knew those were my worst times and feared my pleadings might persuade her to leave. So, during my most apathetic episodes of boredom, I turned to books. Many were assigned from school, so I could take them from the public library. Others I would ask my mom to buy. The ogre liked seeing me reading, so he didn't care for that kind of spending. As my cold soul searched for affection in the written words, I found it in the version of Meg, Jo, Beth, and Amy. *Little Women*, a book my mother bought but never read. Her fault for gifting me the perfect mother's guide. The book became my bible. When I was given the first copy, I tore it to pieces reading it, and requested a second one. My mother didn't expect to see her daughter as an avid reader, so she even went and told the ogre pridefully. To which he replied with approving silence. She then rebought me the first and the second book of *Little Women*, which I devoured in a week. Long after the events of my teenage years, I went and bought a third copy on my own, which I cherished and never opened, simply adored its cover – four girls sharing a sisterly hug. I could relate to each of them. I felt like the fifth sister taking advice from Marmee, the epitome of a mother. I still remember my favorite quote: "They always looked back before turning the corner, for their mother was always at the window to nod and smile and wave her hand at them. Somehow it seemed as if they couldn't have got through the day without that, for whatever their mood might be, the last glimpse of that motherly face was sure to addict them like sunshine." Like sunshine.

After intense *ogrerian* admonishments, I would lock myself in my room pretending to study, but instead, I would lay on my bed, ruffle it a bit and visualize how Marmee would rescue me from my unjust persecutions and envelop me into a hug. So sparse were my mother's hugs that I felt more warmth from a fictitious character. I would then imagine how she would guide me through my life's troubles and smile at me with her compassionate eyes.

Nothing changed, of course. I got no mercy from my mother or any other mother from a fictional setting in the nineteenth century. Thus, I redirected my woes towards the future. I promised myself I would never be like her. I would always share my child's woes and joys; I would build a bond stronger than glue which would last a lifetime; I would never put my needs before my baby's; I would enrich her experience to a sacrificial extent. I would dedicate my life to bringing a smile to my baby's face and keeping it on. I would be an elephant mother with an enormous love to nurture my offspring's early years and lifetime. I would let my mother witness the miserable replica she was by example, by MY example, the daughter she never nourished, never understood. It would be worth it in the end.

Years had passed with one thing to make it easier to survive: a garden. The ogre didn't care much about it, my mother even less, so he let me do whatever I wanted. We went a few times to a nursery, and there I had my epiphany. The multitude of colors, the nectar imbued air, the buzzing, the wing flutters resounding in my ears. I couldn't get enough. Thus, a new journey in my life commenced: amateur gardening. I began with daisies and daffodils. They were the hardest to kill. Then I moved to pink peonies and lilies. Begonias were my choice when it came to butterfly visits. The garden already had some mauve wisteria and white hydrangeas. I added some bleeding-hearts bushes, yellow roses, and white gaura. The pin-spine ogre liked my hobby and would let me garden as much as I wanted but not to the detriment of my grades. My garden transformed into a fairytale in a year, not as luscious as my Hanging Garden of Kenmore but stunning, nonetheless. The love for my plants grew like a mother's love for her children. I cherished my flowers with a profound sentiment of affection. I compared it to having a child. How different and similar would it be? Those were my assuaged thoughts as I watered my hydrangeas and sprinkled fertilizer around my rose bushes.

My favorite occupation often revolved around admiring the bloom of a lily. One of nature's most refined works, the flower, would blossom on a stem and out of a sepal. Inside it, a love story would be concocting. Between the petals, the pistil (the female) looking like an exquisite long-necked vase, and the stamen (the male) with its wobbly anthers declared love to each other all day long. Though so close to one another, they were never able to consummate their love. It came upon fate to bring pollinators to expand their attachment, most likely to a different couple. As such, they lived happily ever after (or till someone would cut the stem and place it in a vase). It was how plants lived, procreating at fate's will. For us humans, the petals were the main attraction like it was intended. The paper-thin but alive sheet looked like nature's parchment with the secret recipe for its most delicate but effective creations. Not only did they protect its love couple, but they also donned bright colors and even fragrances to attract pollinators.

As time passed, I felt more consumed by my garden and the world I had discovered in it. Few things mattered as much as my flowers and the feeling I shared for them. Subsequently, my grades slipped a bit, not much, and my chores were not done to a standard of excellence. I knew of my mishaps, but what followed was nothing short of a nightmare.

One day when I came home from school, I saw the door to the deck slightly open, then I heard some noise coming from the backyard. Near the deck were mounts of ripped flowers and plants. Pieces of wisteria sprawled around the garden like body parts. And no butterflies in sight. When I got a little closer, with great unease, I witnessed the ogre demolishing my hard work in mere seconds. I've never witnessed a massacre before, but this came close to being like one. I grabbed him by his massive forearm, pleading to let them live. He didn't hear. I then started scratching him in an attempt to stop him. He shook me off like a willow branch and resumed his destruction. I then went around, in front of him, begging for forgiveness and another chance. His anger grew visible through the vein in his neck. He dropped the lifeless body of a bleeding heart, slapped me with all his might, and the deed was done.

My mother didn't see anything, but she saw the mark on my face and the backyard slaughter. At first, she tried to downplay it, saying they were only plants, and my cheek would heal in no time, but when she saw my eyes looking like a deer's in the headlights, she understood. She calmly talked to the ogre. He didn't react much, as if he already knew what was coming. The divorce advanced as fast as the wedding but with a hefty settlement, which allowed us to make a down payment for a two-bedroom condo.

Even if I escaped the claws of the ogre, it took me years to overcome my anger and the scars of injustice. I repelled any thought of flowers, gardening, and enjoyment. Any accidental observance of a plant reminded me of the lifeless ones from that day. If we ever were to pass by a flower shop, I would turn the opposite way. If my mother bought some roses, I would put them outside and out of sight. It didn't take long for my mother to notice, so one day, she sat next to me in my new dark-toned bedroom and said, "Laura, I hope you can forgive me. I put you through a lot of suffering."

I didn't answer.

"You know I love you, right?"

I couldn't answer.

"You are the best thing to ever happen in my life."

I couldn't hold it in anymore.

"So this is how you care for the best thing in your life?" I asked, tears clumping in my eyes.

"I am only human, Laura."

"If I could disown you, I would've done it at twelve when you married the ogre."

"You cannot disown me," she said with a hurting smile, "I am your mother. I will be forever in your life, dead or alive."

I glared at her with a disgruntled stare.

"When I will become a mom, I will never be like you."

"I hope so, my dear, I really do."

It seemed weird that even though I threw such harsh words at her, she didn't react. She simply took me to the car and drove to the closest plant nursery. It was a volunteering job. It was where I met Margaret for the first time.

CHAPTER 10

TWO weeks had passed in a severe slowdown. It felt like I dragged the day on my shoulders till it reached dusk, then during the night, I longed for the sunrise to appear again behind the blinds. Now finally, I was about to take a pregnancy test. A process perfected through imposed experience, it became a tool for hope and desolation. As usual, I didn't expect it to be successful. I kept reminding myself we still had two shots. But when the process had been done, I couldn't look. The scaredy-cat in me couldn't muster the courage. I called Gavin. He was in the kitchen cooking some pasta.

"What is it?" He came in, wiping his hands with a paper towel.

"Can you look?"

"At what?" His curiosity piqued.

I showed the elongated plastic device lying next to the bottle of hand soap, silently shouting my results to us.

"Are you sure you want me to find out first?"

"Yes, I can't do it," I said, kneading my hands.

"Okay, I'll look. Is it supposed to be two lines?"

"Yes, hurry!"

He scrutinized the test, and his face fell as if gravity pulled it to the ground.

"It's not clear. Maybe I don't understand? Could you look? Please?"

I knew the answer already. It didn't take a mastermind to realize it. Even so, I looked at the test, and, of course, it was one line. Involuntarily, I began to shed tears. Gavin hugged me like a warm blanket and said, "we can afford a couple more tries. We can do this."

"I hope so," I said, wiping budding tears with my hand.

He gave me his paper towel to wipe them.

"Let's go eat some carbonara. A full stomach makes everything better."

The second day my period knocked on the door. With the doctor called and informed, the process reloaded again: migraines, bloating, and mood swings. This time around, I took the denial route. I ignored my pain and discomfort with vehement valor while giving my body no excuse other than pushing forward. Nevertheless, as the pills disappeared from their plastic nest, the days were even more challenging than before, and my brave armor of indifference was reduced to the facade of emaciated anxiety.

The day for the procedure arrived once again. Gavin went in the late morning for his part, whereas I went to work as things were heating up there too.

I was in meeting after meeting till noon, and my only opening was during lunch, which I took upon myself to eat at the domed terrace. Once again (it seemed unavoidable), I sat at the mother witches' table (where all the childless ladies were under inquisition), which on that day was represented only by Cassandra and outsider Jasmine. Everyone else was probably scurrying around the building, trying to tackle some of the immense workloads. No one was in the mood. I was just better at hiding it.

"Is everything okay?" I addressed Jasmine.

"What a terrible start of the day," answered Cassandra. I glanced at Jasmine as she laughed it off.

"The paperwork I have to do amounts for two weeks ahead. I am exhausted, and coffee doesn't help."

"Yes, it is a big transition for the firm. Mergers are usually pressurizing. Mr. Rogers has his hands full in paperwork while I try to condense as much as I can," I said.

"I'd rather have to deal with merging paperwork than to see the same resume over and over and, somehow, extract the best fitting one. I might need a third eye for this since the ones I have are dulled out," said Cassandra, oblivious to whether we were listening or not.

"What about you, Jasmine? How is work?" I switched the person of interest.

"Intense but manageable, I had to prepare a PowerPoint with all our next steps in the transition. I love presentations. To make them, that is, not to present them." She chuckled. "But I'm sure it will get better once it is all done, Cassandra."

Adorable Jasmine always healed my heart with her positivity. Such a refreshing stance on life gave me a reason to doubt my own. I loved hearing her stories, as they emulated a fairy's journey, full of sparkle and a grand moral ending. Jasmine was similar in many ways to the flower from which her name was borrowed. Fragile on the outside and even more on the inside. Her purity came in the form of blind optimism that every person deserved a chance. An antithesis to my dejected core values, but precisely this radical position enticed me to listen carefully to her personal views on life and bask in the radiance of her innocence.

While her interior self could bear no negative emotion, her outer shell encapsulated a layer of splendor. Her Mexican heritage had been doused in Irish whisky blending two continental endowments into one. Jasmine was a sight to behold with eyes larger than usual, pouty lips, and wavy dark hair with blue hues. In contrast to me, she was curvy in all the right places, whereas I was flat in all the wrong places. We both had long hair, but hers looked like the night ocean and its delicate waves, and mine resembled a puffy mess similar to pampas grass. We both had green eyes, but hers were pale jadeite able to hypnotize with its translucency while mine were two dull stones lying by a riverbank. She, of course, knew she was gorgeous but never used it as a weapon, and it made me like her even more. I couldn't even get jealous of her innumerable qualities. I simply wanted to be close to her in hopes I could catch some of her glow.

Even though she represented a mixture of blood, culture, and language, Jasmine chose to identify as Mexican and spoke out in defense of her community. She preferred Mexican cuisine to any other. She listened to Mexican music and read Mexican authors. She also wore the milkmaid hairdo and jewelry like her favorite Frida Kahlo. You could find in Jasmine a bit of Frida in everything: in her strive to belong, in her fierce cultural identity, in her wistful eyes. She even let her eyebrows reach a more bonding connection but not as close as Frida's. For me, though, Frida's image revived another vision, her miscarriage. The painting "Henry Ford Hospital" took realism to a greater level, an illustrious image of anguish I could unwillingly relate to, though it could easily send me into a spiraling breakdown. But that was not what Jasmine's Frida described, nudging me to believe there were so many sides to one story.

I could imagine Jasmine as a potential good friend. Though, I still needed to make sure she was not one of those clingy friends who called every time Starbucks didn't fulfill their order with accuracy. We went outside the office habitat a few times, but I mainly talked, and she mainly listened. I wished she could open up easier, but fairies were hard to catch and even more challenging to convince them to land on one's shoulder. In the end, Jasmine became a very dear friend, the one who taught me more than I ever expected.

"How do you manage to look so good?" asked Cassandra, aware as I was of Jasmine's splendor.

"I don't do much except some skincare."

"Of course, you don't... But I do know the secret. You don't have kids."

As Cassandra talked, the three-kid mom approached us and sat quietly next to her, trying not to interrupt as if she was saying something of value.

"I used to be skinny as you with luscious, well-defined curls and skin smoother than butter. Then I gave birth, and half of my hair fell off, my skin got brittle, and my weight skyrocketed. It's like I selected the best of me and poured it all into my baby's DNA. I don't regret it, but if I get to have another, I'll probably never lose the weight."

"I used to be the skinniest in the family, but by my third, my weight increased so much I look like my mother," said the three-kid mom.

"Did you try going to the gym?" I asked.

"What gym? When?" Cassandra said.

Again, these ladies with their "too complex to handle" situations. There was never a good enough answer and never enough time to regard it.

"I went to a plastic surgeon to see what he can do with my stretch marks and flabby belly. The doctor said to do the mommy makeover, as in a boob job, liposuction, and whatnot. Hubby almost choked on his coffee when he heard the price. I wonder if he even cares how I look anymore," said the three-kid mom.

"Yeah, I catch Russel ogling on those skinny twenty-year-olds like no tomorrow. Well, I usually make sure he knows exactly how his tomorrow looks like," she said, and both cackled.

"You look pretty good to me, Cassandra," Jasmine murmured.

"Why, thank you, dearie. You always find the right words compared to my husband." Words shining from her mouth.

"Alright ladies, I'm out for the day," I said as I picked my empty lunch bag.

"What? You take the half-day off on a week like this?" asked Cassandra.

"I have some urgent business to attend to." I rose hurriedly from the table.

"Is it that time of the month?" asked Cassandra.

I knew she wasn't talking about my period, so I let it slide. Less talk with Cassandra meant more freedom for me. Let her speculate as much as she wanted; it might bring some joy to her stale life. As I departed further from the table, Cassandra brayed at me like a donkey, "make sure you make that baby today!"

I wanted to go back and strangle the obnoxiousness out of that witch's undefined curls, but priorities were bigger, and saving energy for the more important was vital. My appointment today was a second IUI.

"Maybe this time?"

CHAPTER 11

I'VE shared many warm memories with Gavin. We've flown to a few islands, climbed a few mountains, and visited too many museums to count. We've dined at the best restaurants our wallets could afford and witnessed sunsets with astounding panoramas. But my most cherished memories to this day were our pillow talks in the evening. On one such evening, after my first failed IUI, I laid my head on Gavin's chest while my cup of tea, placed on my nightstand, was cooling off. I heard his heartbeat underneath his soft chest raise, a beat so strong it felt like a call of war. Something about lying on his chest made me feel more feminine, more sensual, more at ease. Of all the ways we expressed affection, this one was my favorite: feeble in the arms of my strong man but with my permission. The sense of security and bonding elevated all my restricted or even hidden feminine desires of weakness. I could never show frailty at work, especially to my co-workers or, heavens forbid, around my mother. It would mean defeat, surrendering my hard-earned boundaries. But under the blanket of masculine presence and muscular body features, I could relinquish all my restraints. I suppose people always searched for those with whom they could set their armor to the side and bathe nude in a lake of vulnerability. It was always a risk, but one we couldn't impede ourselves from trying. Freed of all barriers, I remembered my failure. When I could freely engulf in my femininity, my most basic misdemeanor banged on the door of consciousness.

Had I lost my femininity? Did I become uglier under the pressure of a common goal? Would I still be attractive to him like in the beginning? We've indeed had a subdued libido with all the ovulation tracking we've been doing these years. Nothing ruins one's sexual delight like the burden of obligation. The constraints of having to mate on specific days in an imperative manner strained the overall mood. I wasn't stealing kisses anymore; I didn't need to share the meaningful wink; it was clear and precise when we would engage in intercourse and how. Never was spontaneity such a crucial aphrodisiac as when we tried for a baby. As the fruit of our love's expression, the baby constituted a mood killer from the start. There were months when I ceased all attempts to get us a chance at relaxation and relationship maintenance, but somewhere in my mind, a tiny, guilty whisper would always evoke: "What if you conceive this month and you're wasting it? What if in nine months you could hold your baby, and you could miss it?"

I began investing in makeup, lingerie, all in the style of a light erotic movie, just to keep the fire going. Gavin never said a word, but I felt his desire slip away under the pressure of mandatory performance. The voice of determination had interminable arguments of such sorts till my third miscarriage, but since then, we realized it didn't matter if I got pregnant. The baby wouldn't stay with me. The issue grew more prominent by the growing number of miscarriages. It took two more to finally accept it would not be only the two of us conceiving a baby.

As rumination began to swelter in the back of my brain, I peeked at him from my uncomfortable angle. Gavin was enjoying his rock music; he usually used headphones since he knew how much I despised it. Silence was my preferred music. I pinched him to show I had a question. He immediately took off his headphones and asked:

"Do you want to talk?"

"Yes, I wanted to ask a personal question." I raised myself lasciviously to a seated position, gazing at his face from above.

"How personal?" He grinned.

"Not that kind of personal." I slapped his traveling hand. "What if I never conceive and never have a baby? Will you still love me?"

"What kind of question is that?" He hurried to give me a hug. "At the end of the day, it's you and I in this world. I am still worried about all these procedures. If there would be a day when you come to me and say you want to quit, I will be there to support your decision."

"But you want a baby, and I can't give you one. Isn't it a reason to leave me?"

He released me, choosing instead to gaze into my eyes.

"Your imagination is complicating things. I didn't marry you for kids. It's only the next level, but the present level with you is pretty darn good. Shouldn't you drink your tea before it cools off?"

"What if you found a more beautiful woman who could also give you kids? Would you pick her?"

"You are confusing me with some European king. His choice should fall on a wife who could birth an heir to succeed the throne. Fortunately, I do not have a kingdom to rule unless you consider our mortgaged house. So, with milady's permission, I will stick to modern-day monogamy. Also," he said in haste as if to not forget something of an obligatory manner, "you are the most beautiful wife one could ever wish for, with long dark brown hair, bright green eyes, nice skin, built well in the right places."

Leave it to a data analyst to compliment you. Bright, nice, and well in the right places would be the primary descriptors. Though I knew where he was getting at, I could not help but tease.

"So, like every other girl you meet on a daily basis?"

"No! You make these features work only for you," he said in an exasperated way.

"Okay, okay, I believe you." I raised my head to give him a peck on the lips for his effort, but the mischievous inquisition began rolling so smoothly I couldn't stop myself.

"What would make you hate me, though?"

"Laura, what is it with these questions?"

"Just answer."

"I'm not sure, maybe if you murder someone or endanger someone's life. You know, the never-going-to-happen stuff."

"So, you will not help me bury a body?"

"Laura…" He deepened his tone.

"I'm joking, trying to lighten the mood."

"You're trying to lighten the mood after you deliberately darkened it?"

"These kinds of weird questions keep popping into my mind, and having you answer them makes it a bit better."

He took me into his arms, peered at me through the lens of his glasses, put on a serious face, and said, "number one, I will love you even if we don't have kids. We can always adopt or foster. Number two, I will never hate you. Number three, you would be a ruthless and breathtaking Mafia godmother."

"Well then, I have a proposition you cannot refuse." Innuendoes wooing from my lips.

"Tell me more, madame Corleone."

"You better lay down for better comprehension," I said as my hoody's zipper began unraveling, and he placed his glasses on the nightstand.

The only thing getting cold that evening was, unfortunately, the tea.

CHAPTER 12

THE month after my second IUI, no pollen reached my petals, the stork skipped my address again, and no cabbage seeds germinated on my cabbage patch. Just remnants of migraines, stomach pains, and a few extra pounds. My hope simply shattered into a million mosaic pieces which had imprinted in them all my failed attempts. At first, I didn't understand why I had such a devastating reaction to my second failed attempt. It was only the second. Some tried beyond five. Maybe it had something to do with having so many babies up in heaven? Perhaps, after losing so much, I had depleted all my prowess in grappling with life's challenges? The fear of living through it again grew to an egregious and uncontrollable size. I could only feel exhaustion, my body's and my mind's. I functioned on inertia and Gavin's support. And with every morning's awakening, I heard my internal turmoil repeat the same questions over and over again: *"Till when I will be able to endure it? When will be the time I say stop and change my view towards other viable options? When will this Sisyphean struggle stop?"*

The third time would tell.

***

My body on the gynecological chair, eyes on the bumpy ceiling. Last chance. I had to keep calm, but the earrings were bothering any strife for serenity. The first time I saw Dr. Devi, her earrings were made of glass. On my second try, she had a pair of plastic hoops with a leopard print. Today couldn't be any other material except metal. Metal should make proof of my viability. It had to, for I didn't believe I could do it one more time. I wished and loathed the idea of her coming in.

"Laura, come back to your senses," I told myself, "there cannot be a connection between the doctor's earrings and the procedure. Your mind is messing with you. Get a grip."

The creak of the door announced her entrance. I held my gaze to the ceiling.

"Hello, Mrs. Miller. How are you?" Her voice a song.

As an unconditional reflex of politeness, I lowered my head.

"I'm good." A miserable attempt at showing strength despite the struggle.

My gaze went straight to her ears. The earrings were made of... Yarn. They were symmetrical knots with frayed ends in the natural color of wool, similar to the macrame hangings I'd seen on walls. I glanced at the ceiling again, this time to keep my tears from trickling. It should have been a moment of divine intervention, but instead, my hope was sentenced to the gallows because of the earrings.

When the procedure was done, Dr. Devi, seeing my vexation, came closer to me, laid a compassionate hand on my shoulder, and said, "I hope it makes you feel better, Mrs. Miller. I, too, went through three IUI procedures. The last one worked."

The arid land had denounced herself. Indeed, it made me feel better. She was splendid, but beauty was not a symptom of fertility nor of a happier life. We had to crawl through the same trenches of defeat towards a common denominator.

"Thank you," I said, wiping my tears fervently in hopes to keep face, whatever was left of it.

She left, and I stayed with my legs up.

The weeks went by with a destitute feel. The test was made; the second line didn't appear. End of a chapter. It was time to end my Sisyphean struggle. The harsh reality had hit straight in the center of my heart, producing poisonous puss of defeat and rejection. I began to estrange myself from my failure. I behaved as if I didn't want it at all. I even went up to Gavin and said to never bring up the subject again. We were never to speak of said issue unless for trivial matters. He agreed.

And so, began a different kind of life where a married and in love couple lived a wonderful baby-less life. Walking in the park, hiking on trails, dining in restaurants having a carefree lifestyle. The only issue was that anywhere we went, there was a newborn baby present. In the park, a mom swayed her newborn baby girl. On the trail, a dad was keeping close to his chest an adorable little boy. Everywhere I went, I could hear children giggling and laughing, a contagious atmosphere of merriment I was privy to but never a part of. Scenes upon scenes of picture-perfect parents with their ideal children enjoying themselves. One of such scenes I noticed at an Italian restaurant where Gavin and I were having dinner. A mom, a dad, a toddler son, and a baby daughter were in the middle of their act of mundane life similar to ours with a significant exception: they were exuding happiness. Gavin observed my baby-distracted face and said, "let's try again, Laura."

"Try again what?"

"If you could see yourself from aside, you would understand."

"How so?" I asked, a bit dumbfounded.

"You yearn for a baby. It's written all over your face. You always blank out whenever you see one." He leaned closer and took my hand. "Let's find more strength and finish what we started."

"I can't, Gavin. Another failed IUI attempt, and I will have a mental breakdown. There's no doubt. It's too much failure for two people to go through."

"But we are together in all this. It's what makes us stronger, don't you see?"

I stared down at our linked fingers, listening to his and my heart's pleads, but I could not do it.

"Let's try IVF this time."

My gaze shot straight at him, incredulous of his words.

"We'll skip this year's vacation and invest our spending into our own precious bundle of joy. What do you say?"

"It's a lot of money and sacrifice."

"Together, we can beat the odds."

One nod, and the evening wasn't as somber. It seemed like someone turned on additional lights to congratulate us on our decision to move forward. The night turned out better than I thought.

CHAPTER 13

I usually visited Margaret on Saturdays. Most of the time, I would catch her in the midst of work. That day was no different. With her hands covered in fresh-smelling soil, Margaret was busy repotting a few pansies, but when I got closer, she pushed the pot to the side and rose to welcome me. Tall with wide shoulders, she looked like an Olympian swimmer at their prime, even though Margaret was at a respectable age of fifty-nine and never took a swimming lesson in her life. Her presence demanded admiration; her fierce soul created an aura of awe. Her face had an angular refinement, with eyes the color of obsidian, skin the color of Black Forest calla lilies, and a head full of curls not higher than an inch. When Margaret approached me, her pace was slow and heavy. Heavy with pride and self-acknowledgment. She knew no one would supply her the time, so she created it herself. She wasn't made strong but grew to be so; it wasn't a choice but a necessity. Though her mannerisms intentionally suggested a harsh presence, her femininity would always illuminate from within, similar to the light escaping through the crevices of an enclosed door.

Indeed, Margaret was a bouquet of opposites, and the most obvious ones were in her character. Even though Margaret came from unfavorable beginnings, she did not accept defeat in any form. She was a mere child when Dr. Martin Luther King's assassination happened, but the event transcended her whole life, bestowing it with a purpose. Margaret was from Atlanta with dreams and aspirations her family couldn't materialize. But little did they know that whatever Margaret wanted, she would get. If Margaret wanted to study sociology at Stanford, she did. If Margaret wanted to teach sociology at Stanford, she did. If Margaret wanted to marry a white man (her peer at Stanford), even if the times squinted at it, she did. And if together they decided to become activists in shedding light on racial injustice across the country, they did. Unfortunately, speaking one's mind and fighting for it implied a risk with potentially devastating consequences. While driving home one evening, her husband was murdered at a stoplight on the streets of Atlanta. Most likely retaliation for the work they were doing. It pushed Margaret to turn her stance away from the world and towards her kids. So, she moved to Seattle and opened a nursery business as she and her husband dreamt about, even though Margaret never experienced dirt underneath her nails. Margaret never spoke of her husband openly, but she always mentioned him with affection when she would retell her extensive travels across the country.

"Hi Margaret," I said as I entered the voluminous gates guarded by a squad of trimmed Blue Point Junipers.

"Hi kid, up for some work today?"

"As always."

I grabbed the handle of a large red cart filled with bags of garden soil and followed her into the depths of the potted forest. I always felt stronger at Pots N' Roses Nursery. I could lift heavy pots and carts, plant, and replant for hours and never get tired. It was Margaret's stoicism that propelled me from an early age to find in myself strength beyond expectation. After experiencing life at the nursery, I could never get enough: building something magnificent with plants I loved, alongside people I enjoyed being around. What else could one ask for?

It tugged at my perfectionism, the long rows of white, red, and yellow blossoms. The taller pots like cat palms I would usually place in the back while the finer and shorter ones were placed in front. The arrangement created an image of a choir singing praise to nature's most saturated colors. Aesthetically pleasing to the eye and soul, I could work for hours at arranging a field out of my favorite pansies, azaleas, or camellias, depending, of course, on the season and the choices Margaret made. The potted blossom field was encircled by tall Holly Cones, Emerald Green Arborvitae, Junipers, letting her customers walk through a hidden entrance into a magical meadow of flowers. As the name Pots N' Roses implied (a phrase she chose to commemorate her husband: his favorite band and their love for the flower), there was a great selection of roses, from a multitude of colors to sizes. I usually received a delectable number of mini roses from Margaret as a gift. She made sure everyone working for her could indulge in their fragrance and frailty not only at work but in the comfort of their home.

Besides the numerous plants, there was a great selection of gardening tools, gloves, and ceramic pots. Red carts were placed on their side and arranged in a row, waiting to be of use. Mulch and garden soil bags were stacked in such a manner it resembled a fort wall. Margaret's kids didn't need any other materials to play with. From the time they were in elementary, they had more than enough soil and tools to use in their daily imaginative play and enough soil bags to create fortresses. Usually, after a half day's work, we would have lunch together at their small house located behind the nursery. It looked like a tiny house fit for children's play, and it was planned so at the beginning when her three kids would return from school. But it slowly spread tendrils and grew into a large cottage with a living room, a kitchen, and a small bedroom. They had another house somewhere in Bothell, but, most of the time, you could find them in the back of their nursery.

During summers, we would usually have lunch under a pergola woven with trumpet vines in the front of the house, where she would already have prepared sandwiches and fruit salads. While during the colder months, we would sit in the living room on the ever-present brown sofa with a cup of tea and a warm dish. After a satisfying meal, she would always listen to my uneasiness as if paying for the volunteering I had done. Since my mother was not one to advise, over the years, I found solace in Margaret's wise words. She knew some of my sorrows (though not in detail), and I must've been easy to read since every time I would visit her after a miscarriage, with only a glance at my face, she would bring out the family favorite, Turkish delights. I would munch on them and relate all my quotidian issues but usually, avoiding the giant pustule of pus festering in my heart.

When I arrived that day, tiny blooms of pansies aligned in a row, waiting for attention. Margaret needed to repot them, add more fertilizer and fresh soil. I couldn't wait to get my hands dirty, especially with planting or replanting flowers. She didn't have to tell me anything. I jumped right into work and lost track of time till noon. It was drizzling here and there as the weather couldn't make up its mind, but I was used to it. Few things could deter me from my occupation. After finishing the day's project, we went into the living room since during winter, noon meant the end of the workday. No one ever came to buy plants when it turned dark. That day, Margaret prepared ham sandwiches. As we sat on the covered reclining chairs, it felt like a good day to open up a bit, so I told her about some of my experiences. I told her about the multiple miscarriages (though she suspected), of the illness so hard to diagnose, of the failed IUI's. Margaret didn't say a word or show much facial expression, but I could tell she felt for me.

"I just want to hold my baby in my hands, to enjoy the blissful days, the cuddles, the sunshine in her eyes."

She kept silent.

"Is it too much to ask?" I continued.

Margaret regarded me with some hidden heaviness of knowledge and said, "having a baby, in your case, is the success of expensive procedures but don't confuse conceiving a baby with raising one. It's a whole different story." Her pensive gaze aimed down as if thinking of the right words to say. "The changes that will arise could prove strenuous on your relationships, so expectations between you and your child must be set on equal footing."

"Gavin and my mom will help me. I will not be alone. Together we can tackle any challenge."

"It might seem like having more people around you will save you from loneliness, but it might not be the case. You will feel lonely and alone with your worst fears. It's what having kids is all about, facing your greatest fear while looking into the mirror you birthed," she said as she poured some tea in my cup.

Again, Margaret with her cryptic messages.

"How can I be lonely when I have my baby? Nonsense. I only hope all these efforts bring some result."

"Your child should not be responsible for your efforts, so everything you go through at the moment will be part of your story, never theirs."

"Wouldn't a child be grateful for the life their parents gave them?"

"You would be surprised."

A worker opened the door and began asking questions, to which Margaret gladly went to explain. Always short and confusing were Margaret's words, like she never had time to waste, but at the same time, she was never in a hurry. Still, I always wanted to hear her opinion, even if contradictory to mine.

Interesting how my mother, though oblivious to my actual needs, directed the course of my life on a path where I could find resolution on my own. When my mother brought me here, things were never the same, but it worked for both of us. Maybe my mother's intuitive feel was more cognizant than I expected. Who knew? One thing I understood for sure, the greatest gift I got from her was meeting Margaret. She was the mother I longed to have. Her exterior might've calcified in the face of adversity, but Margaret never let her sense of self get tarnished. She became a warrior statue with a mother's heart beating inside its casing and warmth oozing out of it. It filled my eyes with admiration for the ways she dealt with her children's mishaps. If one of her kids showed a character fault such as greediness or disrespect towards their siblings, Margaret's fury would rise like magma within a dormant volcano. But like a true professional in sociological matters, she would settle conflicts by acting upon previously approved consequences and install boundaries in place. Now, if her child would get a scratch, it would trigger a whole ritual of care: a worried expression would form between her eyebrows, followed by an oxytocin-filled hug and a kiss on the boo-boo in case of profound vexation. Though sometimes I suspected her kids exaggerated their sufferings to receive the endearment, she would always follow suit.

Oblivious of my observational gaze, I could take my time to relish the transfiguration of her character. And after witnessing it on several occasions, I realized I wanted to be part of this visceral experience of exemplary showcasing of motherhood. I wished to learn from her as much as possible before I embarked on my own journey. Margaret looked like a real mother. Nothing like the amateur excuse my mother showed me.

With a rubber spine, my mother would bend to the whims of patriarchy in an attempt to ease her life's tribulations. She kept quiet when she was supposed to stand up for her cause. She let her head down for men to pet it in exchange for a bone of comfort. If Billie wanted my mother to cook, she would whip out the spatula and do so, though she abhorred it. If Bobby wanted my mother to be a car enthusiast, she'd pretend to be so and blabber some information she heard on TV. If Bucky was a sexual pervert, mother would don the most expensive lingerie she was gifted from Bobby and prance like a pageant queen in front of her new benefactor. The sad part was that she never picked them properly. Thus, her efforts would always nullify themselves like the spinning wind that fizzled away and never turned into a tornado. And the whole narrative would start all over again, only with a different character. It was a discombobulated conclusion she had in her mind that only a man could grant her the solace of financial stability and resolve all her problems. Whenever I would accuse her of being a sellout, she would give me the "when you'll grow up, you'll understand" talk. Well, mother, I grew up, and I still didn't understand.

  The first time I stepped through the gate at Margaret's nursery, I was dragged by my mother's hand. Even though I had a strained attitude towards flowers then, Margaret's nursery astounded me with its splendor. But when I saw Margaret for the first time, her demeanor spooked me. The tall figure scanned us with an aloof expression on her face and said, "I am Margaret." She enunciated each syllable as if to make sure we didn't botch her name.

  While my mother talked to her, I kept thinking of ways to avoid this job altogether. I didn't want to get involved with another version of the ogre. But her calm, resolute voice, her patience towards my blunders, and the few words of encouragement she gave assured me. Margaret was pleased with my involvement but stated from the beginning that she didn't have the resources to pay me. It didn't matter since I had gained more than she suspected, and it's been more than a decade of volunteering. At a certain point, my flare to become a botanist ignited again. I knew so much about fertilizer I could teach a lecture. But constraints like risk-taking were never in my plan; I couldn't risk becoming reliant or in debt. I preferred the job of corporate anonymity, a gear in the grand scale of productivity. What I loved and what I needed were two different things. I chose the necessity and sublimation, so I decided to continue volunteering at Pots N' Roses Nursery even after I got my job. It was enough. My best amenities were all the gifted plants I could grow in my own green paradise at home. It was the best of two worlds.

When Margaret returned, I already had my fill of nature's bliss and advisory on my overgrown thoughts. Though I always wanted to stay there forever, I knew the fantasy had to end.

"I'll be going. Thank you for the meal and advice. I needed it."

Margaret, difficult on taking any kind of compliments, stood marble-like in her navy long-sleeved shirt, slacks, and a red apron on top. Then she followed with the same question repeated for more than ten years: "Are you coming next week?"

"Of course," I said as I went on to face reality once again.

CHAPTER 14

THE time had come. We were to embark on the last possible option, in vitro fertilization. A final step on our path towards parenthood; the answer to all my prayers. My excitement reached heaven, but my anxiety boiled down in hell. One moment, my heart skipped a beat at the image of me holding my baby. The next few would leave me breathless at the thought of losing the baby during pregnancy. Thoughts swirled in my head like a vortex of futility.

At the fertility doctor's office, the same plastic uterus welcomed me. Her splendor didn't fade; it presented the same plastic perfection. On the other hand, mine felt like a soldier at war, preparing for its most significant battle yet. The doctor was in a better mood than last time. Thousands of reasons could grant such cheerfulness, but, most likely, it was the hefty sum of money I was bringing in. Frustration gripped at me again, but I shifted my focus to my goal; a baby in my arms. A. Baby. In. My. Arms. At least, with this route, we could pick the healthiest baby and, preferably, a girl. I always wanted a baby girl to play with, to dress her up, and, oh, those big headbands I saw everywhere, I wanted those too. As my imagination roamed free in my head, the doctor's question brought me back to my drab reality:

"So, what brings you in today?" he asked as if unknowingly.

"We are looking to move forward with IVF," I said.

"Okay, since we have all your bloodwork, we will move to step number two, which is ovarian stimulation. It is similar to IUI, except when your follicles mature, we will harvest them through a minimally invasive surgical procedure. We will then produce the embryos in the lab and insert the selected embryo into your uterus. You will be prescribed a progesterone treatment prior and after pregnancy to ensure a healthy implantation."

"Sounds like a lengthy process, but I'm ready. In any case, I feel like the most challenging thing is the price," I said.

"The good news is the percentage of a viable pregnancy is much higher. It's about 40%," said the doctor. "Plus, we choose the healthiest embryo possible, which accounts for a great advantage."

I pursed my lips. I knew he was right, but I didn't want to give him the moment of glory.

"What do we do next?"

"You will speak with our nurse. She'll explain all the necessary medications you will need."

Exiting the clinic, I could not escape the persistent dread awaiting me when we would begin the vicious cycle anew. Pills, syringes, bloating, all would be worse this time, and I barely recovered from the previous procedures. Nevertheless, a new hope emerged in my soul like snowdrops blooming in a frozen field at the end of winter. But after two weeks of injections, I was reminded once again of the previous tribulations. Anywhere on my tummy area was a war zone: bloody punctures, bloating, and bruises sensitive to any touch. Also, I cried, oh how I cried. I cried at the grocery store for not finding my favorite dark almond chocolate. I cried in the shower when the cold water touched my body. I cried at every movie with a dog in it. Pathetic was the suitable description for my state.

When the time came for the retrieval, I was ready to be harvested high and low. The procedure was under anesthesia, so I didn't remember anything. When I woke up, Gavin said they retrieved fifteen eggs. Relief washed through my body when I heard the news, but also because I didn't have to poke myself anymore. When my baby would reach the blastocyst stage in the next five days, I was to receive her. From fifteen eggs, only two survived, and only one was healthy. We had one shot at this, so it had to work.

On the day designated for the embryo transfer, I was escorted, as if for the final time, into the procedure room. Upon entrance, the room smelled different: warmer, sweeter. The orchids swayed along with my steps as if to say farewell. The gynecological chair was still there, waiting with open "arms." I took my well-practiced position and turned my gaze to the melancholic ceiling. I thought about Dr. Devi and her earrings. They had to be metal today. They had to be. The nurse came a few times to check on me. This time it was IVF, so I was able to witness the procedure myself through a screen. I was assessing the image on the monitor when the doctor came in, but there were no earrings. No earrings at all. The ears were not even pierced. It was a slouching man with heavy framed glasses and delicate hands.

"Hello, Mrs. Miller. My name is Dr. Wong, and I will be performing your procedure."

"What about Dr. Devi?"

"She wasn't available today," he said and proceeded to turn on the machine and align his tools.

"Is it going to hurt?"

"It shouldn't, but let me know of any discomfort."

He wasn't as radiant as Dr. Devi, but radiancy was the least of my worries in such issues.

The whole procedure took maybe twenty minutes. Then, another twenty, I spent keeping my knees bent. The only thing bothering me was, how was I going to work today? I was utterly exhausted and didn't have any desire to share my energy with anyone. When I slid off the gynecological chair, I called Mr. Rogers to grant me the day off. After, I took my weary self out into the world.

The light blinded me when I exited the clinic. It was a warm February day in Seattle, not too hot, not too cold, and the fresh blossoms cheered me up a bit. Even though the weather was good, my body felt cold, my lips began trembling, my fingers stiffened, the skin on my back prickled as if a porcupine's. A clear message to hop in the car and go home, but I couldn't. I let myself walk the streets of Seattle, trying to experience them from a different perspective. To feel the city's bustling energy, its amalgam of smells, from coffee to marine breeze, its walls and roads of bricks, and the never-tiring strive to experience. The city lived. It wasn't stuck in its uncontrollable goals. I needed to do the same. In a world where all came together organically, things happened when they should and how they should. I couldn't compete with superior forces, no matter how much I tried. Letting go of my aggressive wishing for a less expectative life could aid me in getting what I wanted, but maybe not WHEN I wanted it. No matter how twisted things were in my mind, I already had all I needed around me. There was my husband, mother, my job, co-workers, and the city. I could connect to strangers on the street as if to an extensive family since, in the city, we were a part of one large community. When Gavin came home, serenity was already nested in my heart. I hugged him, gave him a peck on the lips, and told him everything I did that day.

***

At night, exhaustion took me to bed fast. When the clock struck nine, I was already snuggled underneath my sheets, ready for slumber. Gavin sat next to me to tuck me in and kiss me goodnight and soon left the bedroom. With all the lights off, I closed my eyes, but sleep didn't seem to care about my wish. I shut my eyes and held them tight for a few minutes. When I opened them again, everything was dark. Gavin had to be sleeping. I turned to the side, but I couldn't find him, then suddenly there was a knock at the door.

"Who could it be at this hour?" I thought. I went to open the door. It was Jasmine. She wore a long black dress with colorful flowers all over it and a long velvet cloak in the color of ripe cherries. Her whole appearance was adorned in color, from the embroideries on the dress to the red, pink, and white ribbons braided in her milkmaid hairdo. Baffled, the first thing I thought was how she knew my address. But before I could put my question into words, she grabbed my hand, and we ran off into the night. I was wearing some worn-out pajama dress, which I felt imminent to tell her. She laughed as if I was the funniest person she'd ever heard. Jasmine turned towards me to share her smile, but when I looked at her the second time, she transformed into Frida Kahlo. I opened my mouth to exclaim, but words wouldn't come out. Still holding my hand tightly, she took me through a narrow path into a forest with heavy branches leaning onto us and scratching me all over. Colors of dark green and black were popping in front of our eyes. The noise of the night critters sounded indignant of our presence. When the path ended, we reached an open field brimming with pink carnations. The wind rustled between each flower, making them lean lazily from side to side in synchroneity. Frida didn't hesitate and rushed through the tall blooms. The sky was clear, with innumerable stars forming several spiral-like formations as if galaxies rotating at the speed of a clock. In all that silence, Frida's effervescent laughter could be heard in echo. She rushed as if late to a grand celebration. The touch of carnations on my hands felt like the caress of fine velvet. The smell transcended anything I experienced before, something like honey and a mother's warm embrace. The sprint across the field should've tired me, I knew it in my mind, but I didn't feel it.

After passing the field, we arrived at a giant wall of rock. Frida let go of my hand and ran around it. Fear engulfed me, so I followed her. When my peripheral vision reached the edge of the stone, I could see the lines of a statue as well as the flutter of white butterflies roaming around it. It was a female Buddha made from marble. Her figure emerged halfway out of the giant rock. As I got closer, I could clearly decipher her features: her eyes were closed, her chin was very sharp, with a big nose, and long willow branches instead of hair. She had thin arms, but her hips were vast, and her legs were crossed in a lotus position. Her naked breasts were taut with milk. Two streams of her breastmilk trickled alongside her body into wells on opposite sides of her hips. Another stream connected at her solar plex flowed onto her protruding belly, where it got absorbed into the rock. In between her crossed legs was a fire pit flashing light at a rhythmical tempo. It was a fire that couldn't ignite. It kept bursting into light and extinguishing, but the fire wasn't a usual one since it didn't have flames; instead, beams of light arose like a sunrise behind the clouds. When it would align with the walls encircling the Buddha, it showed hieroglyphs I'd never seen before. I tried to decipher some of them, but I noticed Frida approaching me.

"Who is she?" I asked.

"The mother of all mothers," she answered.

"Is she pregnant?"

"The mother of all mothers always bares life."

"Why does she look like a Buddha?"

"For each of us, she looks different. You chose her image."

"What am I doing here?"

"You have the power of decision."

I turned towards Frida. Her face would illuminate every time the fire ignited. She then wrapped the cloak around herself, threw the hood over her head, and behaved as if invisible.

"What to decide, Frida?"

She didn't answer.

I beheld the menacing statue, climbed it, and kneeled next to the fire pit. What on earth could I do to start the fire? I tried blowing on it, waved my hands at it. Nothing. I looked around for some sticks or leaves. I found a few, but those didn't do much. After all the fidgeting, I turned towards Frida again.

"Tell me, please, I need to know? You must help me."

"Only you know how to birth this light. It belongs to you."

I begged once more till I opened my eyes, and Gavin was there to serve my tea in bed.

"Ready for the day?" he asked.

"Not really, but I guess I should be," I groaned. After a long sip of tea, I said, "I must see the sunrise on the Orcas Island."

"Isn't it a bit spontaneous? We have work," he said with amused bafflement.

"I want to see the sunrise." I tugged at his arm.

"Fine. We'll take a few days' leave."

I couldn't tell him more. There was a power brewing in me. I had to let it happen—the power of rest, of doing nothing. Great things happened in action, but great things happened in idleness as well.

I had to step aside, let my body create while I enjoyed the sun's healing rays.

CHAPTER 15

THE following weeks bore one goal: distraction. I knew I had to keep my mind enthralled with other preoccupations. I completely ignored my wandering thoughts leading me towards that place, the hidden-from-my-subconscious place. I wished not to visit the location or dwell on its ways of affecting me, but similar to how others could not escape the picture of a purple cow once imagined, I could not run from the image of a baby growing in a previously barren place.

I chose to divert my attention with visits to Margaret. She was always happy to oblige in giving me something to do. Good enough to keep my hands busy and away from my pesky thoughts. I, of course, asked for relatively light work, nothing heavy, just in case. She inspected me, analyzing my words, sizing me up and down as if trying to decipher if there was something new about me. It was the first time I asked for light work, so she quickly figured me out.

"How about you pour water in the kettle?"

"Oh, I could do more than that, of course." I rolled my sleeves up.

"The weather is dreary today. How about we rest and have a talk." She placed her hand on my shoulder. "We both deserve a rest."

As I sat at the table, Margaret went to the kitchen to prepare the tea and snacks. The silence reminded me her kids weren't home.

"How's Harriet, Rosa, and Luther?"

"Oh, they're always busy doing their own stuff."

I glanced at the worn-out piano, and a touch of melancholy took over me.

"Remember when you would invite me to their little recitals when they were still in middle school?"

"Yes, I miss those days."

"I miss them too."

***

Harriet, Rosa, and Luther. The first time I met them was when I received harsh criticism towards my complaints about my mother:

"If you want to break that woman's heart, you will continue talking in such a manner. There is no other mother for you, so you might as well deal with what you have. Stop whining like an ungrateful brat."

I was seventeen, and it was my second time working with Margaret. She then left to deal with a customer while I sat on the wobbly chair, ready to cry.

"Please excuse my mother," said the oldest of the three. "She never had anybody to help when we grew up. Dad died when I was in kindergarten, so she had to be there for him too."

I realized having three children and raising them herself would cut one's verboseness short. There was never time for chatting, only acting.

"But we always try to help her. Momma's our rock."

"My dad also died when I was young," I said.

"What's your name?"

"Laura. And yours?"

"Harriet. I'm seven. And she is Rosa. She is five." She pointed at the slender girl with box braids and turquoise rubber boots, "and he is Luther. He is three. "

The way Harriet defended their mother surprised and warmed my heart. I realized I had to learn from those kids as much as from Margaret. Now, they were two young ladies almost finishing college and one gentleman, a senior in high school, ready to conquer the world in their own way.

One time, when they were in middle school, Margaret told me about their familial recital and asked me to follow her to the house. As our footsteps brought us closer to the building, the sounds of a piano became more distinct to my ear. Previously, I heard them practicing many times from the depths of the nursery, but the music was choppier, more dissonant. This time, a melody resounded, a clear tune of classical provenience. My curiosity needed no more invitation. I entered the hallway, all plastered with their photos and drawings, and stopped in the living room. It was Rosa, with her wispy back playing on the piano like a miniature goddess of music. She knew her notes well. She followed the music, or maybe, the music followed her; it flowed like a sad stream of memories. When my presence was observed, the young musician stumbled on her fingers, but as she became used to a stranger's audience, she calmly took ahold of herself and continued. Harriet was seated next to the piano, and Luther sat on the windowsill where he could see his sister's face while playing.

"Rosa, let's welcome Laura first, and then you can perform the song again."

I expected a reluctance to perform for me, but I was mistaken; she was eager to show me her improvements.

"Laura, each of my kids, has prepared a number for their school recital. You will be the first to hear it."

Margaret guided me towards the couch and sat next to me, leaning her torso forward.

"Kids, show us the best of what you've got."

"I'm no music connoisseur, Margaret. What can I understand?" I said with apprehension.

"Then you will be the perfect spectator because you will listen with your heart."

Margaret welcomed my presence with a smile as well as with an air of rigor and pridefulness.

"Okay, Rosa. You can begin when ready."

The girl turned towards the exhausted-looking piano. It was missing a few white keys at the end of the keyboard as if its wisdom teeth were removed. But when she touched the instrument, the music beautified it like an antique relic of the Greek gods. A slow, meditative melody unraveled like a ball of yarn in different colors. Some were sad, some pensive. But most were simply astounding, the ups and downs pouring inspiration into my ears. The melody was so sad. It tugged at whatever primitive sense of artistic perception I had. It flowed from one tragic descent to another, only for it to end in a happy chord. What? So much sadness could end in happiness?

Silence followed. There were few words to be spoken, and no one dared to break the music's spell.

In the end, Margaret initiated a clap with her calloused palms so everyone could follow.

After the initial astonishment, I couldn't help but ask, "What is this melody?"

"It's Bach, Prelude number four from the Well-Tempered Clavier. It's my teacher's favorite and mine," Rosa said with eager enthusiasm.

Her brother hissed as he shifted his stance on the windowsill. She paid no heed to him, being used to his nonchalance.

"It's such a magnificent and sad melody. But how come it ends happily?" I asked.

"Well, as my teacher says, it's called the Picardy third, where only the last chord ends in a happy one."

"After all that sadness, could there be a chance for happiness?" A rhetorical question but to which I got an answer.

"Why not?" said Rosa.

"Thank you, Rosa. Let's see what Harriet has prepared for us," said Margaret.

"Is it another piano performance?" I inquired delightfully.

"An original poem," said Margaret.

Tall and statuesque like her mother, Harriet cleared her voice, emulating any other theater professional. Then she began:

"The clutch of the wheel

The clutch of the wheel.
The blaze of the body.
The force of justice rushing towards you,
But you have no one, no one to go to.

For the life that they ached,
The change that they dreamt,
Is crushed by those who should protect you,
And you have no one, no one to go to.

The anguish of ancestry,
Dunked in present delirium;
These headlights aren't meant for those like you,
Since you have no one, no one to go to.

The tremble, the torment,
A nest of trauma,
But nobody listens to you,
And you have no one, no one to go to.

It was a peaceful afternoon until you came along,
The safe laughter, the innocence of joy
Are not meant for you,
Since you have no one, no one to go to.

A bang, some smoke, some maroon drops,
A dried-up well of hope.
The laws work proper, but not for you,
Since you have no one, no one to go to.

The handcuffs, the booking,
The black bars, the white walls,
The laws work proper, but not for you,
Since you have no one, no one to go to.

Though change is a stream of clear water
Leading you through the paths of dark,
You were told to not judge a book by its cover,
Unless that color is black."

This time, silence was mute as well. There were no words that could follow such a performance. We didn't want to stay num, but there was nothing to add. We couldn't clap either unless for the talent, and for it, Margaret raised her hands slowly, her claps even slower, and then they transformed into a frenetic energy of exaltation. After which, Margaret went and hugged her exquisite daughter.

Later in the evening, Luther performed a musical piece as well. He preferred the guitar and a more modern song I knew nothing about. Nonetheless, his performance was flawless. Of course, Margaret did not hesitate to share the perfect scores and grades of all her kids, as well as the drawings and paintings they mastered. I realized what she was doing when I held one of those papers in my hand. She was preparing them for the world. A cruel world made of only black or white, of only bad or good. She was giving them every kind of tool they could use to their advantage so they would never get trapped in the limited prospects of discrimination. They were supposed to be intelligent, talented, polite, educated, capable. To be better than everyone else, so they were never questioned. To bring to the table more than their peers; to rule instead of becoming followers. To succeed in everything they touched, thus success becoming an imminent occurrence. The forcibility of an unjust life and the excessive preparedness would transcend through the new generations to change the world's shackled views on equality. Margaret didn't change her path. She never stopped being an activist. She simply changed her strategy so her kids could continue to pave brick by brick the path of equality.

CHAPTER 16

THE required time passed by easier. Easier than I anticipated. It plunged me into a state of limbo where things were hanging in the air, but I was enjoying it for the first time. I began liking such an indifferent state. Around me floated an aura of detachment from which I effused great calm around my co-workers and even Gavin. The image of the female Buddha from my dream helped maintain my serenity. Until the day before the testing, when my lotus position and mudras were dispelled like a far-away dream. My Zen started to decentralize, and all kinds of malicious thoughts crawled up into my consciousness: *"What if I am not pregnant? What if I'll never be able to get pregnant? What if Gavin gives up on me and leaves? The amount of time, effort, money, pain, illusions will be all in vain."*

    My worlds of present and future got demolished under the impossible task I put myself in. It felt like I swam through the Atlantic but was drowning in the shallow waters of its shore. As if I climbed mount Everest and froze to death upon reaching its base. Or ran a marathon and fainted next to the finish line. The prize was near but still too far. A step too far. I crumbled under the pressure of a day. I couldn't sleep. How could I? There was nothing for the tendrils of sleep to attach to, only tension. It seemed easier to wander around the house in a vain attempt at soothing.

After two cups of tea, a midnight meal, and ice cream, slumber took hold of me. Not for long, though, as the electric zap of my unconscious' yearn woke me up like an internal alarm. It was past five a.m. I had plenty of time before work. I went into the bathroom and straight to the cabinet underneath the sink. Who had time to brush their teeth when stakes were so high? I took a test from the pink box, fought with the wrapper till all its particles fell on the ground. Quickly, I placed everything on the edge of the sink. I could barely hold my pee with all the excitement and fear. I took a small container designated for such situations, took a sample, placed the tip in it, and let it soak for a few seconds. Then I put it on the smooth surface on the back of the toilet. And waited. Each second ticked in my head as the internal clock from earlier revived under such intense scrutiny. Those two vertical lines of hope took an eternity to appear. The second one was more important than the first, but they both counted as one. My heart banged the beat of anticipation. There was no air coming from my nostrils, and my body, stiff as a board, didn't shift an inch from the hovering position it adopted earlier. My eyes were laser beams burning the stick with trepidation. If there were a tornado spiraling next to me, I would be still rooted to the ground like an oak tree with a hawk's eyes seizing my fate.

There they were, two magnificent cherry-stained marks. It took some time for all levels of processing to reach central systems, but when it did, the excitement took over me. I began twirling in my tiny bathroom. It didn't feel tiny anymore; it seemed like the taupe walls were expanding from the burst of my happiness. The hem of my midi dress was hugging my shins, giving me an extra layer of comfort. I laid on the floor, red-faced, out of breath, euphoria glimmering from every pore of my body. If I ever were to explain the definition of bliss, that was it. I rested for a few moments when I remembered the last time I was like this on the floor. A dark filter covered my eyes. What if I lose this baby too? Even with IVF, with such strong selection and accuracy.

"If I lose this one, I might as well die." I got up, shoulders drooping from sorrow.

"This time around, I will rest. I will not fret about work, my boss, or friends. I will take care of myself and allow my baby to attach to me properly." I went into the bedroom. The thick curtains did not spare enough light into the room, so I decided to take a nap.

I didn't tell Gavin I knew I was pregnant. I didn't want to plant any seeds of hope into his vulnerable soul. I kept it to myself. We stepped into the clinic holding hands. He held my hand when we sat in the waiting room. He also held my hand when the nurse had drawn blood from my vein.

"The results will be today in the afternoon or tomorrow morning at the latest," she said.

We looked at each other with a deep sigh of resignation. No matter what happened, we were together in this, till the last try. He held my hand when we drove home, and I laid down on the sofa. The phone rang very soon, and I picked up.

"Hello?" I asked.

"Hello, Mrs. Miller. I have your result concerning your pregnancy."

"Yes?" I glanced at Gavin and his eager eyes.

"Congratulations. You are pregnant. Your HCG is high."

"I'm pregnant, Gavin!" I screeched.

His face morphed into a surprise while his hands grabbed mine and took them to his face. He kissed them with fervor. I felt wrongly flattered as if I had won a prize I didn't earn. His head lay on my lap in an attempt to apprehend the miracle of life forging inside my belly. Tenderness filled us both. All of a sudden, a shiver rippled between my shoulder blades. A thought emerged which never crossed my mind before: *"From now on, there will never be just the two of us."* I smothered it quickly. Such a wonderful man deserved to be shared; his baby deserved to witness his magnificent wholeheartedness. I should only know happiness and excitement. Still, a tinge of sadness gripped my heart.

I smiled bittersweetly as I caressed the hair of the person I loved.

CHAPTER 17

I was pregnant, an irrefutable fact. I had been pregnant before, multiple times. I knew the feeling very well. The giddiness of knowing a secret larger than my life. The idyllic state of a perpetual mental levitation, where all things seemed mellow and imperturbable like a wheat field in a summer's day. Pregnancy always plunged me into a daydreamer's world in which the imageries I saw around me went through a sunny day's filter. Tiny spheres of light protruded from the lenses of my gaze; the exposure was ramped up to the max, even with the gloomy afternoons of Seattle. Life never felt as precious as when I was the one making it.

On the other side of the spectrum, though, there were the evenings when I couldn't find my place, fearing I would go to sleep and wake up with no baby. I would replay each of my miscarriages as if a horror movie, reminding me I hadn't crossed the bridge yet. I couldn't eat a morsel of food or even drink my favorite tea. Gavin would sense my unrest and try to smooth the spikes on my back one by one as if I was a threatened hedgehog. Only I knew how grateful I was to Gavin, a prince who couldn't sing a note in pitch but could soothe the strings of my dissonant heart.

This disheveled frame of mind persisted for the first two weeks of my pregnancy. By the third week, something new appeared on my incipient pregnancy journey, morning sickness. It wasn't a foreign concept to me the previous times, but it never manifested in such a rigorous way. Driving the car became an invitation for regurgitation. Any smell beyond baked bread provoked an episode of unease and nausea with a propensity towards future ejection. I tried the notoriously renowned pickles, which burned all the way up through my esophagus and straight into the toilet. I tried crackers, ginger candy, and even ice cream. Nothing worked. Sticking to water, lukewarm peppermint tea, and keeping my head busy showed the most results.

Interestingly, during my tumultuous intrapersonal ordeal with the toilet, no one at the office suspected anything. It seemed like all those veiled interrogations were irrelevant small talk, an escapism of boredom. It did not matter to me much as I feared the chance of being found out before I was ready. But it did occur to me how easy it was to hurl my morning breakfast one moment and the second to exchange documents with said curious subjects. The size of my bra had doubled, and my face looked green. Still, obscure was the mind that did not care to search.

As the weeks rolled on, my sensitivities worsened, and I wondered if it was harming the baby. When I researched it online, all articles said it was actually a good thing. The baby was connected to me to a great extent, and assurance should be my consolation. And it was. I welcomed every gag with an agreeable thought and planted crackers and water everywhere I deemed necessary.

When I reached the eighth week, my past dread came rolling back to haunt me. The risk of losing this one was the same as all others. My previous experiences didn't let me forget it. The eighth week felt like a week of loss. On Monday, I lost the first, on Tuesday the second, on Wednesday the third, on Thursday the fourth, and on Friday the fifth. Of course, it didn't happen in that order, but I assigned each a day for remembrance. Today was Saturday. I wore a pad just in case.

But Saturday passed and Sunday too. And when Monday arrived again, it was week nine. I reached my personal viability threshold. Also, I had my first visit with the obstetrician. I already knew what she would tell me, but nothing could prepare my ears for the heartbeat. Those solid and steady beats hidden in the depths of my uterus were such a bliss to hear. I could listen to those beats all day, every day, till I met them in person. The rhythm of life, beating in a duet with my own. What else would a mother want?

As my little raspberry grew into a grape, then a kumquat, fig, lime, it created in my mind an orchard of various trees where I could pick a fruit and stick my fangs into it since I was hungry all the time. The moment the great period of retch ended, a new one commenced: the great period of gluttony. It was undoubtedly for the baby's benefit, but I've never known desire till Gavin accidentally grabbed the larger piece of the pie. I began with small snacks here and there, besides the big meals. But by the time I reached week twelve, there wasn't a moment when I didn't chew on something. Gavin became the ultimate enabler to correct his beginner's mistake, providing me a copious amount of food. At a certain point, I wasn't sure what exactly grew faster, the baby or my belly fat. It was a tight competition. But if there ever was a reason to release the glutton in me, it was now, and I enjoyed every minute of it.

During one of her visits, my mother noticed my insatiable appetite, throwing suspicious comments about ovens and buns. I asked her to keep her opinion to herself, and when it would happen, she would be informed in due time. I knew the weeks would go by quickly, and I had to divulge my secret to the world, but the world didn't care if I succeeded or not. It was just insatiable for the gossip and new revelations worth a single conversation. I feared my precious secret would lose its integrity, being split into a million pieces of information spread out like a computer virus. I didn't want it to affect me, or worse, my baby. The evil eye seemed real when I had so much to lose.

Nonetheless, I had to confront the world with bravery and valor, as other previously arid territories did. I was stepping into the realm of fertility, potency, and prolificacy. I knew of a world of loss. How would a world of gain look like?

CHAPTER 18

AT the thirteenth week mark, we decided to share the news with the world. We told his dad first, to which he responded with an ecstatic reaction and tears of happiness. We then told his cousins, nieces, uncle, aunt, and others that I couldn't care to remember their place in the genealogical tree. And with every tell, I felt sadder and more restless. Sharing such a sanctified secret with everyone already felt like treason, but I felt less and less in control with every person initiated. If the world knew and something happened, I would be utterly devastated. Never in the past did I go so far into the tangible realm and divulge my innermost wishes.

It then came time to tell my mother. She planned to come over and impart everything that happened with Robert in the past few weeks. As if I had inquired. Her smug ignorance never ceased to impress and revolt me all at the same time. She was supposed to come over at seven p.m., but she was late, till the bell rang in intermittent chimes five times in a row. Mother always made herself blatantly aware of her presence. It was a given.

Mother entered the square entry, dressed like a mammoth. During May, the weather in Seattle usually reached seventy degrees, but somehow Svetlana still considered herself a citizen of Siberia and added layers of clothing to avoid the great frost. She placed her heavy blazer on the sofa, removed her purple chiffon scarf, and shoved it in one of the sleeves.

"Where's my tea?" she asked.

I invited her to the kitchen table, where we had some carrot cake and chocolate chip cookies—her favorites. Gavin liked to spoil his mother-in-law, so Svetlana had it pretty good with her favorite child. I didn't mind and, actually, supported it since my attempt at soothing my mother's presence was limited to a kettle of boiled water. She sat in one of the beige chairs, already sniffing something. My mother always had a nose for oddities, but most likely, it was my smile that made her suspicious. She stared at me as I was placing some plates on the table like a dutiful daughter. She then peered at Gavin, who was emanating bliss from all angles, and said, "Laura, you are pregnant."

Her shrewdness surprised me and made the plate slip from my hands which miraculously didn't crash.

"As a matter of fact, we are, Svetlana," said Gavin. "We wanted to make it a surprise, but I guess you took it a notch higher and surprised us."

"Oh, I know my daughter and son-in-law fairly well. It would be my mistake if I would miss it." She rose and hugged us with the power of her Russian ancestries.

"You could at least let us tell you ourselves," I said, eyeing the slice of cake, winking at me delectably.

"I waited too long to be able to control myself, Laura Tatiana. You know how I dreamt of a grandchild. How far along are you?"

"I am thirteen weeks." I mustered a proud smile.

"Oh, the hard part has passed. I remember when you lost the other baby. It was such a hard time. I was so worried. I didn't know–"

"Let's leave the past in the past, Svetlana." Gavin interrupted, and I sighed.

"Of course, the future is what matters." She pondered a bit and continued, "what do you think the gender is going to be?"

I brought myself to a more positive state of mind and said, "I don't care, be it a boy or girl, I will love the baby the same."

Gavin touched my back softly in support of my assertion.

"I think it's going to be a girl. It will be a bliss to have three generations of girls in the family," she said.

I kept my silence as any counterargument could bring frustration, and I wanted peace, not a goose's rattle.

"Did you break the news at your job?"

"Not yet, though I suspect Mr. Rogers might've figured it out."

"It's a pity that Mr. Rogers of yours is married. We could've made a great couple. I remember you telling me he likes strong liquor. I think we could share this hobby in wonderful ways."

"Mother! You and your fantasies. What about Robert?" I shifted uncomfortably in my chair.

"Oh, Robert is good. We had a nice dinner. He remarried." She took a sad sip of tea.

"We'll hope the new bride doesn't have a daughter he needs to discipline. He was too good at it."

"You might've not liked it back then, but it did help you build a strong character and certainly helped in your decision making," she said. "Did you know, Gavin, she made me divorce him? I had never seen Tati here being so decisive. So much fierceness like a true Russian woman."

"He knows, Mom," I said indignantly.

"I do know, Laura is a strong woman, and that is why I married her."

"Only for that?" I asked.

He tried to retouch his phrasing.

"One of the many reasons I married her."

"That's better." I looked at him as a piece of cake slipped into my mouth, dissipating sweetness through my throat.

***

As expected, it was unavoidable. I had to announce it at work and declare my maternity "retirement" to Mr. Rogers. He was quite thrilled. I think he was suspecting something, and now he felt relieved to share his joy with me. Shortly after, Mr. Rogers called his wife and told her the great news, which made her very happy since they could leave for their trip to the Bahamas earlier.

I avoided telling Cassandra and the team till our lunch on the domed terrace. I wanted to witness their reactions and see if anyone suspected it.

They were chatting like sparrows in a birdbath. I sat quietly next to Jasmine, prying on their conversation. It was about kids again. What else? I didn't know how to intervene. My heart began pounding like I was about to give a commencement speech.

"So, I told Russel, 'How about you give Abby a bath?' He stared at me and asked if he needed to watch a video first." She cracked a laugh.

"I have something to tell you," I chirped.

"And I said a few decades ago people didn't have how-to videos–"

"Hey everyone," Jasmine yelled, "Laura has something to tell us."

I glanced at her in gratitude and said, "I am pregnant."

A wave of excitement followed to an extent I couldn't have planned. All of them hugged me as if out of duty or maybe something more. I was stepping into their realm, the motherhood realm. They had to greet me officially and ceremoniously. Jasmine was the last to do it since it was out of sincerity rather than tribal tradition.

"How are you feeling?" asked Cassandra as she was taking a seat.

"I'm good. I'm fourteen weeks along," I said, trying to inform before they ask.

"Oh, I remember the time I was pregnant. It felt like I was the center of attention all the time. People would stop me on the street to congratulate me. I had the best gifts at my baby shower, which was a surprise. Russel was so thoughtful and attentive. Now, though we are parents to Abby, he seems like a stranger sometimes. Love does slip away after having kids."

We were waiting for her to finish her tirade. Cassandra went silent and, for a moment, I thought she was done, but no, she had more to add, "since Laura is with a bun in the oven, what about you, Jasmine? When are you going to share the big news?"

Surprised at the enormous amount of attention directed at her, Jasmine chose to take a sip of coffee before speaking, leaving everyone a bit more curious than intended.

"I'm not planning any time soon, if ever."

"What? You don't want kids?" Astonishment got ahold of Cassandra. "What about your boyfriend? Does he know you are against having kids?"

"I'm not against having kids," she said, pursing her lips. "I believe kids must be brought up in an adequate environment."

"And what is not adequate about your environment, Jasmine?" asked Cassandra.

"Nothing." Jasmine glanced at her hands, fearful she spoke too much.

"Exactly, you're too comfortable with your childless life. I was once like that, but I soon understood life without kids is meaningless. You will regret soon when your eggs dry up, and you won't be able to have kids anymore," Cassandra spoke as if it was a personal affront. She was pushing Jasmine towards areas of significant discomfort.

"I think everyone has a choice to make for themselves," I said as I grabbed Jasmine's hand. "We should respect anyone's wish regarding having kids or any personal choice for that matter."

"I worry about her." She gazed at me and reinstated her victim demeanor.

"So, Laura, what do you think you're going to have?" Marie asked.

"I hope a flower." I laughed.

"As in a girl?"

"No, just a flower, so it could brighten my life with its petals like the sun does with its rays."

Cassandra made a wry expression and probably concluded I was a bit weirder since I was bathing in pregnancy hormones.

CHAPTER 19

WE met my twentieth week with a visit to the clinic. It was time for the Great Ultrasound, a detailed report on every aspect of the baby's body and, of course, the gender reveal. My curiosity mixed with anxiety bubbled up to my throat, limiting my ability to speak. Gavin mirrored my feelings, so we went through the Ultra Sonography door in giddy silence, with hands locked and eyes focused on the future.

The ultrasound specialist poured warm jelly on my tummy and pointed to the screen above our heads. There was nothing much to see for the untrained eye, but when she showed us the arms, legs, fingers, toes, and organs, all became clear. Then came the gender reveal. The lady asked if we wanted to know the gender. We chose from the beginning to keep the gender a mystery, but my curiosity got the better of me.

"I think it's a boy, but let me take a better look," she said.

Our eyes were glued to the monitor, not even blinking.

"Oh, wait, it's a girl. She moved, and I could see her clearly. Congratulations!"

Everything she said after disappeared from my spectrum of intake. I only saw my little girl playing in a meadow with bunnies and deer and laughter and me. Gavin couldn't hold his tears while mine were still lingering at the corner of my eyes. We arrived home floating on a giant cloud of reverie. I didn't even remember when I got home, but I remembered the wonderful dream I had that night—me and my little girl running in a meadow towards each other into an embrace of completion.

After our appointment, Gavin turned into a doting father to his unborn daughter. He would prevent any possibility of me tripping by giving me no other choice than to weave my arm around his. At any point, if I would hiccup any discomfort, he was there placing a pillow under my head, shoulders, or feet. Any meal, any culinary whim, was delivered to my growing belly. We even went on a few shopping trips for our baby girl. He picked the most ruffled, chiffon pink dresses he could find. I knew he wanted to be a father but never suspected him of an inclination towards a girl. Would she be a daddy's girl? We would wait and see, for I would not surrender easily.

Cassandra's experience did actualize with mine. Indeed, I was the center of everyone's attention, not only around my acquaintances but strangers, as well. When we were on a walk together, many would approach and congratulate us. Afterward, Gavin would walk like a rooster with his chest elevated, brimming with pride. His excitement honored me as I finally could give him something he yearned tacitly for so long. I got a glimpse of his utmost blissfulness, the pinnacle of his aspirations actualized in the conception of life. Gavin paid a great price to be with me and stuck close even when the ground seemed to crumble underneath. The feeling of silence didn't suffocate him anymore. He could yell to the trees, to the mountains, to the sky that he did it. He would become a father. He could boast to lake Washington about his plans to bring his daughter to play next to its shimmering surface. He could tell other dads on the street he was about to stroll with his daughter alongside them in a few months. It was a reasonable wish for him to have as he deserved as much as I did the enjoyment of parenthood in the light of surrounding reality.

Most of the attention, though, was attributed to me. It was a spotlight I yearned for years on end, and I let myself indulge in it with absolution. I let myself feel deserving of it. I deserved the helping hands, the congratulatory remarks, the aura of recognition. I paid my price: it went beyond the banknote, beyond the sorrow, beyond what I thought I could endure. But it was when I got the laurels that I could finally rejoice and enjoy.

My mother didn't let herself miss out on the excitement, either. Her visits increased, her opinions on how I should take care of myself had doubled, and all she could talk about with Gavin was, in fact, the baby, who would she resemble, and what name would be a good choice. As if they would ever be given the privilege to name my baby girl? Naïve fools.

As such conversations took place at our house, I felt the urge to find refuge at Margaret's. At least, I knew she wouldn't pretend to control all elements of my pregnancy and more. The second day, I walked through the metallic gate at Margaret's nursery with my belly visibly protruding. As the owner of such an adorable belly, I could not hide it, so the blouse was usually tight. Harriet came running towards me to help carry my bag. I didn't expect to see her. Next to her, a bit further away, were Luther and Rosa. It was on their mother's order to assist me in any way possible, so I didn't protest much. They were not related to me, but I felt part of their family seeing them rushing towards me. The day was hot, and Margaret didn't want me to flop like a pancake, so she sent me into her doll-like house till she was done with the afternoons' work. Her kids came along with me. I took a seat on the far-left side of the sofa, expecting they would follow suit, which they did but only for five minutes. Luther went to fetch some lemonade, Harriet went to bring some Turkish delights, and Rosa rushed to help their mom.

As solitude descended, I noticed the four o'clock streams of light sneaking through the horizontal blinds into the dusty chandelier's glass beads. Through them, the sun bunnies were born.

Sun bunnies or *solnechnyj zaichiki*, as my mother would call them, were those little sunspots reflecting on the walls. Since there were multiple cuts on the glass, the sun bunnies were multicolored. A rainbow of magnificence in which I could lose myself for hours. Nothing could fascinate me more. It was an intricate method of bringing a bit of refraction from the sun's elaborate adornment into a human's dwelling. The same was inside me; the light beaming from my heart went straight to my belly and lightened my whole existence. My daydreaming was cut short as the oldest brought a glass of lemonade, and the noise from the other two returned as if it had never left. Margaret joined us with her smoldering hot coffee in her hands.

"How is the mother-to-be feeling?"

"Better than ever," I said, smiling in rays.

"Your belly is growing so well. I always love to touch pregnant bellies. May I?"

"Be my guest."

She didn't hurry to touch me. Time was necessary to cherish life's unfolding. When her hand lowered, pressing delicately on my belly, I felt the moisture of her fingers and the callouses underneath. Her whole demeanor transcended in front of me. She looked so motherly as if the door of a hidden passage had opened, and Margaret had lowered her Spartan attire. She probably remembered her own memories, maybe those of her own kids or her husband. I couldn't be more delighted to witness such vulnerability from Margaret. Her micro-expressions would intermingle between them, from awe and delight to sadness and anguish, to melancholy and forlornness and again to happiness. I loved observing how her emotions betrayed her gilded guard. She took her hand faster than intended and glanced at me, saying:

"She will be a wonderful girl. Though you will not always relish in happiness, it will make you a better person and a good mother."

"Aren't all kids supposed to be like that? Sacrificial happiness?"

"When we are born, we do not choose our parents, but the lessons shared by them will be most useful for us in the future. The same happens with our children. We do not choose our children like we do not choose our parents. They are given to us for the sole purpose of transformation. Your sacrifice might not resemble other mothers' fate since some bare a branch of the chokecherry tree on their backs, but in the end, all of it will transform into a purpose far greater than oneself." She placed her cup on the end table and fetched the younger one. As she ruffled his hair, she continued, "you might not like some of it. But all of it will be necessary. A sacred transformation."

Again, Margaret spoke in riddles. Wasn't there space for a more straightforward text? Did it have to be so convoluted I could never connect the dots? I knew there would be a transformation the moment I chose to have a baby. The only transformation waiting to happen would be my love's exponential growth.

I left the nursery with a weird question mark imprinted on my heart and warmth from her palm imprinted on my belly.

CHAPTER 20

ONE afternoon, as I was enjoying my pregnant state, I began watching a competition show about people rolling on a hill trying to catch a wheel of cheese. At the same time, I was attempting, for the first time, to eat ice cream with the tub on my belly. As the bits of vanilla ice cream melted in my mouth and slipped down my throat, my only thought was, why would anyone roll cheese off a steep hill? I planned on delving into other mysteries of the human mind, but my phone rang. It was Jasmine.

"Hi, Laura." Her voice icy.

"What's wrong?" I asked.

"I… I need to ask you something," she said, tripping on her words.

"Is it serious?"

"No, no. It's not serious. I only need to talk to someone."

I could hear she was in distress.

"Okay, where do you need me to come?"

"At a Mexican diner in Seattle, at six p.m., I'll send you the address."

"Okay, I'll be there."

I hung up, weirded out but curious.

***

When I arrived at the diner, I could see Jasmine inside, already sitting at the table. Her head, covered with a cap, was turned to the side away from the window. I entered at a faster pace and soon was accompanied by a hostess to the respective table.

"Jasmine, hi. How's everything?" I chirped.

"Hi, Laura," she said while raising her head. I stopped breathing for a bit when I saw the swelling in her right eye. Then I trailed all the unusual tracks displayed across her face and neck. There were bruises, cuts, bumps of different sizes. She barely could open her mouth. I couldn't believe such a beautiful face could get distorted in such a cruel way.

"What happened?"

"I fell." She tried to form a smile.

"You fell? From where?"

"I fell from… Actually, no, I didn't fall, and that is why I'm here to talk to you. It was Brandon, my boyfriend. He beat me up. And… and it's not the first time." Her chin trembled at the last words.

Jasmine rushed to say everything she intended, in case she might change her mind: about the fairy-like beginnings when he behaved like a gentleman; about the time when he had his first sip of whiskey after a long time of abstinence; about the night when they had a fight, and he blamed Jasmine for his relapse; about the first slap, the first push, the first kick, the first fist; about the excuses, the promises, the perfect weeks of sobriety and the singular nights of terror. I kept listening even when Jasmine went silent, in case there was something more to add. But she was waiting for my reaction. Was it going to be judgmental? Ignorant? Since she didn't know, I've lived once with a despicable ogre and had learned the ropes of harsh life under domestic violence.

"Did you tell anyone else?" I asked.

"No. Only you," she answered, a bit confused by my response.

"How much do you love him?"

"I love him a lot, and I was willing to forgive him again, but this time, he beat me when he was sober." Her words drowning in tears.

"You understand him assaulting you when he is drunk is not a good reason either. There is never a good reason. Did he apologize afterward, saying he will never do it again?"

She nodded.

"And every time you forgave him?"

She nodded again.

"You realize your life could be in danger. One wrong move and your lifeless body will be the responsibility of prosecutors."

We stayed in silence for a bit. I saw a waiter coming towards us; I grabbed Jasmine's hand and said, "Let's get some drinks. For you, something harder."

With the tea warming my palm, I once again gazed at Jasmine's face. She still emanated the allure of a goddess; no brute could take that away from her. She also calmed down a bit.

"What should I do?" she asked.

"A restraining order could help. We'll have to go to the police. Fill up some paperwork. Are you ready to move to the next step?"

"Yes, I am. I am done living in fear."

As I comforted her, Jasmine's eyes rose above my head, and terror began to fill her gaze. The air turned ominous as a shadow darkened my peripherals. Turning around, I saw a mammoth of a man with bulging muscles. A red shirt was there for supposed decency, but with bulges everywhere, it looked painted on. His veins resembled snakes crawling under his skin throughout the whole body. Now I understood her fear. As he approached her, his cologne forced us deeper into his presence. Only then, I saw the discrepancy between his demeaning figure and the puppy eyes show he was portraying.

"Jazz, I searched all over for you. I was so worried," he said, kissing her bruised cheek sloppily.

My disgust drew his attention.

"And who is this?" he asked.

"This is Laura, my co-worker. Laura, this is Brandon." Jasmine fidgeted.

"Hi, nice to meet you." I expanded my arm for a handshake he reciprocated.

"Congrats." He pointed at my belly. "Jasmine and I are also thinking of having a baby in the future."

I looked at her swallowing knots like a sacrificial lamb and mustered a thank you.

"Well, we're gonna go since it seems you are done with your little meetup."

I noticed his grin and the shades of pale Jasmine exuded.

"Actually, we are not done. I'm sure you would be nice enough to let us spend a bit more time. We haven't finished our talk."

"I think you can always find time at work to finish your nonsense." He grabbed Jasmine's arm.

"No." I tugged at her other arm. "Jasmine will stay with me. And it would be a good idea to respect our wishes. You wouldn't want to bring the whole diner's attention while maltreating two women, one of which is heavily bruised and the other pregnant."

He glared at me, nostrils aflare, ready to curse the daylights out of me. Then Jasmine grabbed his hand and pleaded, "how about I stay a bit more, and we can talk tomorrow."

"Promise?"

She nodded, knowing at least during that night, she would be okay.

We stayed in the diner for a few more hours, glancing at the wetness of the outside street. Strangely, we didn't talk about Brandon, though I wanted to do so. Jasmine, instead, chose to focus on my baby and me. When we were done, she helped me get up and hugged me. I asked her to text me when she arrived home, then each of us went our way.

I told Gavin all about the encounter at home, but his reaction was nothing I'd expected.

"Are you out of your mind?" His tone a roar.

I sat on the sofa in the living room, trying to find words to explain myself.

"You meet with Jasmine to talk and then try to protect her from her six-foot violent boyfriend? How far do you need to go to put yourself and the baby in danger?"

I didn't answer, as I was still at a loss for words.

"Listen, I understand you wanted to help your friend, but this time for us is the most crucial. What if you lose the baby and will never be able to have another?"

His words poked at a scar, multiple scars.

"I couldn't stay idle. She was in physical and emotional pain. Would you stay there and do nothing?"

He sat on the sofa, gazing at me with some sort of new sense of admiration.

"Come, let's get you to sleep."

***

Two days had passed since my talk with Jasmine. She never called. I wrote a few texts, but no answer. I became agitated as I didn't know any of the events that happened afterward, and my imagination leaned towards the worst. As I was in the garden, watering my roses and trimming some boxwood bushes, my phone kept buzzing on the patio table. The only benefit of living in a small house was the short path I needed to reach any destination point. I wobbled my feet towards the table. It was Jasmine. I answered with an expectant rush:

"Hi, Laura..." Her voice faint.

"Hi. I was worried about you. How are you? Did you decide on anything we've talked about then?"

"I... Well... I decided to give Brandon another chance."

"What?" I couldn't believe my ears. "Why?"

"He was really nice this time. He listened to all my issues and worries. And he promised he will never do it again."

"I hope you understand he's manipulating you, Jasmine."

"I think it was a mistake to involve you in any of this."

"I completely agree. What would be the point if there wouldn't be a difference?"

She didn't say anything, and I immediately regretted my words.

"I didn't mean to be rude," I said with precaution, "I just want you to take the time and reevaluate things. Maybe next time, you will choose yourself and find the strength to move away from this situation."

"I will. I will think about it, Laura. Thank you," she said with a doubtful tinge in her tone.

I sat on the patio chair, exhausted from the talk. I didn't understand how people attached themselves to others as if they didn't have a choice. There was always a choice. I realized it was dangerous to leave in her case, but wasn't it more dangerous to stay?

This was why I didn't want to have any friends. They entangled you in messy affairs with no easy solutions in sight. I wanted to help, but what more could I do? I decided to distance myself from Jasmine, at least till the baby was born.

My soul hurt for her, but I had to focus on Gavin and the baby.

CHAPTER 21

THE second trimester flew by like my twenties, unnoticed and unappreciated. I became aware of it when the third trimester hit me with joint pains, fake contractions, and sausage limbs. And as the days passed through my thirty-sixth week, I began contemplating a potential early labor. I knew it was the worst thing to wish for, but my pelvis felt like cartilage, risking breakage with every step. I barely could see my feet, and bending seemed like an achievement. My nose borrowed its shape from a fat witch with newly added features like a mustache and chin hair. When I typed on my phone with inflated fingers, I always hit two keys which made me throw the phone in anger and stick to calling directly. Peeing every five minutes was fine during the day, but I had moments of falling asleep right on the seat at night, dreaming of my previous body.

During this delightful time in my life, Gavin made me aware of the baby shower my co-workers were organizing in secret. It was an unexpected turn of events as I wasn't planning on having one, though they would probably have to carry me on a stretcher if they were to wait another week. Of course, Gavin couldn't hold off on the secret. He knew how much I hated being taken aback, so I had to rehearse my surprised face in the mirror, and with my recent facial mutations, I looked like a bloated Munch's Scream. Gavin reassured me that my face acquired a rather juvenile plump, and I should relish in it as long as I could. Skeptic wrinkles contoured my face at his words, but I chose to focus on other more controllable things like my outfit for said baby shower.

The Sunday afternoon's weather was decent though still chilly. I was supposedly invited over to Cassandra's for some decaf coffee and scones. I wore a balloon-like dress in forest green, though the fashion side lost its appeal compared to the dinosaur egg I had to carry in front. I clawed myself and the egg out of the car with my newly practiced moves. With a hand to the back, I waddled in a two-beat rhythm to the few steps left from the pinpointed doorbell.

The ding-dong rang as if it came straight from London's Big Ben. It made me expect a butler to open the door. But no, it was only Cassandra. The moment I laid eyes on her, I immediately straightened my back, losing sight of all my aches. She invited me in. I obliged when suddenly I got screamed at by a flock of bleating ladies hiding behind a wall and a couch.

I knew it was my cue:

"Oh, my goodness, guys. I never could've guessed it!" I stepped inside, dinosaur egg first while giving myself notes on paring down my reaction. Her house had a roundabout planning, where the living room, dining room, kitchen, and den could be accessed in a circle. The bedrooms were upstairs, which I never got to see, but downstairs was decorated poorly in a boho style with some eclectic additions. Cassandra, most likely, was the decorator, and, most likely, her husband's opinion wasn't taken into consideration.

"We planned it a month ago, but it was difficult to get all the girls together at the same time."

"Good thing you found the time before I gave birth." I injected some sarcasm but quickly reassessed. "I appreciate it."

With trembling hands, Jasmine adorned me with a sash and an itchy "Mother To Be" crown. Still feeling guilty about our conversation, she tried her best to make me comfortable, showing

Casandra's house as if hers and, finally, inviting me to the dining table. There were three types of salads, deviled eggs, and fish—my kind of food. The hunger monster in me awakened, and I vanished from the social group for a good twenty minutes, devouring my food in a corner. Cassandra came over and asked if I wanted anything to drink, but the food bulge in my cheek didn't let me speak.

"Okay." She smiled. "Let me know if you want anything."

I smiled back and continued the feast. After the famish had been satiated, a few co-workers I knew only visually sat next to me and opened a conversation.

"So, how far along are you?" asked a skinny lady with bleached blonde hair.

"I'm almost thirty-seven, but I wish my labor would come soon," I said.

"Clearly, it would be too soon. I had my boy at thirty-seven, but I wish I could've reached the forty-week mark," said a lady with thick eyeglasses.

"Why? Isn't the thirty-seven week a viable threshold to reach?"

"Yeah, but they say it's best to give the baby time to grow in the uterus." The blonde hid her burnt tresses behind her ear. "Mine stayed with me for forty-two, they said I should do a C-section, but I refused."

"Why? Isn't a C-section a safe way to have your baby?"

"Clearly, you must be kidding me. C-section is the worst. Your baby will absorb all those chemicals from the epidural. You want to have your baby in the most natural way possible." The lady with glasses blinked at me with her frog-ish eyes as if I committed treason.

"I even thought about a doula, but my husband insisted on a hospital birth. Can you imagine giving birth at home in a calm environment by the candle lights with your close ones next to you?

Oh, if I could've had that experience." The blonde gazed longingly at her beverage.

"But isn't it a bit dangerous?" I asked.

"Well, you get approval from your obstetrician, clearly. If they deem it safe, then it should be. But what do they know? I know my baby. I'm his mother, and mothers know best," said the glasses lady.

"I'd rather be with my family in a hospital. What if something unexpected happens, and you could lose the baby?" I said.

"Those are rare occurrences; women had given birth at home for centuries. There's nothing new or strange about it," said the blonde.

"Wasn't there a statistical report about maternal deaths declining to up to ninety-nine percent in the past century? Mostly due to babies being born in hospitals?" I shot a stare at the blonde delusion.

Animosity hit the stratum. Nerves began to crack like thunder.

"Babies love being born naturally, clearly," the spectacled mother frog croaked.

"I think babies love being born. Alive," I said.

"Don't tell me you are one of those lazy moms who want to skip the hard parts of motherhood. Are you also going to formula feed your baby?" Sarcasm appeared in her optically deviated eyes.

"When I get to that point, I'll see, there are many factors to motherhood. There is no specific trope we are all supposed to walk," I said.

They rose from the table, snickering and stirring the straws in their peachy drink.

"I guess she will have a lot of fun once the baby is born since she's going to have a babysitter instead of being a mother," said the blonde.

"Clearly."

They strutted away in a cheerful mood and a well-formed opinion about my position on motherhood. I chose to rule them out of my mind and focus on other people and, of course, the Tetris arrangement of my presents.

First, though, there were the games. Measuring the belly game was decent, but the chocolate in the diaper game repulsed me and potentially disrupted my digestive process. Finally, after hours of meandering around the already known corners of the house, the time for the cake was announced. The chocolate cake soothed my unsettled stomach. But I didn't have time to contemplate on it for too long since I was invited on the throne, a chair with a white wedding cover-up and a pink satin ribbon tied around the back. The presents in front of me awaited eagerly for my unwrapping.

I first opened Casandra's gift. There were funny pacifiers with giant teeth and mustaches, a few cute dresses, and, to my astonishment, a screwdriver set and packs of variously sized batteries. I couldn't understand her intentions. Were these for Gavin? I looked at her questionably.

"Are these for the baby?"

Her horse's laughter resounded across the room.

"When you have your baby, you will understand."

Cassandra always had to stand out as an eyesore. Ignore and deflect. Ignore and deflect.

"Thank you, Cassandra. When I get there, I'll let you know."

Next, I took a box with purple wrapping and a white bow. Jasmine said it was from her. I opened it in rushed curiosity. Besides the cute dresses, socks, and bottles, there lay a plush sunflower with the most adorable face. I didn't know why, but emotions got ahold of me. I glanced at Jasmine; she had the same sweet, warm smile I remembered.

"I'll give this flower to my baby girl, so she can be reminded of my love for her," I said. I couldn't help but hug Jasmine, and she responded in her usual generous way.

The evening went on in endless delight. It felt like Christmas, but I was the only one receiving gifts. Besides the egregious amount of clothes, I got multiple gadgets for my nipples, nursing blouses, breastfeeding pillows, travel crib, bottles, rattle toys, blankets, bassinet, noise machine, baby bathtub, bibs. And these were the things I could remember on top of my head. Besides the basic car seat, stroller, crib, mattress, and diapers, I never realized how much stuff one might need to care for a baby.

I arrived home feeling like I'd won the future mom lottery. Gavin brought the accumulated fortune from the car while I was resting my feet on the ottoman. I dozed off thinking about what potential detriment could an epidural bring to the baby.

CHAPTER 22

ON the first day of my fortieth week, November nineteenth, I felt celebratory. As I finally reached the long-awaited milestone, I assumed my contractions would start any minute. Every time I remembered, I would give myself a quick checkup to assess any pain but to no avail. The baby was still nestling inside my belly, with no plans of coming out.

Truth be told, I didn't quite know how contractions felt. I only knew they had to hurt in an "I cannot speak" kind of way. And let me tell you, I could speak. Oh, how well I could speak. I talked to my mom the whole day over the phone, and in the evening, I uttered an overflow of nothing-in-particular to Gavin. My excitement was bubbling up in the form of words, ready to gush into any willing ear.

The baby moved a lot the past week, leaving me with little to no sleep. But the exhilaration of finally meeting my baby girl shot spikes of shivers through my spine. I kept myself busy nesting and reorganizing the nursery. I couldn't decide how to decorate the nursery for the longest time until it was almost too late. Gavin insisted we make do with what we have and curb down my perfectionism. I had my Pinterest board filled with hundreds of pictures I would have loved to implement, but I settled on one with an easier execution since my capabilities were limited, and it fell on Gavin to finish my biding. He, first, focused on painting her room the color I wanted, a diffused olive green with sunflower wallpaper for an accent wall. After, we hung canvases on the wall, each of them brimming with daisies, buttercups, and cornflowers. The crib, the dresser, and the fluffy rug were white to maximize the effect of the colors. It had the feel of a sunflower field bathed in light, just in a greenhouse version fitting our home. It would be our little retreat of bonding for me, Gavin, and our little girl.

We couldn't decide on a name since no name seemed to fit the image in my head. So, I took it upon myself to wait till after she was born and give her a proper name the moment I saw her. Everything else was ready. The hospital bags like soldiers ready for action were aligned next to the entry door: the car seat (safest I could find on the market), my two-size-larger slippers, and a leather duffel bag so full it was ready to pop just like me.

Before, this trip could only exist in my imagination: how Gavin would take my hand, the bag on his shoulder, and the car seat in his hand, and we would walk out this door as two content members of a family and come back as an accomplished family of three. But the days passed with no significant changes except for the rainy, cold weather. While physically, it got worse. I was in so much discomfort that my ability to think was reduced to figuring ways to ease my pain. The aches grew so intense I could only sit or lay on mountains of pillows and only in intervals of an hour. But there were no contractions, except for an occasional pressure in my lower back. There was nothing worth screaming about. Mother would call me every few hours to ask if my water broke. After several calls, my patience couldn't take it. I told her the only thing breaking would be my phone if she called again and hung up. My mood got a little cheerier after my conversation, so I went to Gavin, who was making dinner, and asked, "maybe something is wrong? Why doesn't she want to come out?"

"You know, forty weeks is just a number. When the baby is ready, it will happen."

"You always have the right answers, Gavin. How could I contradict such a statement?"

"There is no way. I'm that perfect. Now turn around, lay on the sofa, and I will bring dinner and ice cream." He turned my pouty posture around and guided me to the sofa. As I laid on my side, he gave a few rubs to my gargantuan feet and left towards the savory smell brewing in the kitchen.

In my mind, though, setting aside my nagging bouts of pain, I couldn't stop ruminating about all potential scenarios leading to my labor. Could this be an ominous sign? It didn't feel like it. Was there a reason to worry? The doctor said it was expected. So, I didn't have to, but I did, and no sane arguments could diminish it.

At night, I dreamt of the glistening meadow again, my little girl at seven years old, running towards me. I almost reached her and the happiness she was exuding when, suddenly, the colors around us turned somber. The sky turned into menacing darkness, moving fast to cover any light. All the surrounding greeneries drooped as if a dry storm desiccated all their moisture. The meadow turned into a place where all its life was sucked out of it. As she was running oblivious towards me, she fell into a ditch where underground vines of roots began spreading around her. I ran to my little girl, but she was already engulfed in the vines. When I rolled her over, she was suffocating, with a creeping root wrapped around her throat and body, dragging her into the ground. Her face had an aubergine hue of death; the roots spreading on her arms resembled black veins. Her eyes were closed till the moment I tried to free her, then she looked at me with terrorizing intent. I couldn't believe what I saw in her eyes. Instead of pupils, there were tops of wells filled with black water; I could see my reflection in its ripples. The water began to overflow to the eye's edges and then onto her cheeks, disappearing into the root vines digging into her neck. The dark, muddy tears resembled streams of blackness. I drew my breath back, startled from the sight.

"Are you okay, my baby? How can I help you?"

"Hold my hand, Mommy." Her voice trembled like a ghost.

I took her hand already submerged in soil, mud spilling from her nails, and held on to it as hard as I could.

"I am here for you, honey."

She smiled wryly, sighed a deep breath as if last, and opened her mouth from where flew a dozen giant white butterflies tied with a string by their hind leg. In a strive to free themselves, their flutter became manic and disoriented. They began to hit one another, ripping their wings apart and dying one by one.

I woke up, wet hair from all the sweat. I hardly had time to analyze my dream when a wave of pain hit me in the lower back as if a hydraulic press pushed on my pelvic area. I couldn't move, only yell.

Gavin, in a sleepy frenzy, got up and turned on the light. Together we saw the bed. It was drenched.

"I think our baby girl is ready." He said, rubbing his eyes.

My dream still perturbed me, so I could not grasp how the colossal change we so eagerly awaited just began rolling. He helped me out of bed, helped me put a dress on, and walked baby steps alongside me to the door. Since the pain subsided, I had time to realize once more the experience I thought would never come true: Me, Gavin, the yet-to-be-filled car seat waiting in pristine calmness at the door. But we didn't exit the house holding hands. Gavin went and put all our things in the car, as there were too many, warmed it for me as it was a freezing cold night and then, came to the entrance, gave me his prince's hand and out we went together.

CHAPTER 23

THE car trip, though, was nothing I could expect. The pain grew more extensive and more frequent as if an arrow was shot through my body. It would hold me in a straight line for a bit, and after, it would go back to normal as if nothing had happened. My body would get surprised each time, like a torturous game of peekaboo. The road was clear as it was two a.m. It took Gavin less than thirty minutes to get there, but I could feel every bump, turn, and stop sign along the way.

Once there, we were taken to a room where the nurses measured my blood pressure and temperature. They also checked how much I was dilated. It was six centimeters and almost ready for the transition phase. Then, we were transferred to a room, where I was connected to all kinds of wires. All seemed fine. Till the tidal wave of pain would hit, then we had to perform our practiced breathing technique from our birthing classes. Gavin's exaggerated facial expressions were comical, but the grips of agony wouldn't let me laugh.

With the epidural in place, hours flowed at a swifter pace. After the initial alertness, Gavin and I turned towards other more interesting occupations: magazines, books, and ultimately our phones. I texted Mom but got no reply. Most likely, she was snoring while having a dream about a middle-aged prince sweeping her off her feet. A few times during the night, nurses came in and verified my progress but didn't comment on it. At sunrise, Gavin and I were in deep slumber though not for long as my doctor came in to see how I was doing. He asserted I was close but not there yet and went on his merry way. Mother came as quickly as she received the message, which was around ten in the morning, bringing with her a new wave of excitement and fret. But the whole day had passed in disappointing inertia, and our expectations quickly dulled into listlessness and boredom.

The only question poking at my heart was if my water broke almost a day ago, wouldn't it be detrimental to the baby? The nurse said it was completely normal and, in any case, there would be the possibility of a C-section. I completely forgot about it, since for me, there was only one way to produce a child, to give birth myself. I had to do it myself. I asked how they could help with quickening the process of labor. Apparently, I already was on Pitocin, and my contractions were weaker than before.

***

A new doctor came in late that night and announced what seemed to be the worst outcome of my plans.

"Mrs. Miller, you've been in labor for more than twenty hours. Your amniotic fluid has been released for some time. It's best to move to the next option and perform an emergency C-section," she said with a stoic face.

"No. I want a natural birth. It's what I came here to do, to give birth, not for an extraction."

"It's not what you or I want," she said, "it's what the baby needs. But, at your request, I will give you more time."

Biting on my words, I said nothing. Only Gavin was fussing around and supplementing me with water from the gifted maternity carafe. Once more, after two hours, the doctor assessed my exposed region, inspected it, and decided on a C-section without much preliminary thought. I was transported to the O.R. and laid on the operating table with a cloth screen at my waist. Still on epidural, I mainly felt pressure and guilt for surrendering. With my hand hidden in his, I finally glanced at Gavin. His worry was flushing on his face under the contrasting shadows of the operating room. I smiled to alleviate some of it. He smiled back but kept his mouth closed.

When I turned my head towards the doctors, a viscous entity appeared before my eyes. The nurses wrapped her in a white blanket and began cleaning her, but there was no sound. The room fell silent. Everyone was waiting for her. A flood with unwanted thoughts began flowing in my mind; what if she was stillborn?

The nurse was doing something to her when an undeniable raspy cry spread across the room. Gavin looked confused about what was happening in the room. He probably wanted to cry and smile and worry and jump from euphoria all at the same time. But he couldn't choose, so instead, he stood there in a stupor and waited his turn to hold the baby. He witnessed how the nurses wiped our precious gooey mass of happiness, then laid her on me. A new feeling overwhelmed me, a love I couldn't comprehend or grasp. My tears rolled over to her confused cheeks, tears bonding us forever. It was here and now, me and her in our little cosmos of love.

"My baby is here," I whispered to myself.

The way she lay on my chest, I couldn't see her, but I could feel her, this new presence, this new entity who moments ago was part of me. I heard her first breaths of life, her first little wiggles. She smelled like a snowdrop's bloom, with tiny nails scratching at my skin. Gliding my fingers across her back for the first time felt like touching the wing of a butterfly, so frail, so ethereal. I could spend hours feeling her presence, a sweet intoxication. She was my baby. I struggled to have one for so long, and finally, she was here forever in my life.

My mother and Gavin were hovering over me to take a better glimpse at the baby.

"She's so beautiful, Laura. My baby has made a baby. I cannot imagine this," my mother said, wiping an invisible tear.

"Honey, she's perfect. With all the things you've been through, it was worth it in the end. I'm so proud of you," the new father said.

I would have felt prouder if it wasn't for the massive incision across my belly being stitched at that moment. I wished for a normal, natural birth, but at least I got a healthy baby. As I felt anxious about this situation, my mother and Gavin were in a different dimension, preoccupied only with the baby. Gavin, with wonky movements, took her into his arms so I could see her better. She was so small her whole body fit into his palms, like a living doll. With almond-shaped eyes in the color of the deep ocean, her irises left almost no white to be seen. Her nose was borrowed from a baby squirrel's; her mouth emulated a hatchling's beak; she only needed chubby cheeks for perfection, which we would be working on. She gazed straight into my eyes but didn't acknowledge me; it was the most adorable staring contest. She lost the competition going straight to sleep.

"I want to choose a name, Gavin," I said.

"Now?"

"Yes, now that I've seen her, I know her name." I paused, giving myself time to think; my mother and Gavin were in breathless awaiting. "I always wanted a flower for a name. Violet or Lily would work great, but Marigold fits her just right as she is my golden flower. What do you think, Gavin?"

"Perfect name for a perfect daughter." Plenitude in his words.

Meanwhile, the doctor was still stitching me and doing a painstakingly good job at it. Though it seemed odd for him to work so long. When he was done, I asked Gavin to let me sleep, for I wanted to enjoy Marigold in full power. He agreed, and I drifted into a victorious slumber.

CHAPTER 24

EYES half-opened. Viscous substance separating from my eyelids. A misty semblance of Gavin with my infant suckling in his arms. My mother's somber presence. The doctors, nurses speaking. Distress shadowing their faces. A stinging smell of antiseptic. My lips, a tectonic fissure in a desert. Instead of words, an echo of silence. Hospital bed. A bassinet. Dismal walls. A forgotten swaying chair. A solitary couch. My body cumbersome and heavy like a magnet clinging tenaciously to the bed. Moving, an audacious wish. Predestined disappointment. Gavin's voice cutting through the mist.

"How long will she be like this, doctor?"

Doctor mumbling… "Antibiotics."

Antibiotics? An exhausting feeling sneaking around my eyes. Sleep. An infant's cry. My baby. Marigold. Things moving astray. Echo of silence. Gavin. Heavy eyelids… My baby…

CHAPTER 25

THE sun's morning rays caressed my face and then blinded me. The smell of left-over food woke my nostrils and, respectively, my stomach. I looked around. I was in the same room I got admitted. There was no one except my mom. She was reading her usual salacious novels. *"Right after I give birth, mom, really?"* I would have told her all my thoughts about her hobby, but my mouth needed some moisture. She saw me fidget and rose in excitement.

"Laura, you're awake! Let me bring you some water."

Finally, she figured something out without me telling her. She raised a part of the bed with the help of a button, which she seemed unusually keen at, and gave me a sip of the best water I had ever tasted. Like a mountain stream, it trickled along my throat, opening the gateway to my vocal cords.

"What's happening? Why are you here? Where's my baby? Gavin?"

"Thank goodness, you're back to your old self."

"What do you mean? I only took a nap."

"Laura, you've been out for a week. The last two days, you would wake up here and there but not completely."

"What do you mean? Why didn't you wake me up? I might feel tired since my body went through major surgery, but I am a mother now. I must take care of my child." I raised my body from the bed to notice a catheter attached to me.

"You had a severe case of sepsis, Laura. The doctors said it was because the C-Section was performed so late. We were afraid we were going to lose you. Good thing Gavin noticed you were turning blue and shaking in your sleep."

"But I feel good."

"It was the fast treatment that helped kill off the infection."

"Who took care of Marigold?"

"I did, and Gavin. He took care of her during the night and I during the day. We make a great team."

"You always do, Mother."

"Where are they now?"

"Home."

"Home?" And that was how I missed our first trip together as a family. I couldn't birth my daughter naturally. I missed our first trip home. What was next? Formula?

"Dear, if we had missed your symptoms, there would never be a road back home for you."

"What are you talking about? I am fine. You just like to fearmonger me." I interwove my arms in protest.

"I will text Gavin you are awake and ready to fight. Then you will be able to spend as much time with the baby as you want."

***

Those clock arms deliberately held the ticks back, always against me and my wishes. Finally, I heard the door crack. It was Gavin and my little petal. He looked exhausted.

"Are you okay?" both of us asked at the same time. I chose to answer first.

"Yes, all good. Can I take her?"

"She's all yours. She couldn't wait to spend some time with Mommy."

The beam of my smile reached Marigold's blanket folds. She was neatly wrapped in a white hospital one.

"Why didn't you use any of the ones I had prepared at home?"

"I wanted you to use them first."

Sometimes Gavin didn't realize how great he was. I took her in an awkward embrace. She was sleeping divinely. Her closed eyelids looked like a sketch made by a masterful painter; her hatchling's beak resembled the bow of a present, though it would grimace into vowel shapes at any slight discomfort; her nose a little uphill accompanied the mouth's expressions with its own wrinkly movement, and two miniature puffy buns covering the slits of her sleepy eyes. She was the same as I first saw her, somewhat fleshier, but, at the same time, it felt different, like she was different, and I as well. I didn't expect to be bedridden for so many days after a C-section. Maybe I wasn't used to holding her, but I had to learn quickly. I was a mother now. When I tried to release her from the tight wrap, she squealed a piercing pitch I'd never imagined a baby could. I tried all the versions of calming a baby I've learned from the internet, but she raised her pitch even higher. She looked in so much pain.

"Am I hurting her? Why is she crying so loud?" I turned towards Gavin in exasperation.

"No dear, she just wants to eat," said Mother as she took her from me and got a bottle from Gavin.

"What is that? Formula?" Rage rising in me like a thermometer in summer.

"We didn't have a choice, and donor milk is very expensive." He glanced at me with guilt.

"What about me? I want to feed my baby. Breast is best."

"We couldn't risk transmitting the infection to Marigold. Be understanding," said Gavin.

Of all the things I planned, such a scenario never crossed my mind. I lost a week of my baby's life; I almost lost my life, and now my baby was fed formula. What else could go wrong?

"Laura, would you like to hold Marigold?" asked my mother as she was holding the bottle to the baby's mouth.

"Of course. Give her to me."

I wanted to rip her from my mother's hands.

"Watch out for the head. Babies can't hold their heads well."

"I know, Mother, do not start preaching."

I took my precious little petal, with the morning's last rays encompassing her tiny head like a crown of light. But her little face began crinkling again, and soon after, it belted another wail of glass-cracking intensity. I tried to put the bottle in her mouth. She spitted it out. I tried again to no avail.

"Now what? Why is she crying only in my hands?"

"She probably needs to get used to you," said Gavin.

"I am her mother. She knows me from inside. She should know the sound of my voice, the feel of my body. What is there to get used to?"

"Babies change every day," said Gavin, "it's been a week, and she's already a different baby."

"This information does not make me feel better whatsoever." I shot an enraged glance at him.

My mother took her, and Marigold calmed quickly as if she found her comfort spot nested in her embrace while I seemed to have lost my place in my baby's heart.

CHAPTER 26

AFTER two days of prodding and testing by the medical personnel, I was allowed to go home. By that time, I felt closer to the nurses than Marigold and simply didn't want to go home to face reality. A reality where I was not welcomed. At home, despite my sorrow expectations, it felt better. Especially when I saw Marigold sleeping in her crib surrounded by a meadow of my favorite flowers, she was a flower between flowers. Right there and then, it clicked. I had to try harder to bond with Marigold. Eventually, she would get close to me like the first time when I gave birth. I took her in my arms, as gentle as possible; she didn't notice. As I watched her peaceful slumber, my nostrils got mesmerized by something sweet. It was her smell. Many said babies smelled like vanilla, but, for me, Marigold smelled like honeysuckle dew, faint sweetness cloaked in freshness. If you didn't pay attention, you could easily miss it, as it was barely there, but once it entered your system, you could never imagine how you lived up until now without knowing such olfactory splendor. My heart swelled to unrestrainable sizes and turned to mush, just like my knees. It seemed like Marigold got used to me for a while, though she always found more comfort in her daddy's arms. I hoped I could get my milk back, but after hours of pumping, I stopped. It was another battle lost on my motherhood journey, already filled with guilt and doubts.

During her second week of life (our first together), I didn't sleep a wink, maybe closing an eye, sometimes two, when she was resting. Instead, I chose to spend time with her as much as possible: to feed her, to change her, to swaddle her. It was my time to show off my previously practiced skills. She found so much comfort in my care, and I was happy to provide. Gavin wanted to be of some help as well, and I let him but only on our doctor's visits. As new parents, we didn't realize the crib was too big for Marigold; it looked like she had to sleep in a stadium. Also, I had to run from my bed to hers every time she was hungry or needed a diaper change. After several nights of running to and fro, I couldn't take it anymore, so Gavin went to sleep on the nursery sofa, and Marigold went with me in her new bassinet next to our bed. The surrounding squishy walls made her and me feel more at ease.

My mother came a few times, bringing with her jars of *bortsch* and whatever cookery she presented as traditional Russian. Of course, she never forgot to add a few bags of sunflower seeds or *semechki*, as she called them. Mother would always buy a Russian brand from the European store. They looked different from their American counterparts: smaller, darker, rounder. As for the taste, it was so addictive that I could never stop at a handful.

Mother also wanted to help us with the baby and let us rest, but we wanted to do it independently to experience her first few months to the fullest. My mother didn't complain though she itched to say something.

A couple of days later, she came over and said, "are you ready for Marigold's first bath? Her belly button looks healed."

"No, no, no. I am not ready," I said, surprised by the turn of events.

"So, you are never going to bathe her?" She raised an eyebrow.

"By the third month, I'm sure we can do it." I assumed an awkward smile.

"The first time is scary. After, you'll have so much fun, you'll do it morning and evening."

"Fine." I capitulated. "You show me how."

Mother took my brand new baby tub and placed it on the sink. She poured water while preparing the shower gel and towel with a hooded corner. After, she took the baby in her hands ready to place her in the tub, but Marigold slipped and fell in it, though for an instant, since Mother quickly stabilized her head. Fright was all over my mother's face and mine.

"What are you doing! Are you trying to kill my baby?"

"She slipped. She's a baby. They move sometimes."

"I think YOU should move, Mom."

She probably felt my rage at the nape of her neck as she shifted fast to the side.

"Mother, if you plan on doing stupid things, do them at your house."

I could sense her guilt, which transcended to me feeling guilty.

"Fine, you can help assist," I said.

She handed me the shower gel, and I, gentle as possible, washed Marigold until she was squeaky clean. Mother gave me a congratulatory towel.

"I guess you are more prepared than you think," she said with a wink.

I was brimming with pride and thought of those mothers who kept complaining about motherhood. Nothing close to my experience. Maybe it came naturally to me, or perhaps those mothers were not willing to sacrifice their comfort or were simply too lazy. Who knew? Nonetheless, I got the hang of it quickly and intended to do so in the future.

When Marigold reached three weeks, I felt like I needed some rest, so I asked Gavin to turn on his dad mode. He had two months of paternity leave, so we had it all planned to ensure the same amount of bonding happened with Daddy as with Mommy. I prepared bottles with milk for her and snacks for him while he excelled at being a dad. The image of the two of them would forever stay in my memory. But at the beginning of her fourth week, something was off. She was fussy all the time, crying more often. I would feed her, burp her, and she would be calm for a bit, but then the crying spell would start again. I called the pediatrician's office, the nurse said it could be the formula I gave her. We switched to one for sensitive tummies, but no result. I searched the web, they all said it was colic. I did the bicycle kicks; I massaged and pressed her legs on the belly. Nothing. I bought gripe water and some other syrups promising the calm at the end of a rainbow, but no results.

Christmas was approaching full speed, and it felt wrong to celebrate with Marigold in a distressed state. We didn't even want to take the decorations out of the garage, but Margaret sent us two marvelous poinsettias (one for me and one for Marigold), and I succumbed to the festivity fever. Gavin assembled the artificial Christmas tree. I half-assed the decoration between Marigolds cries and asked my mother to bring some food on Christmas day.

On the morning of the twenty-fourth, my co-workers decided to pay us a visit during our final Christmas preparations and Marigold's mysterious wails. I knew they were coming but seeing their presence step into my current state of reality felt intrusive. Cassandra handed me a superb red and white basket filled with wine, cheese, and chocolates. Marie gifted Marigold a Grinch dress with green stockings and a plush dog, and I couldn't help but acknowledge the unfortunate accuracy.

Marigold was sleeping at the time, which gave me hope that maybe she would not cry for a while. I prepared some coffee, and they had already opened the box with the Christmas cookies they brought.

"So, tell us, how is motherhood going for you?" asked Cassandra with undiluted curiosity.

"It's pretty good," I lied. "She's healthy, sometimes smiles in her sleep. It's nice to watch her." I hoped they didn't notice my voice cracking and the hollows in my eyes.

"I knew you would be a good mother," said Jasmine beaming.

I smiled dryly.

"She sometimes cries, though," I added as if on second thought.

"Well, it happens to everyone. When my kids were babies, they cried for hours sometimes," said the three-kid mom whose name I forgot again.

"Really? Marigold has been crying for a week now."

"It's normal. It will be over soon, I'm sure. Just hold on for–"

Out of the blue, the three registers of terror woke up, interrupting Cassandra's talk (the only thing that could). It started with the low register and climbed up so fast, I didn't even have time to reach the door to the bedroom. I took her in my arms, trying in desperation to calm her down, but it got worse as if she knew we had an audience. I laid her back in the bassinet, changed her diaper, but she screeched louder. I swaddled her in a white, fluffy blanket, passed my co-workers, and went into the kitchen for the prepared bottle of divine nourishment, which flew straight into her mouth and halted the lamentation.

"She is so beautiful, Laura!" They all squealed in different versions.

"Can I hold her?" Cassandra chimed in.

"Sure," I said and gave Marigold to her slowly as if we were competing for the slowest relay race ever. The moment she took her from me, all hell broke loose again. There apparently was a fourth register I never knew about. Cassandra hurried to give the baby back. This time the bottle didn't offer the same consolation. So, the wails became an uninterested feature in our conversation.

"Something might be wrong. You should talk to your pediatrician," said Cassandra.

I tried to tell her I had already talked to a nurse a couple of times, but Cassandra continued.

"I think we should go, girls. Keep up the good work," she said and followed with a peppy pat on the back, a brisk hug, and an oxymoronic Merry Christmas.

One by one, they hugged me and shared a smile tinged in condolement and relief that it wasn't them stuck in such a predicament. After, each stormed out of the house with unconcealed eagerness, the last being Jasmine.

"We'll keep in touch," said Jasmine with positive reassurance and a warm embrace, "you've got this."

And off she went, as well. As I watched the door closing little by little, I felt like a broken umbrella left in the rain, not needed anymore, and in search of solace from those who didn't care or didn't understand.

I cried though I knew my tears would not be heard behind the wall of clamor.

CHAPTER 27

AS time progressed, the mild cries evolved into a continuous stream of wails resounding throughout the house. I tried rocking her, singing to her (though I suspect my voice disgruntled her even more). No one could sleep during the night or rest during the day. The only time silence descended was when she slept, and that was one hour every few hours. After a week of ambulance noises, I felt like vinegar was being poured in my ears, and anything I did, was wrong. My precious petal was suffering, and I didn't know what to do. I went to the doctor. She didn't say anything new, so I switched the doctor. The new one said something about purple cry. I didn't understand it at first, but after thorough research, I got it. Babies sometimes cried for long periods for no apparent reason, and you couldn't do anything about it.

So, we had to adjust our assumptive idyllic schedule to a state of emergency. We tackled each day at a time and applied different strategies depending on Marigold's mood. After multiple hours of listening to Marigold's cries, we learned to differentiate them: the calmest one was a whimper, the one I could tolerate and, eventually, found somewhat endearing; then there was the persistent cry, once established it would persist for hours on end. And then there was the shriek, the occurrence of this beast didn't happen as often, but every time it sounded like she was dying, and I along with her.

    The walks in the park were accompanied by turning heads and questions if the baby was alright. Eventually, we stopped going outside. At home, there was no place to hide; wails were shadowing us everywhere. If I tried to let Gavin sleep by taking Marigold out in the backyard, a neighbor would approach and tell me the baby was crying. As if I didn't know the baby was crying?

    A month and a half of trepidation and sleepless nights took a toll on my health. I felt like drowning with every gasp of air. It felt like my heart's arteries turned into stone forcing me to make more effort with every inhale. Spells of dizziness bound me to my rocking chair or any other piece of furniture designed to keep me seated or lying down. My quotidian pass time became a fuzzy, blurry string of ceaseless, dull to-do lists. My only real concern was to keep her and myself alive while maintaining a basic system of care. The novelty and allure of having a baby had long worn off, fallen into a sink of dirty dismantled bottles, mugs with various heights of brown rings, dried unwashed dishes, and unrealized intentions.

    My delirium had crossed all boundaries. I saw my dad's ghost almost every day. I placed the milk in the pantry and cereal in the fridge. I always wore my shirt backwards, and showering was a once-a-week privilege. The worse was when I put the baby in a laundry basket. It was a sign to Gavin to take her and send me straight to the bedroom. The grudge crippling my soul wasn't because of a doubled workload or the remindful tug of stitches at my groin. No, it was the insurmountable degrees of agonizing crying sending me knocking at the asylum for the mentally insane. No matter how much we would discuss with Gavin, that purple cry was a disturbing, yet temporal, anguish, for my unaccustomed brain, nothing could compensate continuous, inexplicable wails. Her sleeping schedule was on a routine of chaos. She still slept for forty-five minutes, maybe an hour, and then again: whimpers, cries, screams. I would never have thought a baby could have such power of resistance to elemental principles of life. You heard such sensibilities as horror stories from lazy mothers who cared more about their abdomen bulge retracting rather than learning why their child was crying.

At some point, I reached a state of voluntary obliviousness when armored with earplugs and headphones. I would pretend my baby was like any other baby, even though I could see her face crinkle in distress every time she opened her eyes. The feeling of being hit and dragged by a never-ceasing high-speed train followed me everywhere, and as things progressed from bad to worse, my baby wouldn't even look me in the eyes. I've seen other babies cooing at their mother's sight or smiling at the very least but not my child. She simply gazed past me while I looked into an abyss of ever-revolving critical complaints. No sweet talk, no cuddles, not even swaying would thirst the afflicted child's perpetual cacophony of lament. The few hours of sleep were rationed equally between Gavin and me. Each of us would take her either to the backyard or to grandma. Those quiet house hours were designated for sleep. When Marigold would sleep or eat, we would take care of basic cleaning and cooking. But with all those tribulations, the biggest one was Gavin's return to work. His two months of paternity leave were up. Our well-oiled plan was crumbling before our own eyes, though Gavin didn't look as saddened by the situation.

On his first day, he had on his long-sleeve black button-down and black jeans, badge, and backpack: already in a pristine state and ready to go. I mourned his leave with streaks of tears along my cheeks as if he was leaving me forever. He kissed both of my moistened cheeks, turned around, and left. I suspected a rather brisk walk on his part, but Gavin wouldn't do such a thing. At the sound of the door being closed, I knew I needed help. But I couldn't accept my weakness, my yearn for instant gratification, my mediocrity.

It took me two days to succumb and accept my mother's help. I wanted (God knew I did) to pull through on my own, but I had reached a level of absentmindedness nearing total collapse, and I was afraid I would slip into a deep sleep and not hear Marigold when she might need me. If Marigold would show a need for me or, at least, she would let me sleep a few hours here and there, I would have more reason to fight, to reach the sky for her. Now I had to revert to my mother's help. She could even say she was the one taking care of her all the time. Who knew how Mother was going to turn the situation to her benefit?

My mother was elated to be able to share her grandmotherly wisdom. Her practice came only from dealing with me, and that was a poorly done job. But she also took care of Marigold for a few days when I was bedridden, a brag I would hear for many years to come. Thus, I felt compelled to trust her with Marigold.

My little petal was sleeping when I chose to transfer her bundled self into Grandma's experienced arms of care, but to everyone's dismay, the moment my mother touched her frail body, Marigold opened a mouth similar to a black hole producing sounds unheard of before. The range had been updated. My scaredy-cat mom shoved Marigold back to me as if it blistered her forearms. My mouth formed a straight line, and my eyes torched the overly confident grandma. She hid her head between her shoulders and said, "I don't know what changed since last time. She was an easy newborn."

"Well, where's your experience now?" I said, trying to get my voice heard from the noisy siren in my arms.

"You know, if it was my child, it would be different. I can't make mistakes with your child. You would send me to the purgatory. Plus, I have a job I can't miss."

Excuses, excuses. I felt triumphant to hear those excuses coming from my "knowledgeable" mother, but, at the same time, I was the one losing it, so we went with the next option, a nanny. My mom knew someone who knew someone, and so, after a few days, we met Clarisse. She was an experienced mom of three and a daycare teacher in the past. It would've been stupid to refuse even with the steep price given all the accolades accompanying her. Her face was a wrinkly masterpiece, most probably pertaining to her kids' doing. She always wore a dark grey windbreaker jacket, mom jeans, and dilapidated sneakers. My bellowing creature lay just right in her muscular arms, and for the first time in what seemed eternal, it was quiet for more than an hour. Premature was my jubilance as the baby began its daily tribulations with a renewed vengeance. But I took my bag and exited the house as fast as possible, not giving a second thought to the quality of a mother I might portray.

 I went for a walk in the neighborhood. My surroundings seemed different, more saturated even though cloudy. The smell of dust floated through the air from a recent drizzle. It was winter in Seattle, but it didn't matter because the same weather denominators persisted throughout eight months of the years: clouds, pitter-patter, and mild winds. A type of weather for people who enjoyed things in moderation and never wished to spice things up.

 As I took my walk on the superficially saturated asphalt, I noticed sounds that have been forever there, but, for the longest time, my ears chose to disregard them. A symphony forged out of conventional instruments but blissful in its resonating unanimity. Afar, I could distinguish the jabbed hammering of construction vehicles. Closer to me were the constant humming of a car's engine, birds chirping their soprano solos, and I, in a rhythmical motion, walked in metronome steps framing the integrity of all miscellaneously pitched noises. Oh, how sorry I felt for being so ignorant before for not cherishing the sounds of life at their most natural. I wanted Marigold to appreciate them too. Soon, one day when all the struggles of infancy would be dealt with.

 I sat on a bench close to a short bridge and took my imagination to the clouds. I loved searching for images in clouds.

Though they resembled a dark blanket that day, I could still relish in their puffiness. A hawk flew past the clouds. Oh, how I wished to have some freedom again. No, I couldn't. I had to think of Marigold; she was my priority. Even though bonding took longer than expected. After the purple cry ended, I was sure we would be able to seam our love. She's a baby. What did she know? All those stories about mothers and daughters developing natural ties from birth were all bogus. The only thing we needed was time and persistence. The buzzing of my phone transposed me back from my reverie to reality. It was the nanny.

"Laura, something is not right with Marigold. She is crying nonstop, and her breaths are shallow. I think we should take her to the E.R."

I didn't even end the call; I was maybe ten minutes away. It was ten minutes too long. I sprinted as fast as I could, though my incision forbade any extra effort. Nevertheless, my determination was straight like an arrow. I knew a good speed was reached when I felt the counter-wind whistling low across my ear. I began to lose my breath too quickly, for those months of idleness had spoken at the most reckless time. I arrived at the house. The garage door was open, and I saw Marigold looking pale as a piece of paper. I opened the car door, took the baby from the nanny, and put her in the car seat. I jumped at the wheel, the nanny next to me. In a matter of minutes, we were rushing towards the main road. The E.R. was close. I parked at the disabled parking spot, took the baby, and let the nanny find an appropriate one.

I showed them my baby, at the reception, and the newbie nurse began to stammer the directions towards the triage. The nurses there took my baby girl to a room where I couldn't see her anymore. Another nurse saw my convoluted face and took me by the lifeless arm to a chair. It was a black lady with intricate braids on her head. She gave me water, kneeled, and said, "she's in good hands. The doctors know what to do."

"I don't even know what's wrong with her." I continued to look at the room where Marigold was taken.

"The doctors will find out. That's what they're for," she said in a calm voice.

"She's been crying a lot since she was born. The pediatrician doesn't have an answer, and I am at my wit's end," I said, returning my gaze to her.

"Some babies rebel against the harsh world earlier than others. But I'm sure she needs your support with what is happening to her, no matter how painful it is for you to hear."

I didn't have time to react as a middle-aged man with a mask on his face approached me and asked, "you are the mom of the baby we just brought in?"

"Yes," I responded earnestly.

"Your baby is fine. She had a mild case of bradycardia. It's when the heart slows down. It can happen for various reasons, including strenuous activity. She will have to be monitored, but she is stable."

"Thank you," I said as I walked the nurse and the doctor with my eyes. I noticed the nanny was listening as well. I couldn't focus on her, I had to call Gavin, my mom, but she interrupted my pursuit of action.

"Laura, I am so sorry. Marigold didn't stop crying," the corpulent woman said. "I tried everything, I fed her, bathed her, gave her toys, sang to her…"

My blank face scared her as I saw her flinch.

"She's been crying for a while," I said.

"Then there must be a reason."

"There isn't." I deepened my tone.

She didn't continue.

I removed myself to a corner and called Gavin.

"I'm on my way," he said and hung up.

CHAPTER 28

MARIGOLD spent only two days in the hospital. I wasn't sure why the doctors let us go so quickly, it could've been protocol, but most likely, it was Marigold. Every nurse and doctor knew her by now. I would imagine they called her a hell-raiser, as no one, including me, could keep her calm or, at the very best, quiet. At first, they tried Benadryl and Chloral Hydrate when they needed to do some tests, and it worked, but after, she would snap out of it in a harsher, more vengeful state than before. To my shameful horror, her punitive squeals were the talk of the staff. I didn't know how to bolt out of there sooner. When we were allowed to leave, her doctor came in holding a heap of papers.

"Mrs. Miller, your baby is healthy. There are no major issues with her heart. The only reason she went into such a state was because of her crying fits. She might have colic or purple cry, but we must find a way to bring her into a milder state."

I glared at him as if his impression of me was stupid. Did he think I didn't try everything in my power? He noticed my face ticking like a bomb and resumed. "I will prescribe her some antihistamines to help her sleep longer, and who knows with time she'll be happier when she wakes up," he said with unintentional sarcasm.

At home, Mom was waiting for me in an aura of worry. Marigold was sleeping, so I handed her over and went to bed. My queen-sized bed, my medium-firm mattress, and my beige overpriced cotton sheets were the ingredients to which I succumbed and fell into a deep slumber.

The square clock on the dresser showed three a.m. when Marigold's voice echoed in my ear. I almost forgot I had a child. With my eyes closed, I went into her room, preparing to feed her. Her cry was different, and I knew so because she cried all the time, but now there was a distinct tinge of pain. She looked fine in the darkness, but when I came closer, my heart dropped like a boulder. Her face was so swollen I could barely see her eyes as if hundreds of wasps prickled her tender skin. I took her into my arm, slowly and deliberately, and with a trembling voice yelled, "Gavin."

I heard him pushing through the doors.

"What happened?"

"She's sick," I said, holding in tears.

He approached us, but he could only see a deformed child and a scared mother in the shades of darkness. He turned on the light. When we both looked at her, her whole body was covered in red spots, some bigger, some smaller. I glanced at Gavin with despair.

"Should we go to E.R.? Again?" I asked.

"Do you think we have a choice?"

"We could search online and see if it's something serious?"

"And risk her health? No, we're going."

***

It was an allergic reaction to valerian root. My mother always swore it could calm my child, so she decided to help us. I knew of it since childhood as it was a usual herbal syrup every Russian family used to calm nerves, help with sleep, and sometimes bond relationships (one of my mother's atrocious lies). Gavin did not appreciate the effort since he assumed it was part of some witches' concoctions.

What the valerian root could not do, I had to: be the bonding solution for their relationship. In the end, after a healthy talk with my mother about restrictions and permissions in what she gave Marigold, we settled for Benadryl and braced ourselves for her awakenings.

After our medical scare, things went for the better. Marigold still threw fits and wailed for extended periods but as time progressed, the periods shortened. And I could finally see the beauty in her calm face. Her coos were a wren's song to my ears. She would still not look me in the eyes, but she would smile on occasion, though primarily to her dad. During tummy time, she would ace all the requirements. It fascinated me how someone who came out of my body could grow at such a relentless speed and learn so fast. Every time something new happened, a tear trickled along my cheek, and I would want to kiss her and cuddle with her even more. I was like a hummingbird sipping little by little from the nectar she shared. As Marigold became closer to us, I felt I could spread my wings even further. So, we decided to take her to a children's museum. It was my favorite place to go as a kid, and I felt honored to show Marigold the best place in the world.

When we reached the somewhat shabby place compared to what I remembered, children resembling scurrying mice were rushing towards the entry door. Once inside, Marigold's eyes illuminated like stars, ready to grab everything with her pudgy fingers. Which she did with plush delight. I let her and Dad roam through various activity centers not designated for babies at all. To be in an observational seat looking at this creature with divine proclivity alongside her father drove me to inexplicable heights of bliss. Yes, she was difficult, but the hardest part was over. I would fulfill my duty as a mother and bond with my adorable petal from this moment on.

The next three days were out of a fairytale. Marigold was crying for justifiable reasons, I satisfied those reasons, and things went on. I kissed, hugged, and snuggled with my little petal all day, but she wasn't responsive to any affection. Unless it was her dad. It didn't bother me much; she was a daddy's girl.

But on the third day, she looked pale, clear liquid oozed out of her nostrils, and she was coughing. Marigold was sick. It wasn't the end of the world but seeing my baby hurting for a usual reason affected me in a painful way. I had a Tylenol bottle prepared since she was born. It wasn't expired, so I gave her some. She felt better. The night, though, became a nightmare on legs. Her cries were relentless for the first half of the night. Her nose was stuffed; her screams became a more significant threat. I fumbled with my phone to find an answer. I had to drain her nose. I tried the bulb given by the pediatrician. It did an excellent job at sucking air but not mucus. As her voice grew in a constant crescendo, I desperately searched for more answers on my phone. Steam. Yes! I grabbed her and rushed to the shower. The haze engulfed us. The warm wetness brought temporary relief to her breath and my sanity. She then succumbed to deep sleep and didn't wake up until morning. I, on the other hand, didn't close an eye; sleepless vigilance was ingrained in my brain. I forgot any different. The only problem with sleep deprivation was the perpetual fog in my mind in which meandering thoughts would sneak up on me at the most inopportune of times. Like that night, as I watched my daughter sleep, I kept having the same idea, the same feeling of envy. Envy of her freedom, which she couldn't even acknowledge, the envy of her privilege, of her power. I remembered my times of freedom. Our trips with Gavin, the ocean coast air, the rhymical roll of the waves, the blazing spirit of adventure engulfing us. The unusual food we tried and then, the second day, would have to fill up on Pepto-Bismol. The trails into the depths of woods, waterfalls, fountains. The many encounters and nonverbal conversations we had with the locals. I remembered walking in the middle of a chiaroscuro contrast of the moving blackness of the ocean and the blaring lights of the adjacent bars. Sweet Mai Tais, creepy narrow alleys, and snug bed sheets.

"Oh, I forgot to put the laundry in the dryer," I whispered, "I'll do it tomorrow, which is today." My eyelids were heavy as if someone was pulling them over my eyes. I barely could distinguish between sleep and my awakened state. I always wanted to be a botanist or a florist, but my mom and the ogre said no. Now I had only one flower to take care of, though this one proved to be a bit more complicated than intended. The moon was stunning on the beach.

My heals were always sunken in sand…

CHAPTER 29

IN the morning, as I walked from the shower to the bed, I noticed something protruding like a sore thumb. My disfigured body in the mirror. Our bedroom's closet mirror doors were one reason for choosing this house in the first place. They expanded across the whole room, creating an illusion of a larger space. But now, my eyes inadvertently caught a glimpse of my body, the reason why I repealed the gregarious reflection of its floor to ceiling feature. I could never hide, especially in the supposedly safest environment in a house, my bedroom. Most of the time, I avoided the crude figure staring at me, but the weird shapes drew me in like a freak circus. My hair resembled a decomposing pile of dirt, half of it laying on the floor, my face full of craters and dried up ridges, my breasts sagging, and my upper body expanded to a larger circumference than my hips. I resented how much I ate for the baby during pregnancy because it turned out it was mostly for myself. My belly looked like three rolls of dough planted upon one another. My stretch marks were dark red as if trenches of lava. My thighs looked more like cow thighs. I resembled a cow overall—a cow with stretch marks and no milk to produce.

I've never been attached to my physical body; I took it mainly for granted, like all things gifted. But seeing it in such a dilapidated form made me mourn its times of glory and modest perfection. The grievance was the price to pay for incipience of life, I guess. I should've been grateful for what I got in return; many never got to where I was at the moment.

I told Gavin about it, but he lied and told me fables about how terrific I looked, like a goddess of those renaissance paintings. But I felt like a used-up factory, with rust along the lines, in the knees, the back, the shoulders. My body succumbed to general physical pain but also became a visual abomination. I needed to change something, go to a gym, eat less. But if I ate less, I wouldn't have enough energy or will to push through. I needed something good in my life. Food was the only one, but I could not accept what I had become. I couldn't wait to get back into shape and forget the horrendous version of myself I couldn't recognize. My face needed a mask, at least, or some moisturizer. Laura, the woman, was covered underneath layers of spit-up, soiled diapers, crying spells, sleepless nights, and under the new version of Laura: the mother.

The day went by like a fog of after-thoughts and immediate action towards Marigold. No matter how tired I was, she needed the same quality of care, but her stuffy nose made her irascible to a greater degree (if that was even possible). The only wish I had was for the night to arrive faster so I could sleep. It was Gavin's turn that night, so when he came home and had dinner, I placed Marigold in his arms, hurried to take a shower, and went straight to bed. I pushed my feet under the cotton sheets, and it felt like heaven was hiding underneath. My muscles were so stiff, I needed a few stretches before I laid my head on the blissful hug of my pillow. I never knew a bed could have a therapeutic effect on mothers. Slumber took ahold of me right away; I knew of nothing better. But after fifteen minutes, I felt something crawling on me: first on my toes, then on my ankles, shins, calves… It felt ticklish and unusual at the same time. When I opened my eyes, I saw only my beige duvet. I uncovered it. There were hundreds of black moths crawling on me. Their wings were burnt, so they couldn't fly. I brushed them off, but the moths kept crawling and climbing up my body with assiduity. I tried jumping off the bed, but my body felt so heavy I couldn't move. The moths were getting higher towards my thighs. My skin begged to be itched, but I wouldn't dare touch the monsters. I wanted to scream for Gavin. My voice was mute. Then the worst happened. They began to jump higher and higher—some on my shoulder, some on my face, hair, everywhere. No matter where they reached, they turned towards my ears. The moths wanted to eat my brain, my mind, my thoughts. I would lose myself. In one last attempt to break through, I screamed as loud as I could. It was then I saw Gavin's face in front of me, trying to wake me up.

"You had a bad dream, dear. Are you okay?"

"A bad dream? That's where all phobias stem from," I said and looked at him, "I cannot do this anymore, Gavin. I need help."

"What do you mean?"

"With Marigold. I do not know if I can endure another medical emergency, another sleepless night."

"I will try and help you. Get some sleep. We will get through this like we always do."

He wanted to tuck me in, but I stopped him, so I could check underneath the duvet. The coast was clear. Gavin's face began questioning my actions but didn't pursue answers. It was too late and too weird. He kissed me goodnight and turned off the lamplight.

I closed my eyes, but all I could see were those repugnant creatures. What was happening to my mind? Was this how one transformed into a mother? Through brain mutilation? I would've tried to find an answer to these questions if I could afford it. I couldn't. Sleep was more valuable than gold. I hoped to dream of happy mothers and happy babies.

The following day, when Gavin came from work, I sat with him at the kitchen table and told him with the determination of an exhausted mother.

"I cannot go on like this anymore. If there is something you can do, do it or else I don't–"

"With all the expenses and medical bills, we cannot afford to pay anyone to help, but I can talk to my manager and convince him to let me work from home a few days a week so you could rest a bit."

I couldn't find my place; I couldn't stop hugging him. Such agitated happiness I didn't feel in a long time. He was my pillar in life, the answer to all my questions, the alignment of my stars. He was one of those rare kids born to good parents. The ones who grew up loved and cherished and with enough support to last a lifetime. He didn't experience the fear of not knowing where he would wind up tomorrow or if there would be food at dinner. Thus, he usually settled for good enough: a good enough house, a good enough job, and, maybe, a good enough wife. He didn't get those spirits, the ones who forced you to show you're valuable to the whole world instead of yourself. He didn't grow ambitions from the rotten hole in his heart, and he didn't have to breathe in the air of not good enough every time he woke up. Weird how self-fulfillment stopped one from wanting more than his means. A curse for the broken ones meant the meaning of life for those whole in the heart. It made him a bit dull, somewhat naïve, overly optimistic, and not as a result of compensation. It covered his eyes enough to not perceive someone beyond the first two layers of their personality.

His form of defense? When you already had everything you desired, the few needs dictated your choices of people and relationships. Gavin could afford to choose the ones who fit his humble structure of Maslow's pyramid of needs. So, he never risked getting involved with the wrong people or walking into a place of dubious interests. His coping mechanism, you might ask? Well, he didn't need any. He didn't obsess over the meaning of life when his mother died. He didn't get an existential crisis when he failed a class in college and went out drinking himself into oblivion. He focused on what could be done and did it. That was it. Ignorance was indeed his bliss, and I liked living in his world. Even as a shadow, I felt replenished. I wanted to pretend I was like him, secure and trusting.

CHAPTER 30

THREE months had passed since Gavin stayed home more. Marigold had bloomed like a rose in the embrace between the sun and rain. Her cheeks looked like they had two slices of apples hidden underneath, glowing with hues of pink, red, and yellow. Her body was made up of marshmallows: marshmallow legs, marshmallow arms, and a marshmallow face. At six months, she reached her sitting milestone, so the majority of times when she was awake, Marigold preferred to sit enjoying her new power. She began babbling more, became more expressive, though still highly sensitive. My sleep schedule had improved, but in the process, I lost my rest. If before, Marigold couldn't choose which parent she could spend time with, now she did. Surprise, it wasn't me. Her crying had the same impulsiveness, but now it would fade away only under Daddy's gaze. No matter how much I tried to calm her, the one true answer wasn't me. Ever. The worst part about it was after she began teething, which resulted in horrendous tears, fever, and diarrhea, Marigold discovered her new superpower: to bite. And I was bitten, oh, how I was bitten. Marks spreading across my arms and chest looked as if I was devoured by savage mosquitos. But she didn't stop there. She would bite my fingers, face, shoulders, and one time, even my toe. The only thing good coming out of this was the sheer pleasure I experienced when she bit Grandma. I rejoiced. I was even more excited when Grandma said she might come rarer as she suddenly became a busybody.

Gavin was never bitten. If I could ever describe the definition of a soft spot in someone's heart, it was Marigold's love for her father. She gazed at him, fawning at every word he uttered, like a bee towards a flower. They both formed the picture of an ideal family, though I was missing from it. He, of course, didn't notice. He thought everyone got the same attention as he did. His ignorance was understandable but not forgivable. We were still a couple: husband and wife. I felt like that part of our life also slipped away on a slope of mundane tasks. Pangs of jealousy were tugging at my heart. On one hand, I was jealous of the undiluted attention Gavin gave her, but on the other, I wanted to be in his place showered with her unconditional adulation.

Days with days, weeks with weeks all had conjoined into one big melting pot of time. I knew little of what was happening outside, just the cries on the inside: hers and mine. The more time passed, the more I became accustomed to a life of the ungrateful and the underprivileged. I slept more, my only comfort. It was what I kept telling myself. I got to sleep. Wasn't rest what I wanted? But at what price?

When she began eating purées and drinking water, we started three meals daily besides the formula bottle. She never took a bite from me, not once. It was super Daddy to the rescue again. I felt like the adoptive third cousin, who everyone in the family felt pity for. It was hard to believe somewhere in the world, motherhood was glorified. Since, in our household, there was only glorified fatherhood. I wasn't supposed to complain since my workload got lighter, but what was the mother's role supposed to be? To birth a child and be done? Would there be something more my child would ever need from me besides life? I couldn't even give her milk. I still did the monthly photos to commemorate her growth over the first year, but I felt as distant from her as earth from the sun. She didn't want to have any connection with me despite any biological theory or survival instinct, and I had to respect her wish, much to my dismay.

When I dreamt of my Marigold, she resembled the ideal version I always pictured in my mind. She always looked me in the eyes with warmth. With a crown of daffodils bestowing her perfect head full of russet waves, she would hug me and kiss my cheek, and smile. A sunlight diffused smile as big as a suspended crescent moon. How I craved that smile. My whole existence would hang from its corner, leaning to her side in hopes Marigold would keep smiling just for me. Her laughter would breathe life into me, but only till the real version would suppress it in grumpy growls.

Alongside her physical growth, Marigold grew more interested in the outside world. If before she despised going somewhere with the car or to the park, now she cried to have the exact same thing. Going to the park became a must and a vital part of our daily schedule. On sunny days, she knew of no better joy than breathing the fresh air while swaying in the stroller. There was only one problem. It was raining all the time, and when we would risk it on a cloudy day, it would start drizzling upon our arrival. When negotiating with Marigold became a preposterous idea on those rainy days, I would strap her in the stroller and take her out in our backyard. Shame was one word to describe the deplorable features my garden had reached. I hadn't picked a single fallen leaf from it. They were all gathered in small circles swooshed by the incongruent wind, along with pine needles and dead bugs. Many of my wisteria's vines were overgrown, spreading to whatever it could latch on. With more dead branches than healthy ones, my Japanese maple tree was in dire need of pruning. The fountain was clogged and occasionally sprinkled some muddled water, and the few spring flowers I had planted had a hard time blooming out of the trash covering it. What would Margaret say? She would, at the very least, express great disappointment. But I learned to accept these anguished thoughts and expectations. My soul lived on promises; maybe one day, when Marigold will be older, she will help me replant and replenish our Hanging Garden of Kenmore. But for the moment, as I rocked my baby to sleep, I let my imagination embellish my garden to its future glory.

On one day blessed with sunshine, we visited the Kirkland Marina Park. During those indulgent days, the park was filled with kids to the brim, and there was no space for a seat. But the statement was viable for any other park around since families eager for sun would flock to any public area. So, my choice would always fall on Kirkland Marina. Across from Washington Lake, a picturesque view spread across with a foggy silhouette of Seattle as background; the smell of algae was embedding in with the smell of freshly cut grass; the ducks with their lustrous feathers were wiggling their tails in the waves of the lake. Some visitors loved feeding them, and the ducks never refused, a delight for the toddlers and the ducks. A few people were paddling, others were canoeing, and I would make a bet with myself as to whom would be first to take in the sweet taste of algae soup.

My theoretical attempt was interrupted when a mom of a rock-throwing toddler sat next to me.

"What a cute baby? How old is she?"

I scanned her up and down. She had time to do her makeup and hair, had gorgeous skin and a toned body. Was this an additional skill I was supposed to acquire? Another at which I was failing miserably?

"She will be seven months in a week."

"Ah, I remember those days. They are the cutest, with so many giggles, cuddles, and snuggles. I miss it. I hope I'm not going to get baby fever." She laughed in squeaks.

"I don't know what you're talking about. My baby does not giggle, cuddle, nor snuggle."

"Maybe something's wrong? You know my friend had a kid like that, and it turned out he was autistic."

"My baby is not autistic!"

"Ah, I didn't mean it like that. It's just if it doesn't fit, then there must be a reason, don't you think? You look so tired and sad. You never know, maybe your baby needs special treatment?" She fanned her immaculate French tip manicure.

"What if she giggles, cuddles, and snuggles with her father and not me?"

She spoke no words, only showed a stunned expression in her eyes, judging me as a subpar mother; pointing at me with her freshly manicured fingers; laughing at me with her whitened teeth and perfect abs. I chose to get up and leave than be ridiculed by the unsophisticated. Being a new mother felt worse than high school with all the condemnation and arbitrary rules: a race for the best mother that inevitably we all lost. Was there really a model of the best mother? The best one I knew couldn't protect her son from the cross. What about everyone else? I refused to accept her explanation for what was happening. What was it with mothers with a little more experience than me, shoving "expert" advice up my throat? Lady, you barely got out of the spit-up stage, and you find the courage to spit-up unsolicited advice? She would do better to keep her son from killing ducks later.

In comparison, I had enough decency to abstain from sharing such valuable information.

CHAPTER 31

TIME passed faster, and the months approached the much anticipated first year with inevitable speed. Marigold kept growing exponentially, but I couldn't distinguish her growth since she always seemed the same to me. Only when others pointed it out, I would notice the need for a new shopping trip for clothes. I made an effort to photograph her each month to show Gavin how she was transforming from a baby into a toddler, and he kept on swooning and gushing over them. Whereas for me, a peculiar feeling nestled in our relationship. A weird sensation, a burn ignited in my heart: the burn of tacit oppression. The oppression when I had to stay, not by choice but by necessity. I had to take care of her. I was her mother. Like it or not, I was the sacrifice. It was about me upon till I gave birth, and everyone weighed on MY every feeling. Now, I was the shadow of a new star. A brighter, younger star which I birthed and after automatically vanished into oblivion. What if I didn't feel the connection? What if I didn't know how to be a mother or, for Marigold, how to be a daughter? There was no book on it. How could I teach someone to enter my soul and create warmth? It was not asked; it was granted. Time went by like a carriage with square wheels I pushed from behind. Oppression turned into surrender, a continuous motion of habitude, a routine of negligence towards myself and my inner needs. But she was happy. Gavin too. It was only I who bore the burden of insufficiency; I was the one who tied myself into a knot of unhappiness. My soul held strong to one hope, maybe, just maybe after a year, she would understand to love me.

***

On her first birthday, I went all out and organized a big party. The theme was what I always dreamt of: a sunflower meadow. I went out of my wit's end to find balloons with sunflowers on them but couldn't find none near me. I had to improvise and went with stickers. I used stickers throughout the whole house. I also bought sunflower plates, cups and napkins, and a sunflower centerpiece: the DIY project of my heart. It was mainly vases from the Dollar Store with glass pebbles and three plastic sunflowers I found at a craft store, but the pride I took in them eclipsed any exhaustion I had from driving all day.

  I invited everyone I knew for the grand day of me surviving a year of motherhood. There was Cassandra and the crew and many of Gavin's closest friends from work. My mother behaved like all those people came to her celebration, greeting them, showing them around, and laughing at jokes if any should come her way. Marigold was dressed in a canary yellow fluff dress with matching sandals, and when she made an entrance, all exclaimed astonished interjections. To me, she looked like a glass statue: exquisite to behold but cold to the touch.

  Jasmine approached me. She looked better than ever. No bruises or cuts, only a glowing face. Curiosity took ahold of me, so I went ahead and asked, "hi Jasmine, you look great. Has anything good happened lately?"

  "Nice to see you, Laura. The party is awesome," she said, radiating joy. When her hand went up to handle an escaped tendril, her finger winked at me with a sparkle. I inspected it closer, and it was a ring. It was a giant, exaggerated ring alluding to some great wealth from those who most likely didn't have it.

  "Is this what I think it is?" I pointed to the jewel.

"Brandon and I are getting married," she said, grinning.

"Are you sure this is the way to go? For both of you?"

"He's been good at respecting my boundaries. So, when he proposed, I couldn't refuse."

"I'm happy for you, but do not rush into things. Maybe take it slow?"

"Yes, I thought about it. We will probably get married next year."

"Good," I said, thinking maybe a year would be enough for her to realize it was a mistake.

Cassandra approached us after finishing her eavesdropping, possibly disappointed in the limited amount of information she got.

"How are you, ladies?" she said, embracing us in a bear hug.

I didn't have the will to listen to her blabber, so I excused myself with the usual explanation.

"Oh, Marigold needs my help. I'll let you two talk."

"But we're here to see you. How is Marigold? Easier to handle?" said Cassandra, eager for some juicy gossip.

"She's been pretty good," I lied. "We have a wonderful mother-daughter relationship. She loves to hug me and kiss me. It's so adorable. Even Gavin is jealous," I said though it didn't feel enough. "She sleeps well, cries very little."

"You must be one of those lucky moms, but what about the dark circles under your eyes?"

A crackling sound reverberated in my mind. Oh, how I despised this person.

"Well, I'm not as lucky in the gene department as you, Cassandra. Tell me more about your skincare routine. It must be elaborate."

"Not really, only some moisturizer."

"Then tell me how your daughter is doing?"

"Oh, Abby, she's great. Her dad took her fishing, and when she cast the fishing rod into the water, it slipped from her hands and fell." She laughed with gusto. "Russel complained for a week about the money he waisted and the fact that he doesn't have a boy. I, on the other hand, had a good laugh and a story to tell. So, I think it's a win-win situation."

I heard some yelling coming from the backyard. I couldn't see Marigold anywhere. So I realized it was my cue.

"Will you excuse me, please? I need to find Marigold."

"Sure, sure." She then turned towards Jasmine. "And I told him, do you really think a boy would hold a heavy rod any better than…"

I began searching around for my little ice princess. Her father was chatting with some of his colleagues. Marigold was nowhere to be found. I went into every room and bathroom. Nothing. I felt palpitations rising steadily. Ultimately, I went into the backyard, and when I opened the door, she was walking towards me. Walking! She never walked before, and now she was. She was coming towards me to show me what she had learned. I squatted and spread my hands to catch her. She was aiming her walk towards me. I couldn't believe my joy. I couldn't believe my eyes. She was there, ready for me to catch her, but right before reaching my embrace, she purposely fell on her buttocks. As happy as she was to learn how to walk, it wasn't me who she wanted to share her achievement. I felt like another crack developed in my already hollow heart. I felt so desolate I couldn't take it, so I went to Gavin and whispered in a ruthless tone, "your kid is walking. Go see. She's waiting for you."

Then I went into the bathroom to calm down. I splashed my face with icy water and looked at the image reflected in the mirror. The outline of my skeleton protruded through my face. I lost all the weight in several months of worry and emotional desiccation. My skin looked saggy. The white in my eyes resembled a red-green palette of exhaustion. The droopy corners of my mouth denoted sheer misery. I always reeked, even when I showered. I reeked of sweat and apathy. When I touched my skin, it was dry, calloused even, with bumps of different dimensions. It felt like arid soil. And if my flowers wouldn't survive in such conditions, then I most likely wouldn't either. I opened the drawer, took my recently bought expensive cream, plopped some on my face, and began spreading. Both hands worked with precision on every nook and cranny as if in a meditative state. I must've rubbed the cream on my face for a long time. I don't remember. I stopped only when I heard a knock at the door.

"Laura? Are you there? Is everything alright?" asked Gavin.

"Yes, I will be right there."

I put some more cream on my hands, rubbed them thoroughly, then walked through the door. I might not be a mother to my child, but I was still a woman.

CHAPTER 32

I hoped maybe after her birthday, she would turn into a loving child but a week into her first year, I realized: Marigold would never change because something had to be wrong. A child who refused a mother's care was an abnormality of basic instinct.

And how in the world did a mother cope with her baby's rejection? Was this a temporary blunder? A hitch in the process of human development? I've never heard anyone complain of such unnatural transgressions. It was always the opposite. The bonding became stronger than glue between the mother and child. Typically, children would cry for their mother after mere minutes of separation. What about those who didn't? I hadn't given birth naturally. I lost my milk, I lost her the moment I got sick, and she never forgave me. It appeared I had lost the thread which connected it all. I became a caricature of what a mother was supposed to be—a misaligned mother with missing components I did not know how to get back. Still, a child who abnegated a parent had to be, by default, unattuned to inherent survival. Unless she had an underlying cause, an illness that could muffle those natural progressions of a child. She had to be autistic, as the manicured mom said.

With the thought still brewing in my head, I fell asleep, that is, till the baby monitor's red light rose up and down, reproducing Marigold's whimper. With remarkable speed, I rushed into her room and began rocking her crib. With so much rocking done during the preceding year, my right hand got quite buff. I might as well become a professional rocker—the uncool kind. When her face was at its most serene, I could distinguish some uncanny features belonging to me, but most were her father's. Her look of a diaphanous color, her honeysuckle smell, her touch was worth a star from the sky. Still, she didn't feel mine. But if she gave me a reason, I could give Marigold the benefit of the doubt; maybe she wanted to connect all along but in a slower manner. I could appreciate her striving to get closer with Gavin since it was the only way she knew how. I would understand and support her unique strive to communicate. The clock ticked three a.m.; sleep refused to weave between my eyelashes. Was it worth trying? I had to wake up in two hours. Interesting how after a child was born and after someone died, there was no night during the wake. It was daytime around the clock. A brighter day, a darker day, but still, there was no rest when a soul had bloomed into existence or a body had dissipated into particles of the universe.

  The following day, Gavin was getting ready for work. I felt blurry from another sleepless night, but I had to speak with him, so I made an extra effort. I pulled at my eyes to help diminish the exhaustion when I saw Gavin all put together. He looked like a person where newly grown toddlers came to address their tantrum meltdowns due to their mothers' incompetence.

  "Are you ready for the project you were telling me about?"

  "I am, or at least I hope I am," he said while shoving a peanut butter jelly sandwich in his backpack.

  "I have a question, Gavin."

  "Sure."

  "I have a feeling something is not right with Marigold."

  "What do you mean?"

  "It seems like she can't connect with people."

  "I've never noticed any deviation from any other normal toddler. Why are you questioning this?" He kneeled to tie his sneakers. He looked at his watch and almost rushed through the door but then returned, kissed my dry lips, and continued, "you've been through a lot. Taking care of a baby and now a toddler would take a toll on anybody. It will take time till the storm calms down. You know she is your daughter, and you are her mother."

"I do. I am."

When his heel lastly exited the house, the wails commenced again. As if she felt when he wasn't home.

CHAPTER 33

MARIGOLD'S first year became a blur like most of her early years, elucidated mainly by pictures and videos. Those, of course, had me missing from most of them, so pretty much there was no evidence of how I looked either. After her first walk, my day surmised Marigold's numerous attempts at hurting herself and me being the big bad wolf saving the Little Red Riding Hood from hospital visits and additional bouts of crying. I knew by heart all her favorite songs as those were our primary content consumption. From Wheels on the Bus, Itsy Bitsy Spider to Twinkle, Twinkle Little Star, I would warble with no restrain my own rendition of the immortal nursery rhymes. Marigold would hide behind her knees and cover her ears in protest. I would sing my tone-deaf heart out and enjoy every bit of it.

Though the house didn't resemble the headquarter of CryingKidsRUs, she still maintained a daily schedule of tantrums. But overall, quietude returned to its previous habitat, like an animal to a newly planted forest. She enjoyed playing with toys I bought at consignment stores for half the price. Most of them were wooden and noiseless, so Cassandra's gift wasn't really needed. On her pacific parts of the day, I found myself a witness of her worldly discoveries, from observing an ant's crossing and an airplane's loud swoosh across the sky to establishing the third Newtonian law by dropping her food or toys from the highchair. Gavin loved to witness her little excitements as well and joined in whenever he had a few spare minutes. He also loved to take her for a walk or to the grocery store. And on rare occasions, we would risk taking her on a trip to Mount Rainier or Leavenworth. Grandma would visit here and there, to which Marigold was mostly indifferent. But unlike me, Grandma couldn't accept such behavior, so she would spoil her grandkid rotten by taking her to all the best indoor playgrounds in the vicinity and bribing her with freshly baked cookies.

As for me, my days as a mother of a one-year-old toddler resembled a bleak voyage between mechanical work (such as feeding, thirst-quenching, changing, and entertainment providing) and tantrum storms brimming with anger and sloppy crying. The epicenter of such tempests was always me, never her dad or even my mother. The blast would usually last five to ten minutes which felt like a short movie of my humiliation. A myriad of reactions would cross my face, from bafflement to smiling at her ludicrous reasonings. I knew she had an underdeveloped brain. I read enough books to understand it, but living through them every day, multiple times a day, especially with a creature who didn't recognize my role as a mother, aggravated me. Like a hurricane, she would destroy in her path my ego, my strive to fulfill my part, and ultimately, my happiness.

To dissipate some of her outburst, I had a tool conventional to the eyes of an adult but an absolute delight for children: soap bubbles. Whenever Marigold would begin her ransacking across the whole house, I would equip my weapon of toddler mind control: the bubble maker. Outside in the sun's rays, those holographic ephemeralities were exceptionally glorious. I would produce dozens at a time, and Marigold would try and catch them, but to her dismay, those spheres of joy would pop into nothingness like one's life in the vastness of the universe. To my relief, her apprehension wouldn't last long since there were many more bubbles. I created as many as I could to appease the little daredevil, and I felt godlike. I held the power of creation for the diaphanous orbs and the power of decision to extinguish the duration of their existence or let them perish on their own. On the windy afternoons, I imagined our playtime with bubbles as a form of bonding, though I was always the maker, and she was always the destroyer. One time, as a form of gratitude, Marigold gifted me a rock for my hard work.

Besides her storms, explosion, exploits, and sloppiness, sometimes, I would notice, in her good days, a unique curiosity towards me. When she would catch a glimpse of my belly button, she unequivocally had to shove her finger in the dimple-like opening. I would ask: "Did you find the hobbit home?" And she would be even more mesmerized with her discovery, trying to figure out who was this hobbit and why his home was so tiny. Other times when she would get scared of a dark room, she would run up to me and pull on my skirt to be held. When I would abide, she would hug me so tight and lean her head on my shoulder like I was the only one able to protect her. We would stay like this for as long as she would let me like a limestone statue of a mother and child. I bathed in her trust, inhaling the tenderness, eager to fulfill the role of the mother I always wanted to be but never quite got the chance. I would ignore the cramps and tiredness of my arms and cherish any second she would entrust me.

When we would lounge in bed on a sluggish day, she would always inspect my body. She would touch my mouth, struggling to pry it open. When I did so, she would observe my teeth and tongue with such bewilderment I couldn't escape a chuckle. The same happened with my ears, nose, or my polished toenails (when I had the time to paint them). Her curiosity over my body and complete lack of personal space mimicked the bond between us I always missed. The bond where our worlds would merge and fuse into synchronicity as if she was still a part of my body, only now I was also part of hers. Alas, those moments were rare. Most times, I felt the sharp poke of failure digging in my back. I felt like a lone tree in the desert longing for those rare drops of dew.

Aside from the daily tribulations of raising a toddler, I had a purpose. I had to make sure Marigold was autistic. First, I googled everything I could on the matter. Secondly, I watched every video of other mothers identifying their offspring as neurodivergent. I could relate to them personally as if they understood me and my grief. Symptoms were many, like not making eye contact, which was true for me but not for Gavin; didn't respond to a parent's smile, the same; didn't show concerns for others, definitely true; flapping hands, rocking, spinning, swaying—she did those, but other kids did those as well (this one needed more research); sensitive to smells, sounds, touch—definitely, especially my touch; would obsess about certain activities—she always talked about Daddy, how could that be a usual activity?

I gave Gavin many reasons to be worried, but he wouldn't listen. After several conversations on the topic, he forbade me to bring it up since, in his opinion, Marigold was a perfectly healthy child. It was true she began talking very early at a year and a half (this was his main argument). So what? It didn't abnegate other symptoms. Those needed answers too. I got on various sites and forums, and most confirmed my biggest supposition, she needed an evaluation. I looked online for many organizations which specialized in diagnosing autism early on. I chose the one with the best reviews, Kindering Sprouts. The evaluation appointment was made two months ahead, I had plenty of time to prepare. I had a list of all the unusual and abnormal behaviors. How our relationship was stunted from her inability to connect; how she was always indifferent towards me; how she obsessed over her dad. It wouldn't bother me if I knew she couldn't do it due to an underlying cause. On the contrary, I would've appreciated her effort (if any) to communicate in her own personal way. It made sense; any professional would realize it sooner rather than later. But for the moment, I had to wait.

Wait and observe for other newly formed symptoms I could add to my list.

CHAPTER 34

THE day of the evaluation had arrived. I was so agitated I almost forgot to grab snacks. That error alone would show the therapist how things were around here. I didn't tell Gavin. No way in hell. He never would accept. But I knew something was wrong with Marigold. I felt it in my heart. There had to be. A diagnosis would make things clearer and appease the corrosive feeling I harbored in my soul. I told Gavin we were going on a playdate with a mom and her son at the park. He would find out in due time. What was the point of making it harder on him? It would take a toll on any dad to find out their child was different and they were ignorant enough to miss it? I knew lying to Gavin made me a vile wife, but I couldn't forsake Marigold's health for a guiltless conscience.

  It was on a Tuesday afternoon, after Mari's nap. She had to be in her restful most usual self, so the therapist could get a clear impression. It was drizzling as per usual. Marigold took her favorite doll, a cute little rag doll with two red braids. I put on her yellow with black polka dots raincoat, along with her eared umbrella in the shape of a panda. She always managed to evoke the warmest reactions from strangers. Too bad she was a volcano ready to erupt at any given moment. If they knew, those erroneous emotions would soon be switched to swarms of pity directed towards her mother.

  Inside, the clinic was rather cold, I didn't even take my jacket off, and Mari had a warm sweater. The first thing I saw were the walls painted in purple with high-resolution frames of children's drawings centered around houses, suns, and families, all in disproportionate sizes. We check-in fast and took a seat. Next to us were two parents seated on colorful chairs while their child roamed around the room, playing with the wooden activity cubes placed in the corner or staring at the tired fish in the aquarium.

It took some time to fill up all the paperwork. In the meantime, Marigold was losing it. I gave her all the snacks, applesauce, and juice I had. I went with her to the wooden toy center, but all she wanted was to run in circles, making it harder to concentrate. After the family was called in, for the longest time, no one was there till a mom with a little girl entered.

Everything seemed normal. Only the girl did not speak and preferred to stay next to her mother rather than roam around. They sat a few chairs next to us. The girl piqued Marigold's interest right away. I tried to stop her from glaring at the child, who was mostly oblivious. When I could not control her anymore, I said, "excuse us, my girl's curiosity is beyond my control."

"No problem, Leila doesn't mind the attention."

I looked at the girl, but there was no reaction whatsoever.

"Leila is autistic," she said.

"Oh, I am looking for a diagnosis for my daughter as well. It is yet to be determined." I glanced at both girls, but Marigold did not resemble her in any way. "Did it help to know her diagnosis?"

"Yes and no."

"How so?"

"It finally gave us answers, but the answers gave us labels. I see my daughter as who she is without anchoring her to a word. Knowing, though, does help create an environment where Leila can feel safe and loved."

As I listened to this mother speak, I noticed her beauty. Not necessarily in a physical way, though her hair was a wavy russet color like a stalk of wheat swaying in the graces of wind. Her serenity exuded the tranquil silence of that land. People who accepted their fate unconditionally had a certain beauty about themselves. I've noticed it in Margaret as well. There were no creases on the forehead from constantly searching for answers on their phone or in their minds. When rumination wasn't second nature and pushing through didn't seem like the only feasible answer. They were never in a hurry but always on time. A flowing body, a floating mind unbridled by heavy thoughts. I always wished to be like her but never knew where to start. Or maybe I just didn't know how.

"How do you manage it?" The impertinent in me surfaced.

"What exactly?"

"To be content even in the face of adversity?"

"At first, I lived in denial. Many doctors have been bothered in search of the one who would argue the diagnosis. But then I turned my gaze towards my daughter, and I realized she was still herself. The way I knew her from the beginning, nothing changed except for my perception. But it wasn't about me or my perception; it was about her. As months progressed, I taught myself to live in the present. Like this one." She leaned over to take the pebble her daughter gave her. She kissed her on the forehead, and the little girl pranced back to the wooden cube rolling one of the beads with fervor. The girl became even more adorable under the gaze of her mother's love.

"What about when she has a difficult time coping with her surroundings?" I asked cautiously.

"I live for moments like this." She smiled and showed the pebble. "Accepting my life in its current form was a journey all on its own. No mother plans for her child to struggle to understand a world unlike her own. It is not her fault that the majority of people see things differently than her. But it is my responsibility to teach her how to live in such a world. It is the promise we give our children, to love them no matter what, and help illuminate the path towards understanding and enjoying life."

"My daughter is also difficult, but she doesn't have a diagnosis yet. I struggle to understand her behavior."

"I would say live by the day and strive to control less of it. Then you will not even notice how contentment will ease into the seconds of the minute, the minutes of the hours, and ultimately, hours of the day."

I would have listened to her advice more if not for the call from the therapist. It seemed for a moment like we had no reason to be there. But I had to go through with it. I grabbed my unlabeled child and went into the office.

Once inside, the smell of fresh pine imbued the air. I took a seat on the navy sofa and sat Marigold on my knees. She, of course, didn't want to stay, so off she went to break something in the good doctor's office. To my surprise, the therapist let her. She asked about my concerns, so I did what any other doting mother would do. I whipped out my diligently prepared list. I spun again and again into those nasty, gut-wrenching stories of my child's misbehaviors. The therapist listened, observed Mari, and after half an hour, asked me to leave so she could examine her in-depth. I felt weird to leave her; what if she needed me. The therapist's glance assured me it would be fine. The serene lady and her daughter were not there anymore, so I began a rumination-less state for about ten minutes till I couldn't do it anymore and turned on my phone to search for signs of autism in two-year-old toddlers. It was never too late to prepare for the future.

After some time, the therapist called me in. Marigold was playing with a few toys on the floor. All was quiet. The therapist told me Marigold took a few tests, though, with one-year-old toddlers, it was always a bit uncertain, as only age could prove or disprove any diagnosis. But in her opinion, Marigold was a healthy, if a bit more energetic toddler. A perspicacious child, she said. There were no signs of neurodivergent behaviors, though time would tell. I wanted to give the therapist more examples of her erratic behavior, like when she refused to eat or when she pushed me or bit me. And why only me? Why was I targeted? But once the therapist's mind was settled, there was no more space for questioning.

    I was rather content with stumbling on the serene mom. Learned more in five minutes talking to her than in one hour with a therapist worth a hundred dollars. More reason not to tell Gavin. He already knew he was right. Why tell him again?

CHAPTER 35

AFTER the disappointing visit to the therapist, my mental state took a turn for the worst. Gavin didn't know why but he still took pity on me and decided to include a few days of rest in our family schedule. I could finally get a break from the mundane chaos. And, sometimes, on rare occasions, when Marigold was in good spirits and grandma was well-rested, we would go on a date. Usually, the date would consist of a dinner, a movie, or a walk in the park. What could a mother ask for, if not for the chance to feel like a woman again?

One of our dates fell on a beautiful spring day. Gavin and I took a walk around the University of Washington campus, where the cherry trees blossomed each year. The trees had several large branches expanding in all directions as if to show off their creation. And since the branches were covered only with petals, they looked like exposed roots with pink snow scattered all over. Alongside the gothic style of the buildings, the scenery turned the whole campus into a spring wonderland ideal for couples in love who enjoyed each other's presence and wished to forget the painful strains of reality. When we commenced our walk on the paved path, Gavin took my hand in his, making me swoon even more for his astuteness. He turned his head towards me and shared his signature smile; I could not refuse to reciprocate. With every step and glance made, it felt as if we were in a slow-motioned movie scene. I could smell each note of the fragile fragrance of blooms. I could taste the faint sweetness of pink cotton candy in my mouth (though I hadn't eaten that day). I could feel my hand warming in Gavin's. I could hear the sounds his steps made in contrast to his contemplative silence. I fell in love all over again, with him, with nature, with life. Maybe my struggles with Marigold, as prolonged as they felt, might've been a short detour in the grand scheme of things. With Gavin, I felt safe and hopeful once again. He had a knack for giving purpose to a derelict situation. I stopped for a second, tugging at his hand. He turned with a question mark between his eyebrows. I embraced him, reveling in his aura of endearment.

When my meditative awareness reached a climax, the phone rang. The ability of a phone call to ruin precious moments like these could only be compared to Marigold's antics. It was Jasmine. She was asking for a meetup. This time, she wanted to try a new Mexican restaurant somewhere in Seattle. I told Gavin about it. He let me continue to enjoy the evening on my own with the promise that Jasmine would drive me home while he would go and take the little burden off grandma's shoulders.

***

The dim light of the restaurant made the space smaller than expected and somewhat secluded. I never knew where Jasmine would plan the meetup, every time a different one, though all were Mexican. This one was in a basement kind of location. The walls had Mexican wrestlers with angry faces painted on them. How could anyone swallow their meal with someone's angry face peering over?

As always early, she kept pushing a mug of beer back and forth in a booth close to the window. Her face was drawn in from the weight she'd lost in the meantime. Still gorgeous, but less color as if her brilliance was toned down a bit. Her pensive demeanor added a whimsical allure. I could admire her all day, or till the moment she would notice me. When she did, her eyes lit up, and all her previous forlorn energy turned electrical.

"Hi, Laura. So good to see you." She got up and hugged me with despair. Before I could reply, she continued, "what would you like to drink?"

I meant to say tea, but she saw the waiter approach us and asked if I wanted a beer as well. I couldn't refuse. I took a seat on the red leather cushion and waited for her to take a gulp of beer.

"How are you? How's Marigold? How's Gavin doing?" Jasmine asked, avoiding even a moment of silence.

"Were pretty good. Marigold is a bit rambunctious, but she changes so often. Her personality is always varied."

"Good, good," she said as if she got all the necessary answers.

Another veil of silence dropped. This time she didn't want to cover it as fast. She simply kept her gaze on the beer mug.

"Jasmine, it wasn't your fault that time," I said.

Her eyes shot straight at me.

"It was your fiancé's fault," I added.

Her chin drooped back to her previous position.

"Yeah, Brandon was a bit too intense with you. I could've defended you better."

"Me? What about you?"

"I'm used to it."

"No, no, no. Unstable behavior is not something you should be getting used to."

"He's a really caring person. Most of the time."

"Most of the time doesn't cut it, Jasmine. It's either always or never."

She crumpled like a piece of paper, trying to distance herself from the message I was implying.

"You must break up with him," I said.

She knew those words were coming but still couldn't accept them.

"I would if it were as easy. We're supposed to get married. He spent so much already on the wedding. I can't just up and leave."

"If you were a happy bride-to-be, would we be sitting here discussing your fiancé?"

Silence.

"No," she whispered.

"Then what's there to think about? There's always some reluctance in such matters, but he's not good for you, at least that you can attest."

"I need time and maybe prepare him for it."

"So, he can convince you to stay? No way. You cut from the root. Chop, chop, and be done. Have you ever thought about what you want to do next? Something exciting?"

Jasmine swallowed shallowly as if her throat muscles got paralyzed from the thought.

I might've been too pushy.

"I'm just thinking of your well-being. Nothing more," I said.

"I know... I know. The idea of moving to Bellevue makes me excited. I always wanted to move to a smaller city or even the suburbs. And open a diner, just like this one." Her eyes wandered around the premise. "I would start with a coffee shop where I would sell Mexican coffee. I would decorate it with Frida's pictures, *sarapes*, *papel picado*. There wouldn't be a corner unadorned by color. Every day, I would teach my customers a new Spanish word. No one would tell me what to do, not my mother, not my brothers, not even... Brandon." Her smile turned sad and made her quiet again.

"It's a good start. Then again, whatever you do, I will be there next to you for support."

She felt safer. Something in her gaze reassured me.

"I am afraid something is going to happen to me, Laura," she said as her fingers trembled on the mug.

"I'm sure he won't be capable of a heinous act. He loves you in his own way."

"Yes, you're right. Thanks."

My hand hugged hers, though a bit cold and moist from the beer mug, my warm message of support reached her anxiety. The evening felt lighter.

CHAPTER 36

WE celebrated Marigold's second birthday in the family. Mom came over with a chocolate cake and a candle in the shape of a two. I wasn't in the mood for slapping a fake smile for more than five hours, was the explanation I gave when Gavin asked why I didn't want a party. He seemed a bit surprised, if not disappointed but didn't contest. As plausible as my wry mood could be, in reality, I couldn't show to the world the hideous character my child possessed and expressed illustriously in my house. I left her to her means, and the means she made were over our heads.

On the outside, her dark blonde hair, squarish face, and peachy cheeks resembled a child actress at her prime. Though hard to believe, since her main diet was animal cookies and applesauce, she still stored some baby fat on her neck and joints. The extent I went to assure her a rainbow diet went from mixing applesauce with hidden bananas, strawberries, and blueberries (which were received with convulsions and a purple puddle on the floor) to kneeling in front of her with fast-food French fries, which she adamantly refused and requested once again her applesauce and cookies. We once tried a different brand of applesauce. The look in her eyes put a fear in me I would never forget, somewhere between betrayal and repulsion. One time we succeeded (Gavin did) in convincing her to eat a real apple. The masticated bits came crumbling on the floor like my determination.

After, I went to three different stores and bought all the applesauce they had and all their cookies and laid my weapons down. It was clear as day; the cake was for me. I even blew the candle to congratulate myself on surviving two years of terror. For her, the range of my tonality did not matter. It didn't change when I yelled, even if it was in her ear, when I pleaded on my knees, when I cried in desolation, when I whimpered, when I threatened with Daddy or time out. Only, at times, she would throw me a demeaning look and continue her activity, be it a book (which she read on her own or with Dad), a cartoon, painting a wall, peeing on the carpet, throwing food at me, ripping my hair and, of course, biting.

I downed my cabernet after a full spoon of chocolate cake and with it all my sour memories. Gavin was elated. I really didn't get him. He saw the atrocious behavior towards me but turned a blind eye or two since she behaved like an angel with him. He simply refused to talk about it. A fairy tale of denial, where I was the defeated dragon, and they lived happily ever after. A father and daughter duo. I chose to love her no matter what, but how much could a mother do? Till where do I reach the stop sign? I poured myself another glass and looked at the adorable, picturesque image of a father and daughter. Who needs a mother to such perfection?

"Are you sure you want to get drunk on your daughter's birthday?" said my beloved mother.

"If not today, then when? Besides, who's gonna see me?"

"At least hold it till after the photos."

"So we can smile and make a cute Christmas card which says look at us were so happy and fake?"

"Laura…" Her head moved from side to side but in a blurry way.

"I'm having a great time, Mom. Let me enjoy."

"With that sour face? Who are you trying to fool? Yourself?"

"Maybe. Is it working?"

"You know the answer."

"Gavin, let's take a picture for the Christmas card."

"Sure." He smiled with his fatherly content. "But first, let's give Marigold her present."

"Oh darn, I forgot to wrap it." I ran to the bedroom and back in a sprint and gave her a tiny box with a logo of an unknown brand. "Here you go, sweetie."

Marigold pushed herself into her daddy's chest to avoid me potentially taking her away from him. I opened the box, and to my astonishment, her eyes glowed as if the sun reflected on her green ambers. We knew we were leaning into her obsession, but we couldn't help it. Those were her first pair of ruby slippers. Many more were most likely to follow. Her obsession was something new, but the degree and fulmination it got were growing by the day.

Some weeks ago, I stumbled upon the "Somewhere Over the Rainbow" video where Dorothy sang. Marigold seemed intrigued. So, I decided to show her the whole movie. Since then, there was no rest in the household. Only wizards, witches from the East, witches from the West, scarecrows, lions, tin men, and Dorothy. She learned more words from the movie than from all the books I ever read to her. She would mumble the song from the moment she would wake up to the moment I had to fight her to go to sleep. So, expectedly, we bought her a version of the ruby slippers.

"Dowophy, Dowophy!" Marigold squealed.

"Yes." Her excitement tugged at my heart. "Dorothy."

"Do you want to put them on?"

I was getting a bit tipsy, but I hoped to be able to open the clasp. Success!

"Here you go, dear."

She put her foot in the shoe like a delicate Cinderella. One of those few magic moments in life, which one cherished forever. Her heel, though, didn't cooperate with the creation of my magic moment. It didn't fit. I pushed and pressed, but there was no way her foot would fit. Either she grew two sizes larger in the last week, or the company was garbage. I messed up.

"I'm sorry, Marigold, they don't fit. Mommy will buy you a larger pair."

Apparently, the explanation didn't fare well with her (no surprise there), but I wasn't prepared for the fury she ensnared upon me. First, the shoes were thrown at me, with a speed no two-year-old should possess. Then she threw herself at me, banging at my chest and kicking me with her feet. Shrills, tears, screams. A horror movie encapsulated in a toddler, and I was the first and only victim. Gavin grabbed her and took her under his fatherly wing while I was bringing myself together. But not for long, she threw herself at me again like a feral cat ready to scratch me for insubordination. Along my spine traveled a shiver I never expected to feel from my own blood. The roars grew louder, epitomizing her hatred towards the one who birthed her. I didn't know what to do. I froze while Gavin played the circus tamer.

In the end, Grandma showed mercy upon us, took the shoes from me, grabbed a knife, cut the toe caps, and shoved them on the distraught child. The sky was clear again. We breathed out a long sigh and began to clean up from the table.

"Happy birthday, Mari," said her grandma and presented her with another gift box. They went into her bedroom to unwrap it. It seemed weird when mother decided to go to Marigold's room. Only when Marigold returned, it became clear why she chose obscurity. While Mari presented us her new doll, all I could see was the red thread tied around her wrist.

"Leave." I ran towards the door.

"What are you saying?" Mother asked.

"Leave now." The soft creak of the door resounded. "You are not welcome in this house anymore."

"Is it because I told you to not drink too much? You should know that."

"No, because you have no sense of boundaries, Mom."

"What do you mean?"

"You are not the mother of this child. Thus, you don't decide what she wears and what she should be protected from."

"I might not be her mother, but she clings to me every time I visit."

An atomic bomb exploded in my head. Firstly, because she was lying, and secondly, because she did it to my face.

"In this house, Mother, we do not believe in voodoo. My child will not be following in my steps. I don't even want to imagine it."

"What did I do? It's just a red thread with an evil eye."

"It starts with a thread, and then it ends with untrimmed braids and salty backs."

"We don't want her to be cursed or something. Or maybe she already is, with her behavior and all–"

"Stop it. She is not cursed. There is no such thing. She's just a difficult child." I pointed at the door.

"You will regret this. Without my help, taking care of a sensitive child like Marigold will be hard."

"It might be so, but I don't want to pay such a steep price for your care. I could never afford it."

"Fine." She flung her purple scarf around her neck, and as a last exaggerated move of a terrible actress, she passed the door's frame, turned towards me, and said, "you will beg me to return, and I will laugh in your face," and slammed the door.

Relief relaxed my shoulders.

"Maybe it wasn't a good idea to fight with your mother over such trivial things," said Gavin while holding Marigold, both in a bit of a stupor.

"Trivial? If you knew how much damage this woman has done, you wouldn't consider it trivial."

"Your mother wants what's best for Marigold, in the only way she knows."

"Listen, I've had enough of her superstitions to last me a lifetime. My daughter will not go through the same. Not if I can do something about it."

Me fighting with my mom was already a strenuous moment for a child, but when Marigold saw us fighting, all hell broke loose. She began to flail and wail and didn't want to detach from her father's neck.

"Now, now, Marigold. Mommy and Daddy are not fighting. We're talking. Don't be scared," I said.

I tried to pry her from her dad's neck, but she didn't give in. Rage filled me up again. Fine.

"I have a headache, Gavin. Can you take care of Marigold? I'll go lie in bed for a bit."

"Sure." He took a seat on the sofa with the despotic sloth still attached to his neck.

I lay in bed looking at the popcorn ceiling, thinking about the Christmas family photo we were not sending that year.

CHAPTER 37

DURING the second year of Marigold's life, my misery continued in the same bleak silence, with the same schedule pertaining to whatever I could do to avoid a merciless tantrum rather than a joyful experience of bonding. On a usual morning, her favorite breakfast consisted of waffles with blueberries and syrup, which she would make a point of taking a few bites of and then throwing them on the floor. She loved listening to the splat maple syrup made on the tiles and how the blueberries made tiny hops or, even better, got squished. Every time I admonished such behavior, she laughed in my face. After my black coffee (a warrior's drink), for tea was to be enjoyed (and I didn't have such bliss anymore), we would play a bit in the living room. Most of her play was to open drawers, to click on any button, to jump on the sofa as hard as she could while the mountain of toys remained untouched in the corner. My main activity was keeping her from breaking something, including herself. When the days were blessed with the sun's rays, we would go to the playground where her main activity was to take other kids' toys, and mine was to apologize profusely. We would have lunch, cookies, and applesauce (the only thing she ate, still). Then came the dreadful nap. She hated sleeping next to me, so I tried to let her sleep in her room. Marigold, of course, wouldn't. I, nonetheless, tried to manifest a semblance of a schedule by reading a book, giving her some juice (she abhorred any kind of dairy products), and letting her nap. She usually fell asleep two hours later than intended by the schedule. In the meantime, I had to prepare dinner for Gavin and me, bring the house to a somewhat decent state, and, maybe, take a breather. Marigold slept very short naps, so my breather seldom substantiated.

The second part of the day we spent in various places like grocery stores, the mall, or any random stores since one of her favorite activities was gawking at other people. Of course, she always made a tantrum about not getting a toy or a pack of cookies, but I couldn't spend the entirety of Gavin's paycheck on Marigold's whims. At the same time, I couldn't find any other activity which engrossed her so much. So, I pushed the grocery cart, fully aware of what was about to happen.

Evenings were considered sacred time since Marigold had the opportunity to cuddle with her precious father. When Daddy was present, her entire focus gyrated towards him. I was a mere shadow of resentment to which she didn't pay much attention. Unfortunately, it meant he could not eat his dinner, so the only time he could ingest his food was when Marigold took her bath, another moment of dreadful anticipation. At first, there was the battle of wits on how soon she was supposed to get into the bathtub since separating herself from her one true love, aka Daddy, was a task of unimaginable hardship. With much crying and flailing, contrasting with a newfound biceps power in me, we would find ourselves in the bathroom. She would bite me every time I undressed her and would kick me when I would put her in the bathtub. But once she felt the warm water and the opportunities of destruction surrounding her, she would forget her vexation (did I mention this happened every day?).

While in the bath, the water looked like an unforeseeable storm had struck. The dolls, rubber duckies, and rubber fishes were at the mercy of the humongous wave about to drown them. Giant splashes would move them around with forces beyond their knowledge. The force was Kraken Marigold. Was I happy to see her enjoy herself and I not bothered for a few minutes? Yes. Did the bathroom resemble the outcome of a gruesome marine battle? Yes. I had to pay the price of cleaning, repairing, or replacing Marigold's aftermath for every minute of resting my bones.

Our night routine resembled any other happy family. Pajamas on, teeth brushed, story time with Daddy, kisses, hugs, good nights, and a closed door. But once the door would close, the dramatic wailing similar to her babyhood time would commence. We would take turns to check up on her. When the door would open, she would be fine, calling us "Mommy, Daddy" in a sweet way. When the door would close, her devilish spewing of noise began again. After half an hour of summoning the devil, she would drop and fall asleep. Gavin and I would hug in celebration of another day of survival and go to sleep. There was no time for talking, no time for intimacy, no time for ourselves. Just sleep.

When Marigold reached two years and a half, she was officially ready for potty training. Well, that's what I told myself since I couldn't deal with diapers anymore. I wasn't sure if she was ready. She didn't show any signs. Even though all books I've read told me to look for them, I couldn't wait. I bought her the most adorable potty I could find in the store. I bought books about potty training and showed her cartoons on how it should be done. But on the day of the intended training, Marigold refused to even sit on the potty. I showed her how I would do it. She didn't even look. I put some cartoons in front of her while I tried to coerce her to at least sit, but all she did was stand up and watch cartoons next to the potty. I realized she wasn't ready, so I gave her another month, but she behaved the same when we resumed.

I couldn't let it go for too long; she at least needed to try to sit on it. So, I sat her in increments of fifteen minutes, but Marigold didn't show signs of willingness to pee in the potty. I tried for several days, never losing hope, but then when she seemed done with my insistence, she went and peed next to the potty. The second day she did the same. Even if I was right there next to her, she would pee next to the potty. Then I changed the method and switched her to pull-ups. Marigold hated those so much, she would remove them and pee next to them. One time she even pooped right next to the pull-up. Seeing my fretful face, Marigold understood exactly how this affected me, so she used it against me. She found a purpose. Every time I scolded her for throwing food or not wanting to take a bath, the next moment, she would take off her pull-ups and pee next to them. Defiance was her nature, and I was her main target. I de-escalated and put her in diapers, but she did the same routine of defying me. I begged her to stop doing it, I even bribed her with candy, but she only listened to her daddy. He asked her nicely once, and Marigold never did it in his presence, but once Gavin went to work, I would experience it all over again. Eventually, I hid the potty, and she forgot about it for a while since there were other ways to torment me. Only on her worst days she would pull a stunt like that to show her power. Thus, one could draw a single conclusion from the whole ordeal. I was thoroughly tamed by my own daughter.

As my days became a monotonous burden, I silently yearned for sleep which was still interrupted, but, at least, I got some hours of separation and readjustment for the next day's battles. Then there were those nights when all was silent, but my brain couldn't relax, being in a state of electrifying wakefulness from the day's events. On one of those nights, thoughts of freedom crept under my blanket. The thoughts of freedom crept up in my mind when no one was watching; they crept up when I least expected while remembering a positive highlight of the day. But most imposing of all, the thoughts of freedom crept into my dreams. I dreamt of the same sequence, made out of scraps of memories throughout my life: gathering poppies on the hills of Oklahoma; braiding a crown out of daisies; the juicy bite of a watermelon slice; running through the aroma of lavender rows; observing a butterfly on my shoulder; an evening's breeze as it ruffled my hair; heels sinking in the sand by the seaside's twilight; the taste of his salty lips on mine; my skin turning into the color of golden vivacity as the sun heated my body and soul; hands intertwined as stars flickered in the waves; bouts of deep laughter…

The dreams would appear over and over again like an incessant reminder of all things I couldn't enjoy anymore. The things I missed doing in solitude. I missed being alone with my dreams, with my soul's flutter, with my heart's universe. A wistful wish for the freedom I was so privileged to have before. Freedom to get out of the house alone without needing to take her with me and not be forced to decide when I should return. Before, time flowed freely like a waterfall compared to the afflictions of my daily responsibilities at the moment, which drawled any ephemeral joy out of my life. There were times while she slept, and I would enumerate all the things I could be doing at that very moment. Something more efficient, more effective, maybe even pleasant.

But I couldn't live out my wishful thoughts. Those were forbidden territories I could never long for. I had to give her the benefit of the doubt. I had to forget about my intrinsic needs and focus on hers. I had to vaporize as a person so she could thrive on my droplets of dew. I had to shadow her so she could shine greater than a star. I had to fade in color so she could be a rainbow; to turn into a dry branch so she could bear the ripest fruit; to become fertilizer so I could nourish her into a marigold so she could radiate back to the sun. They all said, "it too will pass," and in no time, it would become easier, lighter on the soul.

"She will understand, and I will be understood," I whispered.

Gavin didn't even notice my lamentation; he trusted me with his precious Marigold to become the perfect family, with picture-perfect love, care, and future. He called me "Mom" now. Once I had a name. He asked only how she felt or behaved or did. I was never a topic of conversation. Where was I in this equation? I missed him so much. My Gavin, my perfectly imperfect husband, which I let love me. I only got bits of him, the scraps from the love and attention he gave Marigold. But, at the end of the day, even with a thirsty soul, if Marigold needed the sacrifice of my obscurity, I would give it to her. If motherhood represented sacrifice, I was willing to abdicate my most precious element. It was the only way for her to like me so I could like her back. It will be worth it in the end.

    Nonetheless, when all was quiet and shades of darkness were ruling the house, dreams of freedom still crept up carelessly into my mind. Dreams of poppies on hills, crowns of daisies, rows of lavender, watermelon bites, a butterfly on my shoulder, evening breeze in my hair, heels in sand, salty lips, tanned skin, hands intertwined, ocean swirls, and never-ending laughter.

CHAPTER 38

"WHAT'S been bugging you lately? You always seem preoccupied with something. What's going on?" Gavin asked me one evening (the first time since forever) while I was watching the news about an orca carrying her calf on the back for several days.

"Nothing. All is peachy dandy with a cherry on top," I said, turning off the TV demonstratively.

"I don't know what I've done to deserve your sarcasm–"

"That's the thing, you've done nothing. Don't you see you are still living the dream before our child turned into an unruly, ungrateful monster?"

"Laura, there are some lines you are crossing which shouldn't be crossed."

"So, it's only how she feels, nothing about me to concern yourself? She's been ruthless with me every step of the way with not even a speck of love. I feel like a childless mother who must yearn for a random bone of affection she might throw at me. She is not the daughter I wanted to have."

"Maybe you are not the mother she wanted to have," Gavin responded, fire in his eyes.

"There is no mother she wants. She wants you. A father. Maybe a grandma for diversity."

"How can you speak like that? She is just a naïve child."

"It's not what the therapist said. She is above average smart and perspicacious."

"You went to a therapist without telling me?"

"What was the point of telling you? You're simply going to undermine my opinion and pretend like everything's alright."

"Laura, I've never heard you talk like this before. What's got into you?" Worry sketched across his face. It took me off guard, him worrying about my mental state.

"I, I-I, I'm tired." I sat back down on the sofa.

Worse than living with a malicious creature under one roof was Gavin questioning my sanity. He did not understand. He was Gavin. He lived in a world of primary colors. He didn't see all the hues of red painted on my face. He just saw red. It made him worry. I couldn't let him doubt me. I needed him. I cared too much about him. How could I let Gavin discover another world underneath my surface? No, no. I would lose him. I might lose him for good.

"Gavin? Remember when we went on a vacation in the Caribbean."

"Yes."

"I want to go there again. Only the two of us."

"We will, honey. When I get a raise and a week off. We'll go." He kneeled next to me, looking at my lowered face. He caressed my cheek.

"How soon?" I asked.

"As soon as possible."

I knew he didn't know when. I knew it wouldn't be soon, but I wanted to believe him. Maybe he knew something I didn't.

"Gavin, I changed my mind. I want to go to work."

"You will."

"And we'll send Marigold to daycare."

"We will."

"Am I a bad mother?"

"No, you're like any other mother."

I snickered when he subjected me to the mediocre comparison.

"Like any other…"

***

It took me a lot of courage to tell Gavin I wanted to go back to work, maybe by placing my mental stability on the table. My mother would've been an option, but I could never ask her, especially after our fight. My only solution was daycare. After my previous encounter with a nanny, I refused the idea straight away, plus they were too expensive. We were already in too much credit card debt, but I simply couldn't stay with my kid in the house all day. She had to go to daycare for socialization, discipline, and other people she could hate besides me. Yes, yes, it seemed like a good plan. From what I remembered, many moms were on a waiting list since they were pregnant to get into the school of preference. I, of course, did not expect to ever send my child to daycare, so it didn't even cross my mind. Before I could even open this discussion with Gavin again, I had to investigate the matter. After multiple calls and unflattering begging, I found one in Redmond. A bit of a stretch to drive, but it wouldn't be a problem if Marigold would be sent safely into the hands of professionals, and I could ultimately find a job.

I told Gavin Marigold would go to daycare in two weeks. He felt somewhat sad as if his child had reached a new milestone of independence. Gavin, Gavin, she wasn't going to an actual school. Only a daycare where people with experience take care of kids whose parents had no choice but to work. Even though it was a matter of choice for me, another paycheck would improve our financial situation (what was left from Marigold's daycare payment). I imagined what I would do when Mari would be busy all day. I would take care of myself with Epson salt baths and face masks, shopping in complete self-absorption, revive my garden's deplorable state. And then, put on my dusty navy blazer and go to work. Oh, the bliss.

Monday arrived, and we were ready as if it was my first day of vacation. Marigold looked like a doll in a floral dress with gold leggings and her ruby slippers. The staff's smiles resembled promising lands of perpetual silence and calmness at my house. I went home and drank tea, lots of it. I watched my favorite shows and ate all the chips I could find. Then, I took a romance novel I never had time to read and went straight into the bathtub. The next day I began looking for a PA job online. One time, I even thought of calling Cassandra; maybe she knew of some openings. With all my favorite things happening, the week went by like a long deep yoga breath. On Friday, though, I got called in by the daycare director for a small chat.

A somber face greeted me, a stark contrast from the first day.

"Marigold is a wonderful girl," said the director, "she is very smart and bright, but she doesn't listen to the teachers. She refuses to eat or sleep at the designated time. But most of these issues are solvable. There is another thing she does which complicates the situation."

"What is it?"

"Marigold bites. She bit several kids and two teachers. Every time we try to stop an undesirable behavior, she retaliates with biting."

"And there is nothing you can do about it?"

"Unfortunately, according to our policy, if a child bites, we have to let them go."

"Aren't you supposed to be the professionals? To teach my daughter how to behave?"

"There's only that much we can do," the director said with fake sincerity.

"You select kids based on your personal preference and choose to discard others who don't fit. Is that how you manage your institution?"

"There are more issues at stake than keeping in a child who doesn't obey. A group setting contains more rules than one on one. Plus, it might take only a short while till she grows up a bit and can return."

"I'll make sure we never return. My daughter and I will never step foot in this so-called professional facility."

I stomped out of the room and straight into Marigold's classroom. I took her in my arms and, without uttering a word, went straight to the car. My daughter might've been uncontrollable, but she was my daughter, and no one was allowed to tell me if she deserved to be at daycare or not. It was my decision to make, and I decided my daughter would not be a victim of such humiliation.

CHAPTER 39

THE dreary Saturday morning seemed to get worse by the time it reached eleven. The weather app confirmed what I already knew—rainy with no chance of sun. Though we were in September, the gloomy weather had already spread through the windows of my house and my soul. Gavin noticed my apathy and lent me a free Saturday to visit Margaret, a privilege I hadn't taken advantage of for many months. When Marigold was a baby, I often brought her to the nursery between the Blue Point Junipers. As Margaret was holding her, we got the opportunity to exchange each other's mundane with each other's novelty. Since Margaret had enough experience with babies, her arms automatically formed a perfect cradle. For me, pots felt closer. Playing with soil, pruning trees, planting fragile forms of life, what could be better? Things looked just right, me gardening and Margaret mothering. But the somewhat good times didn't last long, as Marigold became an unsurmountable creature forcing me to keep her home in the realm of baby-proofed drawers and plastic plants.

  When I stepped through the iron gate, I was welcomed by the same Juniper soldiers, though not as many. As my eyes wandered across the territory, I continued to see fewer plants spread around. Was her business picking up all of a sudden? Did more people find out about my hidden oasis? Or maybe Margaret was renewing her inventory. I was glad to witness a boost in sales, though a bit jealous of Margaret's successful business endeavor.

Margaret was at her usual, muddy gloves, muddy knees while replanting a palm tree. No drizzle could stop her from working.

"I see you've got clients who still yearn for some make-pretend Florida. Did you tell them a palm tree will not make the rain stop?"

"I only provide the tools. They choose the fantasy," Margaret said as she stood up. Her knees were not only soiled but also damp from the perpetually moistened ground.

"Haven't seen you in a while. How are you? How's the family?"

"Gavin's fine. Marigold, as usual, capricious, incorrigible, and self-aggrandized to extremes."

"So, you're saying just like any other child?" she asked as she took a turn towards the house.

"I wish. She takes everything to the next level. Marigold would get the trophy for the unruliest child in the area. I wouldn't dare go beyond. Who knows? There might be someone else worse than her, but I doubt it." I kept walking after her.

"Let's pour some water in the kettle."

Margaret looked a little worn out. Her broad shoulders were a bit slouchy, in her eyes a bit less sparkle, and her spirit a bit less vibrant.

"I see you've been selling more recently." I took a seat at the round table after I peeled my wet trench coat carefully.

"Actually, I haven't been renewing my orders. Harriet is looking for a job, Rosa is settled at the college campus, and Luther left for college recently. Whereas for me, I'm not sure where my path might lead me."

"I'm sure you will find a way to stay. You are wonderful at your job. Why wouldn't you?"

"Just because someone's good at their job doesn't mean they're meant to do it. Plus, I always planned on traveling once my kids go to college," she said taking a longer pause to think about something far away, then as if woken up from a dream, she looked back at me, "but enough about me, better tell me more about Gavin and Marigold."

"Oh, Gavin, he is doing great. Always coddling his daughter. They have more fun than I had with him in all seven years before her. While I am the fidgeting observer," Margaret settled the cup of tea into my hand as I continued, "I can't understand why she never pays attention to me? I feel like a complacent servant sometimes. Most of the time, actually."

"A child's world should never revolve around her parents. It's an individual cosmos. A world built out of everyday things she discovers. She doesn't have time to spend following your rules. Your role is to keep the biome of her world intact, a haven for exploration. She shouldn't worry about food, water, or shelter. It became your responsibility the moment you gave her life. It might seem like servitude, but it only follows the natural cycle of life. You got to explore your world only because your parents made sure you did. Now, it's your turn to protect Marigold's world even if it doesn't befit you. Someday, it will be Marigold's role if she chooses to mother kids. We are not giving life to our kids for our own needs, though intrinsically, we get unconditional love and affection in return. We give life to raise good, conscientious people so they, in return, raise good, conscientious people in the future, which leads to a better society and multigenerational growth. For, when your kid will be your age, she will make decisions for your present and future alongside others of her generation. Raising kids is the epitome of delayed gratification; the results will show only when it is too late to change something.

"But let's think of the kids who do not get their universe protected. Their biome cracked and damaged. Those cracks will design their way into the world. They will become invisible as they grow, but every time they encounter a trigger, those wrinkles of adult failure imprinted on their soul will haunt them again. And consequently, affect us as a society. Remember Laura, if your kid is still curious about the world, then you're doing it right."

I always knew Margaret's career as a university professor of sociology would follow her everywhere, but bewilderment and embarrassment had struck hard when it affected me directly. I complied with my silence but, in my mind, I felt a misinterpreted. How could my kid and I be on opposite sides of contentment? How could my wish to be a good mother be refuted to such a strenuous degree? I had to lose myself to let her flourish. It's either I get the trauma, or she does? And there was no middle ground. Defeat was a mild word for how I felt in that moment, and I wished to not discuss such matters ever so much. Margaret made a long pause to let me absorb the information. She knew me all too well and didn't pressure me into an open discussion, but I couldn't stop pondering on all she said. As if Margaret read my flustered mind, she added: "Listen, I get where you're coming from. All mothers, at some point, get disappointed in their offspring. And trust me, it is for the better because we finally realize our kids are just as human as us. I know. I've had three of them. It ain't no easy business. As much as I like to see things from above, it becomes difficult to disassociate when it comes to the nitty-gritty. Parents must give more than love. They must set boundaries as well. Sometimes, giving too much can have the opposite effect. Boundaries are a necessity for a child, a guide into the social world we have to share. But parents were not taught how to instill them, so they either choose to be permissive in fear of being too harsh or turn the rules of common living into reasons for excessive punishments befitting them personally. The assertive middle is where every parent should strive for. Because at the end of the day, every child is a good child and every decision made by them stems from one need–the need to belong. Many books have been written on the psychological theory of social inclusion developed by

Dreikurs and Adler. You should look into it. They might help understand Marigold's behavior better. Or maybe yours."

It seemed like a sound explanation but, more so, like a waste of time since Marigold was the exact opposite. She didn't want to belong to me, but I didn't want to offend Margaret with my opinion.

"I better get going. I need to buy some diapers for Marigold. Thank you for the tea," I said as I put on my still-soaked coat.

Margaret didn't say anything. She simply followed me to the gate. As I was preparing to bid her goodbye, she asked, "are you going to visit more often?"

I heard an unusual pleading tone in her voice.

"Sure, I would never miss an opportunity to visit you."

And out of nowhere, Margaret gave me a hug. A strong, somewhat desperate hug. One, she wasn't used to giving, and I wasn't used to receiving. Baffled but honored, I pursued my walk towards the car as Margaret kept seeing me off motionless. Out of all the people I knew, Margaret always proved to be one unique lady.

CHAPTER 40

IT happened on an ordinary Tuesday. Marigold was grumpy for whatever reason; I could never guess. It came as a matter of fact like leaves falling in autumn and flowers blooming in spring. But was it normal to expect it from a being whose mood mattered more than her family? Did dictatorships tendencies start young? Were tyrants a result of nature or nurture? I would be the first to raise my hand and say nature.

Again, she refused to eat anything except cookies and applesauce. Again, she chose to wear the same ragged ruby slippers. Again, she chose to pee next to the demonstratively removed diaper. Nonetheless, I felt a bit better, or I wanted to feel like it was better that day. Maybe I got accustomed to all her outlandish behavior, so it proved harder to derail me from a state of contentment. It was all in the brain, after all. Contentment was the modest cousin of happiness, but the latter felt like a cloud floating further and further the more I tried to reach for it.

So, I settled for contentment through a routine of disaster avoidance. When she attempted to spit toothpaste all over me after brushing her teeth, I would have a paper towel ready for protection. When she deliberately threw food on the floor, I had a sheet of newspaper prepared. All her attempts at biting me stopped when I lathered all the vulnerable parts of my body with hand sanitizer. One step at a time. One step at a time. During nap time, she wouldn't sleep but would stay quiet in bed, and it felt like a true success in the making (if you were to set the bar relatively low, that is).

As I drank my tea at my desired temperature, I decided since I could manage her every whim, I might get braver and take her to the zoo. A place she'd never been before. Maybe it would act as positive reinforcement towards her good behavior. And Margaret said positive reinforcement was efficient, so it was what I wanted to do.

Though it was a weekday, the zoo was packed with kids of all ages with parents of various degrees of disillusionment. Some even looked happy. A rare case of denial. I took Marigold to see the monkeys first. Her little eyes, like tiny beads, were fixated on every move of the animals as if to absorb all this new and fascinating information. She did not move for about five minutes. As a proud mother who did something to make her child happy, I couldn't help but experience elation. The first one in a long time. I tried to pry her from the first introduction of the zoo to show her more animals. To my surprise, she followed. My daughter followed me! I could jump there alongside the monkeys from the burst of emotions swarming in my heart. We saw the zebras, the birds, a few cougars. Marigold could not believe the cartoonish animals she usually saw on TV were now in front of her, live and in full size. A day to remember. I even took a few pictures when she reached to touch a parrot.

Our final destination was the lion. The big, indolent lion. We were lucky to see him so close to the fence. When Marigold saw the majestic animal, she went bonkers. She wanted to pet the lion.

"The cowardly lion. I want. I want," she squealed.

The sad creature lying on the ground reminded Marigold of the lion from The Wizard of Oz, and she desperately wanted to pet it. Out of all the animals, she chose the one who could eat her whole. I explained that the lion wasn't the same as in the movie. This lion could hurt her, but there was no compromise. She wanted in. And then it began. Her eyes began to bulge out. Her face turned into various shades of purple. Her mouth opened wide, but there was no sound. Yet. When it finally emerged, it rattled all the animals around. Everyone looked at us in case the innocent lion indeed took a bite out of the distressed creature resembling a little girl.

I wanted to take her to the side, but more and more people gathered to witness the commotion, leaving me no privacy. I knew there was no stopping the train of the tantrum, so I had to get to her. To reason with her. I would've agreed to give her anything at that moment. But having everyone looking at me, it felt like a million eyes judged how horrible of a mother I was. They didn't have to tell me explicitly. I knew as much. So, I did the unthinkable. I tried to stop the train. I kneeled to comfort her, to hug her, to attempt a kiss. The devil's child snapped. I saw it in her eyes. The ferociousness. The viciousness. The hate. And for the first time in my life, I was terrified of my baby. I felt all levels of fear, from stupefaction to sheer terror. I could not comprehend what would follow and waited for her to make a move.

She distanced herself from me, and then, with forceful speed, she launched herself onto me, hitting me with her fists like an animal fighting for dominance. The first few I felt, the rest I caught. Kneeling, I went in for a bear hug from the back. Maybe it would calm her a bit, so we could at least reach the car. The crowd was silently cheering for the weaker party, which I presumed was me. Marigold began wailing, so I automatically let her go. She slowly and deliberately turned towards me, several inches away from my face. She looked me straight in the eyes with the amount of hatred worth a human's life and slapped me as hard as a toddler could.

"You not my mommy," the creature growled, enunciating every word.

I knew not what to do. I knew not what to believe. I felt like a shot of venom spread across my body and straight to my brain. I felt a bit dizzy for a couple of seconds. Marigold was lying on the ground, crying, stomping, and hitting with her elbows. I questioned if Mother Earth felt the same pain as I did.

The pitying crowd scrammed to avoid eye contact with me. I saw no one when I turned. I grabbed my insolent child, put her on my shoulder, and ran. She kept the same rhythm in beating me as when she was hitting the ground. Consistency was key with her. I shoved her in the car but precociously to not hurt her. Some older kids followed us to glimpse a potential continuation of the previous altercation between a toddler and her misfit mother.

"Let them notify the news," I whispered.

When we reached home, the wail subsided a pitch or two but still was going strong. Gavin had just arrived from work. I stormed into her room, threw her on the pink bed, and closed the door. Marigold didn't come out. She simply continued to scream in tears.

"What happened?" asked Gavin.

"Nothing. A misunderstanding."

"I'm sure you will figure it out."

"I'm sure." I turned around and went into the bedroom.

It was one thing to live in a pond of disillusion by myself, and another was to experience a sea of eyes witnessing the unnatural: the strange relationship of an unloved mother and a cruel daughter.

Night fell, and with it, I fell deeper into groveling thoughts. I couldn't help but think what motherhood could be if not the apotheosis of creation. What painting or melody could compare to the gift of life? Who has ever recreated the first breath? There was no terrestrial tool that could compare with the power of divine creation. But after birth came another side to motherhood. The side no one could explain, but it became the denominator through evolution, the main descriptor of motherhood. It was not the process of creation but the course of formation taking the leading role. The sleepless nights, the self-sacrifice, the willingness to do everything for your child, but also the joyous moments of sharing a kiss on the forehead, the rambunctious giggles, the spontaneous hugs, the message of love sent through an inexplicable bond packed with oxytocin. What could be more motherlike than a mother's bond with her child? Or so they say.

But not all mothers had it. Some never crossed the bridge between one's selfish individuality and living for the greater good of others. It wasn't easy to take a step back into obscurity and let new life shine its miracle on the path of life. I accepted that truth as well. I went beyond myself in ways I never knew I could. I forgot my essence so hers could flow freely and in abundance. Since there was no greater sacrifice than self-sacrifice for the better good of a child's happiness. One would expect the child to appreciate, or at least, acknowledge the efforts of her mother. To share some gratitude through the healing powers of a hug, the radiant energy of a smile, the motivating strength of a kiss. A mother would blossom under the intertwined net of a child's need for her. How could a mother say no when her child asked for a kiss on the boo-boo?

But what if the child repudiated her mother? What was a mother, then? If she was not acknowledged for her sacrifice, what was her value then? What role did a mother have when her child didn't need her? What would happen if Jesus rejected His mother? What would happen to Marmee if her girls would refuse her not out of spite or stubbornness but because they deemed her inessential and her teachings futile? What would Hester do if Pearl, her daughter for whom she experienced ignominy in front of their whole town, would relinquish her need for her mother? What meaning would she find at the bottom of her shame? It was how I felt. What I needed. Like a drop of water for a dying plant. My wish became so ardent and confusing. My fulfillment stood in front of me, but my wings flew too close to the sun. There wasn't enough of me to reflect the sun's rays. Could one give too much love? Could one give more than they had and turn into a bleak version of themselves? Like an overmilked cow? What were the guidelines for boundaries where every fulfillment of need felt like chipping at one's self-actualization? Could you give while remaining the same? While still embracing yourself? Was giving and receiving a zero-sum game? I loved giving, I knew I could give too much, but the problem was that no one would see the difference. The difference between giving out of abundance and giving out of scarcity. The intrinsic value of the given did not change, but the giver did. It changed their perspective from the giver sharing their last morsel of self-worth and the taker not knowing the difference. The taker's level of awareness had to be equal to the number of times the taker was in a position of giving. Thus, the taker could understand the value of giving under scarce circumstances only when they experienced scarcity. The taker had to walk in the crippled and destitute shoes of the giver to appreciate the gift. But what about underdeveloped humans? How to translate your love to those who took but never experienced giving? And how could they understand to appreciate the gift if they've never experienced scarcity? One could limit the amount given or talk in perpetuity about the values of a gift. Still, chances were awareness would never be possible. Thus, the only way the giver could experience self-fulfillment was to become the taker. Where giving would turn to gratification.

But I simply couldn't imagine a mother sacrificing herself and sharing the child's love within herself at the same time. A transcendental loop within the self for oneself. A glorified internal rabbit hole. I knew of no such power. The glory of love had to be shared by two individuals. There was no other answer. Photosynthesis happened between multiple components, not just one delusional sunflower.

Nevertheless, I was all alone—a childless mother taking care of an autonomous and self-contained monster. She held the power of my happiness but chose instead to trample on every bud's bloom. I wanted her no harm but wished her no well-being. I simply didn't care. I didn't care if she loved her father or, worse, her grandmother more than me. Probably she merely didn't care about me at all. A servant who gave her life. That was about it. A thankless job, being a mother.

I've had many final straws since Marigold was born. Many of which began way back when she was a baby. Yes, she was little, there could never be any premeditation, but she did something I could never imagine a baby could do, reject her own mother. As if by instinct, she thought of me as a rival, an enemy she had to disarm and torture with ignorance, malcontented, and insufferable wails. I tried my best to understand her, to give her the benefit of doubt. God knows I did. For she was a mere baby, she couldn't have known better. With silent tears, I prayed it was only a phase, a blimp in the path of our bonding. She, of course, proved me wrong and the day we visited the zoo became the final straw that broke the back of my yearning.

One couldn't reach a lower abasement than a complete abnegation of the mother's role. The public execution of my motherhood. I would understand a hormonal teenager fighting for independence and even a feisty ten-year-old grappling for the first taste of self-discovery, but what toddlers had to fight for? What forced a two-year-old to malignify her relationship with the closest human she could ever be in contact with? Inborn meanness? Cruel curiosity? I probably would never find out, but I knew a child's bluntness could scratch deeper than any adult's attempt, as their claws were new and sharp, not yet dulled by grown-up needs and experiences.

I gave up. I, indeed, was no longer a mother to her. Maybe a little bit at the beginning, when I first met her, but something had happened, and I lost my baby girl forever. She had to learn how it was to be without a mother. She had to see how life would be when there was no one to satisfy her every whim. She needed a lesson of gratitude, of humbleness. Since she was so perspicacious, she would learn quickly. Nothing terminal, of course, but something to teach her a lesson of appreciation. It should take place in a large, crowded area, it'll be more effective.

The following Sunday, there was supposed to be an Autumn Festival at Seattle Centre. I planned on going anyway. A perfect spot. The weather predictions on my phone showed luminous skies, unusual for the end of October. It would be temporary, a half a day at most; not longer for sure. Maybe it would become the much-needed cure from her obnoxious self-entitlement. My lips curled up into a crescent, the first one in months. I felt my bones relaxing as I imagined the aftermath of my plan. But what if it didn't work? She could reinstall her tyrannical ways. No, no, thinking in such a way would only make it harder to go through with it. I imagined her desperate face running, searching for me, but I would be nowhere to be found. Oh, I wished the day would arrive sooner.

The next day, I felt giddy about my plan. I was singing a happy song when Gavin entered the house with his keys in one hand and a few grocery bags in the other.

"You look happier today. Did something happen?" he asked.

"Yes, I've come to a reconciliation with myself," I said in a pool of contentment.

"Wonderful. I knew you would. Where is Marigold?"

"She's asleep. She said she was going to wait for you but ultimately fell asleep. Look," I said, showing him the baby monitor.

"She looks so precious when she sleeps. I could watch her sleep forever."

"I made dinner. Want some?"

"Wow, you are in a good mood today. I'm sure tomorrow's going to be a sunny day."

The next few days, it rained.

CHAPTER 41

"TODAY is the day. Today is the day." I kept repeating to myself to avoid intrusive thoughts about potential desertion. It felt wrong for a while. To do such a thing to my child would be horrifying and outright despicable. But she wasn't my baby. She was a *Rosemary's Baby*. A child who fed on others' pain and torment. A spawn of evil set to get me and Gavin and our happy marriage. There was only one way out, and I had to adhere to it, even if my knees were turning to jelly.

  I entered the living room, opened the blinds to reassess the weather for the millionth time. It wasn't as sunny as predicted, but the blurry clouds didn't seem to carry rain in them. A great day for a revolution. Gavin wanted to come as well, but I said it was girls only. A time for bonding. He couldn't contain his excitement seeing how his two favorite girls spent time together and even bonded. Whereas my elation ran through my veins like tiny lightning bolts of electricity. But for a different reason. Little did he know the actual motive for our trip would improve our lives far better. I knew he would appreciate the effort I made for the family, even if not right away. I opened the door to her room; a rotten smell attacked my nostrils. She removed her diaper and defecated on the floor again. I wanted to yell but contained myself; a conflict could undermine my plan. Marigold was ripping pages from a picture book about insects.

On the floor, there were pictures of butterflies. She deliberately chose to pull butterflies from the book like a psychopathic kid.

After I cleaned up the mess and took her to the bathroom for a wash, I kept thinking how no one was aware of my scheme, and my mind became intoxicated with frenzy. I could almost touch the wings of my freedom, like an eagle stepping out of his cage. I would spread my dormant wings and roam the skies in delirious wonderment. I would finally behold what has always been mine: myself. My body would be mine again, my mind would be in my control, and the people I loved would cherish me once again. Today was the day.

After bathing and drying her hair, I grabbed the nicest blue dress gifted by Grandma, a blue cardigan I bought, two white socks with lace at the edge, and, of course, her favorite ruby slippers. I combed her frilly hair into pigtails which made her look like Dorothy, but there was no need for a Wizard since she was also the witch. When Gavin saw us, he exclaimed his appreciation for our outfits (I wore a black long-sleeved shirt and black jeans). Marigold went and hugged her beloved daddy, and I gave him a bashful kiss. We were ready to go.

When we arrived, I parked the car on the closest and most convenient spot I could find in the parking lot. A lucky spot to find in a never-ceasing arrival of vehicles. As we got closer to Seattle Centre, I noticed the number of visitors grew exponentially. The festival brimmed with people who confirmed my hopes and expectations. My disposition instantly got better. No one could wipe the smile off my face; it felt tattooed. I looked at the devil child, and she seemed to like it as well. She wanted to drag me to the Museum of Pop Culture, but I couldn't waste too much time, so we went further, climbed a few steps, and found ourselves near multiple stands. We turned right, and there were even more stands surrounding us: a stall sold numerous wooden bead necklaces, rings, and other jewelry, another sold t-shirts unbefitting for the colder weather to come, and another sold candy of extreme variety. Upbeat music was roaring across the area from speakers attached to trees. However, it had competition from the musicians playing live for large groups of people, which encircled them. Across the asphalted pathway, we witnessed some kids busking on their violins, a fake golden statue gaining more traction, but the most popular one was the magician who was fooling everyone for their cash.

I looked at the time on my phone. It was past one. I had to wait till two p.m. when it would be the most crowded. It was time to choose a place. It proved to be more difficult than expected since it had to be closer to the car, but it had to have enough people. The only thing I knew was I had to avoid reaching the fountain. It was too large of an area and too easy to be found.

"Lauren, that, that." She pointed at the cotton candy stall.

"Yes, dear," I said, the corner of my mouth twitching up, "whatever you want, dear. You can eat as much sugar and colorants as you want."

I got her a lollipop, cotton candy, some rainbow gummies just to contain the *Rosemary's Baby*. We sat on a dark green bench where Marigold began eating her unhealthy snacks, plus some applesauce I brought from home. I looked at her. If she wasn't my child, I would've considered her cute, dare I say, adorable even. Her wheat-colored hair got longer; her green beaded eyes grew bigger. There was something beautiful in this Machiavellian being. If I didn't despise her for all the detestable things she did, I could've cared for her. It wasn't my fault she was the devil's spawn. I tried; God knows I tried. She had been fed, changed, dressed, washed. I told her I loved her, I used positive verbal reinforcement, I tried to hug her. Everything required of a good mother. And still, she never reciprocated. I never got a touch, a hug, a loving word. She even refused to call me Mommy after a while. She only liked her dad, and there was nothing I could do about it. Who knows, if it were her choice, she would force him to leave me? Over. My. Dead. Body. I haven't slept for three years. It was time to get a goodnight's rest. I got up spontaneously from the bench, she still didn't finish her meal. Why did she always have to be like this?

"Let's go, Marigold, let's get you a balloon!" I exuded false enthusiasm.

She looked at me with complete childlike happiness. I almost wavered with my decision. *"No, do not succumb to her manipulative behavior. She has to be let go."* We reached the balloon stand. A guy with a crooked tooth gave me a crooked smile and, in an attempt to impress us, took a long-shaped balloon and transformed it into a poodle. He did a poor job at it. Nonetheless, he tried to sell us the mangled caricature of the animal, but I refused. I needed the most colorful one, and it had to float. The crooked-tooth man grabbed a string out of many tied to a rod and handed me the perfect specimen. A giant balloon splattered in the brightest colors, able to float for days. I thanked him and left as fast as I could so he wouldn't remember my face.

We reached the most crowded area where a guy was playing the guitar, and his dog would bark at the music. Perfect. I squatted to her level, grabbed her hand, looked her in the eyes, and said, "I am giving you this balloon because you are a great... girl. You can go play wherever you want. Go now, go!"

She yanked the balloon forcefully and turned around to leave. I was still holding her hand. I couldn't let go right away, but as she tugged at them, finger after finger, I let her go till she wasn't attached to me anymore. She interwove with the crowd quite well, and after a few moments, the only thing I could see was the psychedelic balloon. It slowly moved across the horde, bopping up and down, simulating her steps. It went down from being tugged by its master but up because it always yearned to be set free. How thin was the line between the control we gave others and our strive for freedom?

Maybe the balloon wanted to fly upward, experience heights no human would be able to do on his own, but, alas, it remained shackled to a string at its root and tamed into bobbing to its master's rhythm. I've never realized the beauty of a wandering balloon, the feeling of being on an aimless path guided by the wind's currents. How incredible freedom tasted! When the shackled balloon reached a good stretch of distance, to my surprise, it was released and liberated from its confinement. Elated and encouraged, I turned around, and with precise determination, raced towards the car. In reality, it was a fast walk to not create suspicion. My tote was held close to my body to gain more traction, and, of course, I had my well-worn slip-on shoes for extra aid. I didn't turn around. I pressed on further with sheer determination. I didn't question where she could be. She could've been behind me. A kid rushing to get to the lackluster magician bumped into me, but I didn't lose my stride. There was only one objective on my mind, I had to push further, no matter what.

The parking lot was filled with cars. The smell of pot descended on the whole area, but I didn't have time to care. I had to find my car. In my mind, my car was somewhere closer to the road, but in my flustered state, it seemed like every black car belonged to me. I almost went and opened a few. I had to use the sound-producing button to find it. I got inside. Closed the door. Locked it. Put my seatbelt on reflex though not necessary. And waited. Frantically, I looked at the time on my phone, counting every minute, filling up half an hour. After the half an hour was up, I planned to go back. I kept convincing myself to go back faster to end this preposterous idea. At the same time, I retorted with the undoubtful fact: even if she did get lost, the police would find her promptly. Who would choose to keep such a burden?

The half-hour was up, but my feet wouldn't let me take a step. I couldn't move. The fear of seeing my plan reach fruition glued me to the seat. I didn't know which was worse, success or failure. With the last flutter of will I had left, I forced myself to unbuckle the seatbelt, unlock the car, open the door, and push one leg at a time. I dawdled in my steps, each leg heavier than the other, my tote almost dragging on the road.

When I reached the spot, the crowd had already dwindled. There were only a few groups of people scattered here and there. I couldn't see her anywhere. I almost jumped out of excitement. I finally escaped, but I couldn't relax; there was another thing I had to do. It was time to introduce the second part of my plan.

"Excuse me, sir," I said, imitating a voice tremble, "have you seen an almost three-year-old girl? She is in a baby blue dress, blue cardigan, and red shoes."

He looked at me in a panic.

"No, is she lost?" said the bearded guy with unusual care for a stranger.

"Yes, I've been searching for ten minutes now and cannot find her."

"Oh no, let me call my friend. He is on the other side of the area. We will help you find her."

The bearded guy stepped away to call when a wrinkled hand touched my elbow.

"Excuse my eavesdropping, but I heard you lost your daughter. You poor thing," said an old lady with a cane.

She wanted to help search for my daughter, but I asked her to stay there in case my daughter would return. I preferred to exhaust fewer people due to my personal decisions.

We searched the premises for around fifteen minutes, and with each additional minute, it struck me harder and harder. Somehow, I still didn't believe it had happened. My inner state was nothing like I expected. There was a sort of relief that I didn't have her near me, but also something was missing. For almost three years, I had someone in my personal space on a twenty-four-hour watch. It felt empty around me. As I walked towards the fountain with my wandering thoughts, I stumbled on a piece of a colored balloon. It was my balloon, her balloon, and it was ripped. But I saw it ascend into the sky. How could it pop? There was no sun today, not even peeking behind the heavy clouds. Could it be the atmosphere pressure? Or the same winds which were supposed to lead it towards a free state of wonder had destroyed it? I was ruminating on the question when a sturdy voice called out for me, "Excuse me, are you the lady who lost her daughter?"

I turned around to see a police officer. Who had time to call the police so fast? And why wasn't I the first one to do it? He began interrogating me about everything. Where was I when she disappeared? In what direction did she go? What was she wearing? What did she look like?

I answered all questions diligently, as he was writing them in a notebook. The officer then hid the notebook in his pocket and said, "Mrs. Miller, my intention is not to scare you, but we must prepare for the worst-case scenario. I suspect your daughter might've been kidnapped. We will escalate this issue with the department and send an Amber alert. I am sorry. It's a terrible situation to be in."

The officer went on to say I didn't need to write a missing person's report at their precinct as he had all the required information and would take care of it. I had to say the police force was doing their job quite well. In a day or two, I'd have the rascal back. Wait a minute, I forgot to tell Gavin. He was so excited this morning, the poor guy. I decided to call so I could control my voice better. He was about to get the news of his life.

CHAPTER 42

WHEN I returned home, Gavin was decomposing emotionally on the sofa. I expected him to be at least a little bit relieved. But no, he looked like a mess spilling slowly out of a cracked jar. He sat deep on the sofa; his head leaned back on the cushion edge contemplating the ceiling's abyss. I could see his neck protruding, all red and patched, possibly from a drink he had earlier. His arms were lying lifeless next to him, and occasionally he would form fists which he raised to his temples as if blaming the gods for such a tragic plight. Get a grip, Gavin. Are you so easy to disintegrate at the thought of spending a few days without Marigold? I wished to say those words, but he might misunderstand in his state of anguish.

"Gavin?" I said with whispering guilt. He didn't answer. I pleaded again, "Gavin? Are you okay?"

"Oh, Laura," he said raising his head as if he had returned from a place that wasn't our living room. It was then I had the chance to see his face. His eyes looked like swollen onions drenched in tears and despair while the corners of his mouth reached his chin. He tried to speak, but his words sounded like a sore throat. When he realized his vocal cords were betraying him, he dropped his head back on the top cushion and wept in silence. In short, he behaved like someone had died, and she didn't die. She got lost. Temporarily. Evil could not perish with such ease. She was a parasite sucking blood, plasma, and air from its unknowing host. How could she not survive? It was preposterous!

I sat next to Gavin, laid a hand on his knee, and stayed like that for a minute, him succumbing to apathy, me inhaling his existential crisis. Unexpectedly, he stopped and looked at me.

"What happened, Laura?" he said in a cracked voice as if able to speak for the first time ever.

"She ran away from me, and then I couldn't find her," I said.

"Did you say something to make her run?" His despair palpable.

"Are you out of your mind? How dare you say this after all I've been through?"

"Exactly, after all you've been through. Maybe you couldn't take it anymore. But she is my little girl…" His voice collapsed at the last word.

"I didn't say anything. She simply wandered off at the festival. I searched for her along with a lot of other people. You can ask them." His words hurt me. He felt it.

"I'm sorry. I can't believe she is not here."

"Well, she will be. Don't worry, your beloved daughter will return to you. And you will live happily ever after together."

I got up, grabbed a cup of yogurt and chocolate chip cookies, and went to the bedroom, shutting the door after me. I would not let him ruin my liberation. Even a short-term one. Pfft. He feared the girl was lost. Ha-ha. She could revive from dead ashes for all I knew. I'll see her prancing in her obnoxious way by tomorrow.

"You wait and see, Gavin," I thought.

For now, though, I've suffered enough, so I would like to celebrate quietly by myself, thank you very much. After my improvised dinner, I took the most exquisite bath, moisturized my face and body to keep wrinkles at bay, put on the whitest, silkiest nightgown I had, and went to bed. The light in the living room was still on, but I didn't care. By midnight, the ruffling sounds told me he had come to bed.

The whole night I slept in a dream. I dreamt I was the queen of clouds, and I ruled over the skies. I was riding on a golden chariot with four winged horses across a reversed ocean of blue. Birds followed like an army of devout soldiers. I wore a long pearlescent robe with a trail fluttering across the sky. My body toned, my hair full and long, and my skin smoother than a statue's. The wind blew through my hair as if it combed every strand. My nose inhaled air of divine nature; I felt more alive with each intake. As a goddess of the world's upper realm, humans brought offerings of white camellias and orchids at my altar. They sang hymns in my honor, reverberating throughout all the corners of the world and straight into my ears.

When I opened my eyes, the room was inundated in light. I couldn't believe I slept for so long uninterrupted. I looked beside me; Gavin was in a deep sleep, but his face looked tortured. For me, though, life seemed more prominent than before. The walls retracted to give more space; the ceiling seemed taller. The kitchen could fit more people. What a great life I lived in.

The tea steeped in the cup as I was concocting some pancake batter. Gavin found me trying to flip a pancake while managing the drip coffee machine. His face looked like a wrinkled mess.

"I am making you breakfast. Take a seat."

He didn't listen.

"I don't have time for breakfast. I took a week off from work and will aid the investigators and police officers in finding Marigold."

"How are you going to do that if you starve to death? Please take a seat."

"The bigger question is how can you eat when our daughter is missing?"

"I don't see how one has anything to do with the other."

"And I don't see how you can smile when your daughter could be in danger at this very moment."

"Oh, Gavin. You're exaggerating. I promise you she'll be back by today. The police department nowadays works consistently and efficiently. You'll see."

"What if she won't? Policemen are not magicians."

"It's not possible. You'll see."

One of my pancakes began to burn. By the time I flipped it and turned towards him, Gavin was gone. I enjoyed my breakfast alone, in divine silence, inhaling those last moments of my freedom. It was good while it lasted.

The day went by fast. Gavin called once, saying there might be a lead. I wanted to tell him, "I told you so," but bit my tongue. He also told Mom about Marigold's disappearance. I almost cursed under my nose. Why did she have to get involved? Only one thought made me reconsider: if Marigold was found soon, the old bat would fly back to her cave, and I wouldn't have to meet her again.

The evening settled eagerly behind the window. There was no sign of Gavin or Marigold.

"They could be stuck in traffic," I thought. I was sure they were to get here any time soon. But with each minute, darkness occupied all the nooks of the house as well as mine. The chicken parmesan sat on my plate untouched, alongside Gavin's and a smaller pink plate for Marigold filled with cookies.

"It makes sense to wait for them, but if they take so long, I might as well eat," I said and proceeded to devour the lukewarm food. It turned completely dark by the time I finished. They were still not home. I pressed the phone's home button. It showed nine p.m., and its luminosity lit the whole kitchen. The key in the lock turned, and when the door opened, the phone's display dimmed.

"Why are you sitting in the dark?" asked Gavin.

"I was waiting for you two, and when I noticed, it was already dark," I said, but he didn't seem to bother with my reply. He turned on the light which presented his whole miserable demeanor. He looked like a miner, with his clothes dusty and muddy. His hair was covered in a few spider webs, and his hands were grimy.

"Where have you been? Where is Marigold?"

"Where have I not been? We've been all around the area Marigold was last seen. We've tried the sewer holes, under the bridges, in homeless communities. No one saw anything. As if she was swallowed into earth's crust."

"How can it be? She was supposed to be found by now."

"As if things would be so easy. Even the police officers were reluctant to share an opinion."

"I'm sure she will be here by tomorrow. There's no doubt about it."

But he didn't wait for me to finish my sentence. He went straight for the shower.

"Come eat. I made chicken parmesan."

No answer. He was punishing me for my sin, and I couldn't reproach him for it.

"No worries, though, tomorrow Marigold will be home, and he will mollify. He will return to his happy dandy self in no time," I whispered.

The second night, I had the same dream. It was glorious. I was riding my winged horse-driven chariot guarded by ten eagles at each side, forming a triangle of protection. It looked the same as the previous night, but it became peculiar when the humans brought the offering to the altar. Instead of camellias and orchids, it was marigolds. It woke me straight up. It was around six a.m.; Gavin was gone already. In the kitchen, his and Marigold's evening meals were still there waiting. After I cleaned everything, the kettle was ready for me. I poured some into a cup over a teabag and went back to the bedroom. I stayed in bed till about eight a.m., looking up different recipes for today.

By the time it was noon, I had cleaned the whole house, and the meal was prepared: chicken nuggets and salad for the hungry adventurers. Gavin opened the door with my mother by his side.

"Wait a bit, Svetlana. I'll grab a jacket and be right back," he said, and indeed the weather got chilly very fast. It was supposed to start raining again tomorrow.

"Hi, Mother."

"Oh, Laura. How are you feeling? Gavin said you were very depressed."

She looked older, less agile from the last time I saw her, with a few more wrinkles on her forehead and arounds her eyes.

"I'm okay, Mom. Trying to keep it together," I said.

"Would you like to join us for the search?"

"I will, but I'm sure she will be found today. So, it won't be necessary."

She looked at me in an observing way, with her eyebrow always raised.

"Let's go, Svetlana," he said in a rushed tone. Gavin turned towards me and said, "do not wait for me," and left.

Besides his scolding ignorance, his monotone words cut through me deeper than a knife. Dejected, I ate all the nuggets with no salad, then put everything in its correct place and delved into the glories of the internet. The content was as per usual, about everything and nothing in particular. Suddenly, it struck me; maybe I should google how fast kids were found. A quick search showed the worst outcome I ever thought. The more days passed, the less likely a child was to be found. I knew, of course, of kidnapping, but those usually happened within the family, by one of the parents. Cases of serial kidnappers were sporadic, and this wasn't a kidnapping. She simply got lost. If I ever got lost in Oklahoma, I would've been on my house's porch by dusk. In any case, it shouldn't have come to this.

Darkness reached our home again when the keys turned. Today Gavin came earlier.

"Did you find Marigold?" I jumped off the sofa as he turned on the light.

"No, it started to pour, and we couldn't continue our searches. Out of all the days, it had to rain heavily today."

"It's okay, dear. Marigold will appear soon."

Gavin's face after my words looked as if I poured vinegar all over it.

"Wake up, Laura! Marigold will not appear soon. Can you not understand this?" He came closer, his eyes crazy with exhaustion and despair. "She is lost. She could be kidnapped, already sold to some traffickers."

"But usually kidnapping happen within the fam–"

"You don't seem to understand," he growled, "it doesn't matter how Marigold got lost, but the moment she did, she became dependent on the world's mercy. And the world, as you know, is a cruel, cruel place."

I took a seat back on the sofa to recover from his words.

"I didn't mean for this to happen."

"I simply want you to realize the delusion you are living in." His demeanor mellowed. "It's not helping you, me, and, for sure, not helping Marigold. We have to push now to find her. Otherwise, we will lose her forever."

Without saying anything else, he turned around and went straight to the bathroom. I felt so tired and confused, I went to bed. My newfound exhaustion took me straight to sleep.

The same dream appeared, with the same glory flowing through my veins, but now the clouds were charcoal, the thundering lightning almost pushed me off the chariot, and my surroundings turned into menacing colors. The humans were still singing hymns, but now there was fear in their voices, and their offering at the altar was a bouquet of marigolds and baby's breath. Attached to them was a color-splotched balloon. The same balloon! My breath froze. Was she infiltrating my dreams? I opened my eyes, sat up, and looked around. It was still dark and a bit chilly. Gavin slept profoundly; the unsuccessful events must've drained him. I went back to bed. As I fell asleep, the same dream continued from where it stopped. The offerings tied to a balloon multiplied. There were so many; I couldn't see anything. They all gathered at my neck and began to suffocate me. More and more. Never ceasing balloons covering my face, I could not produce another breath. They pushed me over the chariot, and I fell from the sky. I rushed out of bed and straight into the bathroom. I looked at the ghost in the mirror and washed it to bring some color back.

    I tried not to think about it, but there was a new feeling chewing at me.

CHAPTER 43

I didn't go back to sleep after the nightmare. I put on some raggedy clothes and waited in the living room for Gavin to wake up. When he did, he didn't even notice my silent intention. He walked past me and straight into the kitchen. I went after him.

"I want to join the search today."

"It would be nice," he said as he managed the coffee machine. "It will be cold, so you should be prepared for the worst conditions."

"Do I look like I'm incapable of taking a little bit of cold when my daughter is freezing somewhere under a bridge?"

He stopped and looked at me with a cold stare.

"I'm not saying that, but you must be prepared for the long search."

Marigold's disappearance made me look at us as a couple again. Being next to him as my husband and not the father of my child made me realize how much was lost in the relationship. We were not the same couple as before. We were two people in a dispersing marriage, too busy to notice it.

"What has happened to us?" I whispered.

"Did you ask something?"

"No, not at all."

***

The weather in November could fool anyone. It seemed reasonable at first, but the longer one was exposed to it, the humidity would eat up through one's clothes and reach bone density. I began trembling in the first half an hour, but I couldn't show it to Gavin, who looked more like a fierce soldier than my husband. The officers led us to three homeless encampments on the outskirts of Seattle. The scenery made me fear and pity those people who lived in such precarious conditions. A few of them were rummaging through their meager belongings in their tents. Others were outside, looking intently at us without moving a muscle on their faces. And one guy tried to sell us something. Shrieks and laughter were resounding intermittently from distances further away. The smell of unclean bodies and pot mixed in a unique, long-lasting way. Some were smiling with their brass half missing teeth and dead eyes. Others were crying in a way I felt like I had to do something. I gave a twenty-dollar bill to an elderly lady and my bottle of water to a young man with a fresh scar along his jaw. It was all I had. They were not wearing more clothes than me, but they had to be homeless all the time. I remembered watching the news when the city reported, they were trying to deal with this issue in multiple ways, injecting thousands in temporary solutions. But these people needed their inner wounds healed, not quick answers. The most pressing thing was that the encampments were not suitable for a child. Marigold could be in grave danger.

"What have I done? What. Have. I. Done."

After an unsuccessful day, we headed back home. I tried to talk a bit with Gavin about the following trips where we could look for Marigold. He didn't answer. His mind was always stuck on something to which I didn't have access. At night, the nightmares kept crawling back into my subconscious. Every morning, I woke up at five a.m. feeling breathless after being asphyxiated by balloons and unnerved from the sky fall ending with my impending death. During the day, we would visit encampments, and my mother would call up different shelters to ask about an almost-three-year-old with green eyes and russet-colored hair, wearing a blue dress, blue cardigan, and red shoes similar to Dorothy from Wizard of Oz. Mother, as well as us, had this phrase memorized to automation. We shared fliers with one of her recent pictures and contacted the police every day.

By the end of the first week, I gathered enough courage to enter her room. It felt eerily uncomfortable; it was never this quiet. Her dolls sat on their regal pink chairs, waiting patiently for her. The giant teddy bear's beady eyes seemed like they were asking me questions about their owner. All the other toys: multicolored blocks, shapes, trains were simply objects for dust accumulation. The room became an image stopped in time. Even in twenty years, her toys would still be here waiting for her to play with them. It was excruciatingly hard to live with her, but a new wave of despair began once she disappeared.

***

A few days went by when we got a call from police officer McDowell saying they found her. My heart skipped a beat. I didn't know if it was from fear, relief, or joy. We rushed to a shelter named New Beginnings, which primarily worked with mothers and young children. For the first time since Marigold disappeared, Gavin's two red onion eyes sparked a ray of hope. His low-hanging cheeks gained some muscle from his inner smile. Gavin couldn't control himself anymore. So the moment I parked the car, he sprinted out of the vehicle like a starving cheetah. I caught up with him only inside, where his beaming smile was eclipsing the whole reception, including officer McDowell's inscrutable face. I wanted to contain him a bit, but it was useless. The matter absorbed him so much, it seemed like he could wait forever for a hug from his daughter. But for me, the wait was excruciating, like one rotation around the sun. Finally, we got summoned to a room with a purple door. When we got there, it was locked. Our confusion was settled when an elderly man approached us and lead us to the correct room.

There were a lot of kids running around trying to avoid bumping into us. My eyes wandered around the hallway out of curiosity, but when we reached the definitive door, time had stopped. Every second seemed like elephant stomps while I felt my breath underwater.

"Here she is," said the man pointing at a little girl.

For a second, I really wished her to be Marigold. But she wasn't. We began frantically searching among other kids, even though the elderly man had already pointed to us the person of interest. Of course, we couldn't find her. Marigold wasn't there, and Gavin was destroyed. He couldn't speak or cry. When I glanced at him, something broke in me. I couldn't hold it in anymore. Tear buds began appearing at the corner of my eyes. One by one. Then they formed a continuous flow, relentless and unstoppable like two treacherous waterfalls. I cried when we said to the man the girl wasn't ours. I cried when we said goodbye to the lady at the reception. I cried in the car as Gavin took me from the wheel and sat me in the passenger seat. I cried in the garage, and I cried when I laid my head in bed.

As I lay like a fractured glass statue, one question flashed continuously as if a neon sign: *"Why did I let her go?"* Dark. *"Why did I let her go?"* Dark.

CHAPTER 44

THE following day was Marigold's third birthday. Gavin looked sour as he marked on a map all the places we'd already been at. I wanted to bring it up but didn't want to make him feel worse.

"Where are we going to search for Marigold today?"

He kept silent for a few seconds without removing his gaze from the paper.

"Someone called the police station and said they saw a girl fitting Marigold's description next to a gas station up north from her last sighting."

"Then let's go there," I said, hyping up his words.

"Your mom is already there."

"Already? Why does my mother have to be involved in everything?"

"Do you hear what you're saying? You refuse a helping hand because of a minor spat you had ages ago?"

"I, I didn't mean it this way. It's just she's so nosy all the time. You don't understand."

"Laura, you really think I don't understand. Do you really think I don't see beyond the words you speak? Take a seat."

He pointed to the chairs from the kitchen table. I took a seat, fretful of what was about to happen. Gavin sat on a chair next to me, folded his map meticulously, took off his glasses, and looked straight into my eyes.

"Along the years of our marriage, I chose to see the best out of everything, including you. My love for you stemmed from your sincere earnestness, determination, and strong will. I even accepted your yearn for the aesthetically pleasing though not always profound. But you've built a world around you that sometimes had nothing to do with reality, a sort of make-believe story of your life. I was happy to be a positive character in it. I felt it wouldn't matter much as most of the time, it was innocent and charming. But as time progressed, you constantly formed fixed opinions about other people, transforming them into villains or princesses without delving deeper. No matter what those people did and how much they evolved, your opinion never changed with their actions. You always believed you understood people far better than you did. You simply decided how to react in certain situations, and only those decisions were the correct ones. But for the most part, they were and are a mere figment of your imagination.

"I might seem like the good guy for you, but I've been through the same doubts and fears as you. I've shared the same sleepless nights, medical scares, hospital visits. The same fears of being a subpar parent, a weak provider, an inconsiderate spouse. I've had moments when I wanted to quit all of it, to choose the easier way, to lose myself in alcohol. Things you chose to brush off because, in your world, I could never do such things.

"Similarly, your mom is not the villain of your story. She is an actual human, just like you and me, who makes mistakes and lives to accept and deal with the consequences. At the moment, she is dealing with your consequences. So, if you will let us, we would like to resume our search. If you want to join, feel free to do so. If not, we will gladly take on the responsibility."

After finishing his speech, he put on his glasses, took his folded map, raised from the chair, put on his jacket and scarf, and exited the house without looking back at me. Stupefied, I sat in the chair, glancing at the door, hoping he might return. That he might come back and kiss me and say he didn't mean it. That he loved me and would never leave. But he didn't. The door stayed closed just like he left it, and my paralysis wouldn't let me move from the chair. I turned around and looked at the scratches on the table. An uncanny resemblance to my state. I didn't remember how long I sat, ruminating on Gavin's words. The only thing waking me from my catatonic state was my phone. It kept ringing and ringing in my bag. The first time I let it ring the Bach song, it still brought back good memories. The second time, I figured it was Gavin, so I rushed to take it out of the bag. It was Cassandra.

"Hello?"

"Laura, hi. It's me, Cassandra." Her agitated voice responded.

"Hi, Cassandra. You sound different."

A moment of silence and a short cough followed.

"I heard about the disappearance of your daughter. I'm so sorry."

"We hope to find her soon."

"I remember it's her birthday today."

"Yeah," I said in a nonchalant way to show her she wasn't hurting me.

"Listen, Laura. I have something to tell you, but before I do, I want to apologize to you."

"To me? Why?"

"I might've been harsh sometimes, but know I never meant to be mean."

Why was she suddenly apologizing, and since when did Cassandra apologize?

"It's all good, Cassandra. It's all water under the bridge. So, what did you want to tell me?"

"I hope you find Marigold soon."

"Thank you, Cassandra. I appreciate your words. I'll call when we have her home."

"Yes, it would be wonderful."

"Well, I'll be talking to you soon."

"I have something to tell you, Laura." She was back to her icy voice. "I don't know how to tell you this. So, I am going to be direct."

"Okay."

"Jasmine passed away."

"Who passed?" I asked, hoping that what I heard was wrong.

"Jasmine," she paused. "The funeral will be tomorrow. I meant to call you earlier, but I thought you knew…"

I couldn't say anything.

"I'm organizing a wake tonight at my house. You are welcome to join. It will be mostly people from work."

"I-I'll try, but what happened?"

She released a long sigh, not wanting to divulge the reason.

"Apparently, something happened between her and her fiancé."

"He murdered her. The monster stomped on the flower. I can't believe it."

"He is in custody now, so he will be punished."

"But the flower will never bloom again."

I heard Cassandra sniffle and take a deep breath.

"I hope you take her death easier than me. They might need you to testify. When was the last time you talked to her?"

"A few months ago. She looked sad but nothing out of the ordinary. She said she wanted to move somewhere in Bellevue."

"Yes, she told me the same during lunch one day. I still can't believe she is gone… I, I hope to see you soon," Cassandra said, unable to control her tears.

She hung up, and I went straight for the pantry and picked the first bottle of alcohol I could find. It was some whiskey Gavin had prepared for guests. I downed a shot of the fierce beverage like it was lemonade, breathing out hot air from my throat. I needed a numbing tool; this was the fastest and most accessible one. I sat on the floor next to the couch with my drink next to me. Jasmine died? Was this some kind of gruesome joke? An incongruence in my mind. A cognitive dissonance. She was supposed to live. She was better than me. No, no, no, it couldn't have happened. She said she would break up with him. I supported the idea. He murdered her because I told her to leave him. No, no, it was not possible. How could I go to the funeral, knowing I persuaded her to her death? Marigold was still missing. I could lose her too. No, no, she couldn't die. She had to be found soon. I did it only to scare her a bit. To show her life with me was better. Not to let her die.

The whiskey reached my logic and made slime out of it. The room got larger and warmer. What would Gavin say? I needed to call him. When he answered, I said, "Jasmine is gone."

"Who? I can't hear you," he said, his voice covered by traffic noise.

"My Jasmine is gone. My Jasmine. My p-precious Jasmine," I said, tears muffling my words.

"I am so sorry, Laura. I'll be home soon. Let's talk then." His voice was a bit concerned, a bit distant.

The blur held me in one spot and put me to sleep on the floor. When I woke up, it was afternoon. I had to talk to someone. Gavin and Mom had left me. I had to speak with someone who understood me and always gave me the necessary advice. I took the keys and the phone and thrust them into my bag. I grabbed the first coat I could reach and rushed out the door. Behind, I left anticipative silence.

CHAPTER 45

WHEN I reached the nursery, the drizzle stopped, but everything was drenched. As I got closer, the two gates were connected by a heavy chain obstructing the entrance. I never noticed them before. The gates were never closed. I pulled on the icy handle; it barely moved. I strained on my tippy toes so I could see what was behind it. There was nothing, a desolate scene with a few leaves swooshed by the wind from here to there. I never imagined this place would ever close. In the fifteen years of helping Margaret, I didn't remember her ever mentioning she wanted to close the nursery or if they ever struggled. I didn't notice anything different the last time I was here. I pushed even harder at the gates but nothing, only the menacing clouds still hovering above me and the day's last dispersing light. I turned around and realized I didn't have anywhere to go. The only person who could help me was gone.

"And I never asked for her personal phone number. I don't even know where to find her."

I looked up a phone number online. It was the nursery number, the one I already had. It said it was disconnected. I leaned on the cold and slippery gates and slid to the ground.

"Where do I go from here?"

The cold beam of the streetlamp was aiming straight at me as if I was in an interrogation room. A guilty inquisition. I looked at the fuming clouds; they threatened to spread the message. I simply plopped my head on my knees and wept. Tears regained their strength again. There was no point in getting them in control. For tears were the only thing to offer me a cleanse. Though many tears were needed.

When did I become the villain of my story?

Is it still my story?

The cold had crept under my skin my fears into my mind…

I know of nothing and of no one…

Freedom has a steep price but guilt is steeper…

I always wanted her but I didn't know how to deal with her…

How to love her how to appreciate the good not only the ugly…

The d-d-dreams I once aspired had molded into a swamp…

My feet feel the cold of it as well as the drab…

It's getting colder my jaw can't control itself…

The street is empty those who see me I don't…

Marigold is lost…

I d-d-did it…

I am a childless mother…

It's so cold I need some warmth…

The sun will never shine…

The moon will always gloom…

The sunflower's petals smell rotten…

I am rotten…

But I didn't want it this way…

I wanted to bid bright goodbyes at the window just like Marmee…

I wanted to stand with her in the same circle of seclusion from human society like Hester did on the scaffold to suffer the pains of ignominy together…

I wanted to throw the pearl like Juana for my Coyotita…

To hug my baby into the muted colors of Klimt's mother-daughter painting…

I wanted to be an orca mom who carried her dead calf more than a thousand miles…

The Orcas Island waters hide more motherly love than I ever did…

The dream…

She turns three today…

Happy birthday to you….

Marigold's morning smiles…

Her sweet way of grabbing my pinky…

I still have the rock she gave me…

Her dancing…

Her long eyelashes…

Juvenile curiosity…

Instead I used the wrath of Medea…

I killed in order to make way for more darkness…

Who knew I had enough darkness within to poison my daughter's livelihood?

N-n-nightmare…

It's a variant of Sophie's choice where I choose between her happiness and mine…

I chose wrong…

Oh how I chose wrong…

Because I was already happy under all that dusty delusion were sprouts of motherly happiness barely showing their heads…

I could not distinguish…

My scar looks like a shadow compared to the rest of my arm…

I remember visiting a museum with my dad once…

D-d-dad had nice clothes all bright colors I wish I could be like his clothes…

I can buy clothes but can I buy light?

Icarus couldn't...
He flew too close to it too bright to handle too much swelter to breathe...
What's the point of having wings if you can't fly where your dreams are?
I looked at my feet...
Muddy sneakers...
In front of them a puddle...
A puddle large enough to reflect my contour and the darkness which has filled those lines... It is muddled muddy and alone...
At the gate...
I lost the ability to smell rainbow to touch the light see the resilience taste the music hear the true path...
I now have to eviscerate my ideals... the colors of pride...
The street is empty...
The day is closing down on me...
The sky is still gloomy not a trace of a star in sight only the probability of rain...
I feel like the skeleton of an umbrella without a cover unable to protect unable to do what I was meant to do...
The crook of her finger unclasping...
The wandering balloon...
The splotched balloon...
The shackled balloon...
The sun the bird the fall...
I am guilty streetlamp you don't have to yell at me with your blaring light...
Moths burning their bodies to the sizzling crave...
They will die for the thing they want most ...
My toes are ice...
Where are you Margaret?
I miss our talks... your Turkish delights...

Instant gratification…
My naked heels drowning in sand to swallow my discomfort…
A headband of daisies a breeze of lukewarm zephyr…
Me and Marigold in a field of poppies…
A dream never to come true as the poppies are the color of blood…
Blood is on my hands reaching my mind…
A sparrow just flew by…
Such freedom…
This wasn't freedom it was transformation…
If Cassandra is a bear an elephant a sloth…
What am I?
A lizard a cuckoo or a snake?
I might as well be all…
My blood is turning cold…
I am guilty…
I killed Jasmine…
I knew and didn't do anything…
A debasement a crime against humanity…
Jasmine will you ever forgive me?
Your radiating face will never give me hope…
Marigold's face is also radiant…
When she smiles the flowers bow to her…
A majestic creature perfect all on its own…
Some kids don't need their mothers because they got all they needed in the womb…
My womb…
A disfigured womb could produce such glory…
Why did I want to change her?
The tears are coming in…
They will turn into droplets of ice in no time…
Cleansing tears like those of a mountain creak…

If I cry for the rest of my life will I ever find atonement?

Darkness fogged up…

No light inside or out…

Silent repentance for the sins I've never thought of being able to commit…

I recon my debasement existed long before I ever committed any crimes…

The layers of clothes and my body stiffened to a hardened degree…

Though it wasn't enough to move me from my scaffold…

Or maybe I didn't want to be moved…

I feel like my tear ducts are drying out now…

I am probably gonna stay here tonight if I am to freeze so be it…

I deserve worse…

But then a voice reached my numb ears.

"Laura, Laura…"

It might be an illusion, a joke of my subconscious. Then a hand touched me. I raised my head. In a fuzzy cloud, I saw my mom, the younger, more beautiful version of her.

"Mom?"

"I called a million times, Gavin too. We didn't know where to look for you. On a wild guess, I came here. I'm so glad I found you. Let's go home. I'll make some tea. It'll warm you up."

"I don't deserve to be warm when Marigold is out there freezing!" I snapped with the last bit of energy left.

Mom didn't expect it, but it didn't stop her.

"Would you want Marigold to see her mother sick when she comes back?"

"She will not want to see me if she comes back. I am not a mother."

"Of course, you are. Even bad mothers are mothers. And all mothers can become better. Aren't you better now than before?" she said naïvely. "Give Marigold a chance to see a better mother."

"It's her birthday today."

"I know dear, I know. Let's go and warm up, have some tea, cookies, and your favorite *semechki*. I have a bag full of them in case of an emergency."

I let her move the iceberg from the ground. When I was on my feet, I was so stiff, I fell on my mother's lap like a drunk. Stiffness in my body, stiffness in my eyes, stiffness in my mind. All was dark around, with one streetlight reflecting on all the puddles nearby. And my dark reflection in all of them. I dragged my feet to the car with the help of my mother. She felt unusually warm and bright like the evening star. I lay in the backside of the car and fell asleep; I dreamt of puddles and a crystal-clear waterfall splashing into the puddles. How the crystal water got contaminated and became dirty. My derelict never left me. I was its prisoner and would not know of any other.

That night I slept in Marigold's room.

CHAPTER 46

NO nightmare visited me during the night. I relinquished all control between two rails attached to a tiny pink bed. There was no sense of suffocation or fear of falling from the sky, only black before my eyes and paralysis in my heart. As my inner world experienced a state of blank numbness, my body succumbed to complete exhaustion. Not from the cold I felt the other night but from the effort of catching sun bunnies with a butterfly net, crashing myself into a wall in the process. In all of that was something tangible, my baby. A child I could touch, feel, and share an experience of existence. Even though different from what I expected, my daughter was still part of me and not a chimera. But I took her natural fleshy body and turned her into one. A bubble of delusion which could burst into reality. The reality of death.

At the crack of dawn, Gavin peeked through the door a few times, unsure what to do or what to expect, but he probably figured this was my way of grievance, so he did not disturb my dysphoric state. I whispered a thank you I hoped he didn't hear, as I realized more than ever, Gavin was the most sensible man I've ever known. When the door from Marigold's room closed, I shut my eyes and slept for what seemed like an hour. Gavin came in again and turned on the light, making me squirm like a worm after rain.

"Are you okay, Laura?" He sounded concerned.

I raised my head to meet his bloodshot eyes.

"Yes, I am okay," I said and laid my head on the ruffly pillow with my back to him.

"Do you want to eat?"

No answer.

"Do you want a glass of water or a cup of tea?"

No answer.

He sat next to me in worry and caressed my hand.

"We will get through this, Laura. We will find her."

No answer.

He simply sat there next to me in a duet of silent solidarity for what seemed like forever.

"I've done a terrible thing, Gavin. I did more than one terrible thing," I said.

I expected him to move away from me, but he didn't.

"You deserve to be free from someone like me," I said.

"Everyone deserves a chance at forgiveness."

"I don't."

"Yes, you do." And with those words, he got up and left for the door.

I turned towards him in fear that this was my last attempt at a confession.

"I killed Jasmine and, and I potentially killed Marigold. Can you live with a murderer?"

"You didn't kill Jasmine, Laura. You cannot take the burden of the one who purposely killed her. And Marigold will be found soon."

"I let go of her hand. I wanted her to want me as much as I wanted her. I craved for a sliver of the love she had for you," I said as my chin trembled.

"You let her go? What does that mean?"

I couldn't explain.

"Life is much more complicated than the definition of an action. Whatever happened, it was a mistake you will have to live for the rest of your life. But it can wait till after we find her. At the moment, it is all about her and neither of us."

With that, he left, leaving me bereft of any hope at explaining myself. Then again, was there any way to do so? Before, I had so many reasons to do what I did, and now all had flown away like a flock of traveling birds that never returned. I continued to ruminate on my own decisions and meanings the entire morning, but I could only see the face of a child trembling intermittently between cold and fear.

***

In the afternoon, I went back to the place where I last saw her. I managed to park in the same spot, though the streets were crowded with cars, homeless people, and office workers hurdling to their jobs after the lunch break. With a steep pace, I hurried through the park, now half-deserted. I stopped at the spot where the balloon stand once stood. It seemed different. I was the same, but everything else was different. It was as if years had passed with Marigold absorbed in the minutes, hours, and weeks, living forever in the notion of time. But I stayed the same. I began looking around the park. Maybe she was still hiding behind a tree or a bush. Perhaps she was still there looking for the balloon that floated away but never realized it. Or maybe she was still crying "Mommy, Mommy" on top of her lungs, but no one got to hear her, especially me. I found nothing except used and crushed beer cans, syringes, and half-used cigarettes. A ringing sound appeared in my ears. As well as a buzzing headache similar to a rose stem being attached around my head spreading poison through its thorns. And the poison had one message: "You are a killer. You are a killer." I called Mom in an attempt to run away from it, but she didn't answer. I then hurried into my car and locked the doors.

"What if she dies?" I said to myself. "What if she's drugged? What if she's raped? Or trafficked? Or killed for the mere pleasure of it? Oh, what is this cruel world children live in? And I am a part of it. Instead of protecting her, I handed her to the wolves to be devoured by the devious and the perverted. No, no, no. Don't let negative thoughts put you down. Think positive. She is at a shelter waiting for us to get her. She knows we're looking for her. I'm sure she is. Though she probably hates me. I am an undeserving mother. Anything a child does is the parent's fault. It was my cross to bear, and I capitulated. If God, the universe, or whoever is listening can give me another chance, I promise I'll do better. I'll make it work; I'll adapt. I'll love her for who she is: difficult but resilient, stubborn but determined, and just because she's MY child."

I hunched on the steering wheel, hitting my head on it, hoping to alleviate my mental headache with more pain but also, I was running out of ideas on what to do. Mom and Gavin were roaming across the city. They didn't need me; Marigold needed me. And I didn't know how to help since the only thing I could do was nothing. Only wait. No, no. I couldn't accept it. Maybe I was the reason she was not coming back. Perhaps I had to die so she could live. We were unable to live together, like magnets with similar poles that repulsed one another. If I disappeared, then Gavin and Marigold could get a chance at a happy and peaceful life. I was the black hole ripping everything apart and infesting our little cosmos with dark matter. I had to do it faster. So Gavin, Marigold, my mother, and the world could live on better. But how should I do it? Pills seemed like the easiest solution. Sleeping pills would be accessible for a suicidal person in a rush. Feelings of exaltation surged within me, I had the answer in my hands, and my headache didn't hurt as much since I knew it would soon go away. With that thought, I drove to the drugstore closest to our house and bought two bottles of Unisom. As I took the bag from a twenty-year-old cashier, she told me I looked lovely today.

"Might as well look lovely the day I die," I thought.

When I reached the house, I got out of the car and into the garage. I noticed the neighborhood's ubiquitous tranquility as if it was listening to my every move and breath. I cared about my neighbors as much as they did. Usually, we met up sporadically along the street and shared a disinterested greeting. But at that moment, it seemed like they knew, like they sensed what I was about to do. I closed the garage door to curb the curiosity of prying eyes; it made a grumbling sound disturbing the serene ambiance.

The house was so quiet, I could hear the blood pressure in my ears. It knew my decision would mar its reputation. I turned on the TV to muffle the silence and kept the lights off, leaving in only natural light through the blinds. I took the pills and opened the first bottle with haste. Half of them dropped on the floor. Now I had to gather my own suicidal tools? I couldn't even kill myself properly. I picked them in a numb motion of my arm and put them back in the bottle. It didn't matter if they were dirty; I was soon to be dead.

I heard a short vibration in my bag. It must have been a message, but I couldn't deter from my plan. I had to push forward. I was done ruining people's lives. Primarily my daughter's. I wished to have her for so many years, and now I wanted her to have many more. It was why I had to free her from myself. To release her wings from my grip. She was the daughter I needed to have, not the one I wanted to have. And I ruined it. I got a large glass from the cabinet, filled it to the brim. Took two pills and swallowed each at a time. When I prepared the next two, the phone began to ring. I looked at it; it was Gavin. I debated on whether I should answer or not. Suddenly it stopped. I put the phone aside. But it rang again. An unusual persistence from Gavin.

"Hi, Gavin?" I hoped my choking voice didn't get through.

"They found Marigold!" he said as his jubilance protruded over the phone. "She's at the police station."

CHAPTER 47

"I CAN'T believe it," I said, looking at the bottle of pills. "How did they find her?"

"I will tell you when we come home."

"Do I need to prepare some food?"

"No worries. Your mother took care of everything. You just wait for us."

As I pressed the red button, I rushed to the toilet, and in an unskilled manner, tried regurgitating the pills. Nothing came out. I returned to the kitchen, hid the remaining pills, even the dirty ones, into one of the kitchen cabinets, and turned off the TV. If I couldn't do anything about the pills, I might as well go to sleep so I could be ready to meet Marigold when she'll arrive home. I laid in bed and closed my eyes for a bit but woke up in a dream-like place. I was dressed the same as in my other dreams. But this time, I descended from the sky into the realm of the humans. I was in a sunlit garden full of purple hyacinths. Everything around me was of a diaphanous nature, in white and bright green colors. Next to me appeared Jasmine, in all her fragile beauty. I wished to touch her and hug her, but she was more like a hologram: turning into the wind, then into an image of herself, then dispersing again into a million molecules.

"Jasmine, is that you?"

She didn't answer, but I couldn't lose this opportunity.

"Will you forgive me?" I asked.

"Laura… You are your forgiveness. I live through you."

She became wind again; she became the leaves' rustle of a blossomed cherry tree.

"Jasmine, I'm sorry. Please forgive me. Jasmine."

"Lauren, wake up." I heard Gavin from afar.

I opened my eyes and saw his figure in a haze.

"You're here. Where is she?"

"Your mom is washing her; you take your time."

When I rubbed my eyes, my vision became clearer. With a smile able to illuminate a solar eclipse, Gavin scurried around the room to find a fresh towel. I heard my mother talking with an upbeat tone echoing from the bathroom. I could not hear Marigold, but her presence was felt melancholically throughout the whole house.

"But if she is home, is my death waived? Do I get to live? Do I get a second chance at life?" I thought.

A life of misery knowing I almost killed my child. I didn't know how to look her in the eyes. How did an abuser look in the eyes of her victim? I deserved my eyes poked and the hand that let her go cut. There was no way one could find redemption in the eyes of a child's abandonment. Still groggy from involuntary sleep, I stepped out of the bedroom and close to where the sounds were coming. In my walk, I stumbled on a pile of clothes. It was her blue dress now the color of ragged with no cardigan to be found. Her tiny socks of a previous white color were now dark and full of rips, dried grass, and thistles scratching at my guilt. I picked up her clothes, the ones I dressed her in, gripped them to my chest, and fell to my knees. I tried in a desperate attempt to feel part of her experience, to remove the cold of those dark nights, and to smooth down the fear of the unknown, the hunger. I brought them to my face. The smell of neglect and disillusionment engulfed me. My tears turned sour, and the knot in my throat strangled my breath. I definitely didn't want to live. The trauma I caused would live with her forever. But could my death be an easier way out? Wouldn't life be a more appropriate punishment for my wrongdoings? I deserved the life of a camel's carcass, with a desert inside.

While I still clutched my precious girl's clothes, the knob on the bathroom door turned. I panicked. I was not prepared to see her. My skin got prickly, my breath got stuck in my lungs, and my blood coagulated in my veins. How could I confront her? But then a little princess in a fluffy pink robe appeared before my eyes smiling like a queen. Marigold looked older, taller, skinnier, wiser. Suddenly, I could see the same cherry blossoms from my dreams float, levitate around her. She looked like an angel. My fear evaporated, and I felt the urge to kiss her feet. Instead, I rushed and hugged her and kissed her cheeks. When I noticed the scratches, I kissed them, trying to alleviate some of the pain, like a healing balm. She seemed a bit taken aback by my stormy excitement, which I assumed was normal. Only when she looked at me, I noticed something unusual.

"Marigold, look what Grandma bought you," Mother said presenting a large box hidden behind the couch, "it's a dollhouse."

Marigold ran to her grandma, already enamored with her new present. Gavin helped with the unpackaging and assembly. It took him at most ten minutes, during which Marigold didn't even flinch. She sat and waited patiently for her present. I never met this Marigold. Was it a repercussion of her experiences or early signs of trauma? Or both? I decided to sit next to Gavin and help.

Looking from afar, we were a picture-perfect family. A little girlt, a dad, and a mom putting together a gift from grandma. But who really was a picture-perfect family? As a picture was only a moment in time. Life instead resembled a vertiginous mountain river filled with sudden waterfalls and hidden rocks. I wished no such thing as picture-perfect; I hoped for discernment. To distinguish between the necessary and the imposed; between genuine emotion and shallow yearning; between what could be given and what had to be taken.

After completing such a prioritized project, Marigold rushed to hug Daddy for his contribution. I followed with a hug as well. Then I extended my arms to Marigold; she came close to me but did not extend her arms. She leaned for a hug and returned back to her initial state only to look at me. She was searching for my eyes to tell me she knew. She knew I sent her away. Her whole face told me so: a few micro-expressions in her brows, the upturned line of her lips, the sparkle in her eyes. She knew. It struck me like a bolt of electricity.

My dread came back, along with my wish to die.

CHAPTER 48

THE day settled to an end. Marigold went to sleep soon after her bath and dinner. The rest of us sat at the celebratory table with the food mother bought before meeting with Gavin and Marigold. Mother and I took a seat as per Gavin's request. He had energy for all of us as he rummaged through the cabinets for plates and cups. When he reached for the salt and pepper shakers, he found my stash of sleeping pills.

"Honey, why so many sleeping pills? Did you get too many sleepless nights?"

Mother turned to me, prepared to scrutinize my answer as she very well knew I hated using sleeping pills.

"CVS had a deal; buy one, get one free." I smiled bashfully.

"Don't you love those kinds of deals?" said Gavin humming a nursery rhyme under his nose.

I looked at Mom as she didn't move her gaze for one bit. She could smell my guilt like a hound dog. I knew it, and she knew it as well. But I couldn't let her in on my desperate decisions. It was better for all. I looked down on the plate Gavin settled before me, leaving my mom searching for answers on my forehead. As Gavin kept placing more bowls and plates with food, I realized mother bought so much food it could feed us for a week. There was potato salad, slices of pizza, deviled eggs, rotisserie chicken, chicken nuggets, fries, cookies, cake.

"Did you really think Marigold would eat so much?" I asked.

"It doesn't matter. The child has been starving for days. I wanted her to choose what she liked."

"Mother, she always chooses cookies."

"Well, the rest is for us. Or would you have preferred to cook?"

"No, I appreciate what you did. Thank you."

My mother was taken aback. How rarely did I express words of gratitude towards my mother for her to react like this?

As we were sitting at the table with a chocolate cake as a centerpiece, Gavin poured us some champagne and said, "today, we celebrate our Marigold's third birthday but also her return which feels like a rebirth. Let's toast." His emotions were bubbling up similar to the champagne in his glass.

After we cheered with our glasses, I remembered I never got the chance to know what happened to Marigold.

"Gavin, who found Marigold and brought her to the police station?" I asked.

"A homeless woman named Luz brought her to the station. She was wandering from one homeless community to another when she stumbled upon Marigold. Two women were fighting over Marigold as she kept crying and calling for her mommy. One of them wanted to take the money from begging since she trained her during those two weeks. The other one wanted some since she had brought her to the encampment. As the women kept badgering one another, Luz sneaked between them and took Marigold straight to the station. When asked if she could share information about those two women, she refused, stating she still had to meet them in her community. The woman said Marigold was well taken care of as much as a homeless encampment could afford."

Tears kept rolling one by one on my cheeks, in an almost unperceivable manner but also impossible to control. In a way, this was an excellent outcome to a potentially horrendous experience.

But the image of her starving and begging at the side of the road was being hammered in my brain with two-inch nails. I could feel the blood seeping through my ears.

"Is the woman still there at the homeless shelter? I want to find her to thank her. What was her name again? Is it too late to go now?"

Gavin and my mom looked at me, surprised by my verbal spurt.

"Her name is Luz."

"Then we have to invite Luz to our house for dinner."

Gavin chuckled at my eagerness.

"We will, dear."

***

In the morning, at around six a.m., I opened the door to Marigold's room. She was still sleeping. I rushed to close the door and headed to make some tea. I barely got to turn on the kettle when a little hand tugged at my sleeve and startled me.

"Oh, you're awake."

I looked at her with apologetic eyes, wondering how she would behave around me. In what form would I take my punishment? I was willing to take it all.

Instead, she took me by my sleeve and pulled me softly to her room. She sat me on her bed and proceeded to play with her new dollhouse by placing all her dolls in it. Silence followed for a long time. I wasn't in a hurry, and neither was she. We enjoyed each other's presence without interfering, and I couldn't be happier. The rays of the morning sun permeated her room, illuminating her strands of wheat hair, her glimmering green eyes, her calm smile. She was my gorgeous little girl, my beautiful flower, the one I always wanted. It just happened that some flowers needed a different kind of care, which made them special. I noticed how she sat all her dolls in different rooms of the house and presented me with the final result.

"Yes, they are all one big family, Marigold. Great job."

She turned to her house for a second, then rushed back towards me, hugged me by my waist as tight as she could.

"I forgive you, Mommy," she said and jumped back to playing with her new toy house.

CHAPTER 49

AFTER Marigold's return, our life turned for the better, though I couldn't say we settled our differences. Oh, there were plenty of them, especially when she was a teen. Her strive for independence knew no limit. There were moments when Gavin had to separate us from ripping out each other's hair. You could say there definitely were sparks flying around (though we would reconcile quickly). This time around, though, we tried to live with the present and cherish the moment, exactly like the mom of the autistic girl said. I learned to love Marigold not in spite but because she had an independent and strong personality. A rambunctious, adventurous, curious human who never bent to anyone's rules but her own. In reality, she never changed. I did. I learned to appreciate her qualities and support her form of expression.

We kept a close relationship with Luz. She became Marigold's godmother and our dear friend. In the beginning, our wish was to help Luz because of her kindness, but in the process, she taught us much more about how we could give back to the homeless community. We grew to understand how complex the situation was. How homeless people were not they, the other people; they were us, an integral part of society. It was easy to shun them away and put a barrier between us because they were uncomfortable to look at. Similar to an abscess, the longer you tried to hide it, the longer the healing process. In the years after Luz returned Marigold to us, she got on the right track through rehab, AA meetings, and our support, but mainly because she wanted to help other kids. She found a job at a shelter and never looked back. She wasn't the only one we decided to help. Gavin always drove to different encampments and donated shoes, clothes, blankets. And if someone would ask for help to get a fresh, clean start, he would always oblige.

Gavin, after Marigold's return, became even more of a doting father. We had a schedule for all our walks and visits; we always knew where each of us was at a specific moment. It didn't bother me since I knew how much my actions had hurt him, and I wished to placate some of my wrongdoings as well as the trauma I put my whole family through. Gavin never spoke of the incident again, he never mentioned any form of blame towards me, but something was lost in his gaze, a flicker of innocence, the embedded belief that everything would be okay. He had learned to live with the fear of tomorrow, the fear of the unknown towards his dearest beings. We mended our relationship slowly with a sincere approach to even the most challenging issues. I promised myself I would never bend the meaning of words, speak untruths, or ever deceive Gavin again. I never told Gavin my promise, but he became more attuned, more perspicacious as if the colors of his palette had diversified, and he could feel the meaning of my unspoken apologies I bid every day since Marigold's return. His tenderness grew, and our love's blossoms bloomed once more.

Our garden had gone through a renewal as well. I had to remove all the dead flowers and bushes. This time, I wanted to plant trees: apple trees, peach trees, and, of course, cherry trees. I wanted them to grow deep into the ground and spread solid and long roots underneath our tiny backyard. I also added strawberries for Marigold to pick. I planted roses to acknowledge Margaret's presence in our lives and a jasmine tree in memory of Jasmine. I wanted to have a sacred place for all the dearest people in my life. A different kind of Hanging Garden of Kenmore.

We didn't make it to Jasmine's funeral as it was on the day when Marigold returned. Her death ripped my heart to pieces, and only my daughter's return stitched it back together. On Jasmine's birthday, I went with Marigold and visited her grave. I brought her the most opulent bouquet of daffodils, peonies, and calla lilies. We turned our visits into a tradition when we would sit beside her grave and tell Jasmine about everything we did that year. My friendship with Jasmine became immortalized through me as her memory followed on my shoulder throughout all these years.

As time passed, I always wondered where Margaret disappeared. At one point, I questioned if I imagined my visits to her nursery until I read an article about gerrymandering, and the author was none other than Margaret's daughter, Harriet. I searched for her contact information and succeeded in talking to her. She told me her mother went on a trip through the African continent, and they lost contact. Last time Margaret was seen in Ghana, but Harriet didn't get a call from her in over a year. I thanked her for letting me know and asked her to call in case her mother would return. I never received a call. My mind didn't want to go to a dark place. I preferred to imagine Margaret enjoying her life to the fullest from helping kids and supporting legislations contributing to a better education in Nigeria to finding love. For Margaret had a spirit stronger than anyone I'd ever seen, but she also had a kind and beautiful soul. I still had the Dreikurs and Adler books she recommended me back then. When I was prepared to read them, it gave meaning to her words and my story. I missed Margaret a lot. But as my mother used to say, "always remember the best moments you spent with that person, and sadness will go away."

Speaking of my mother, I began looking at her in a new light from that day at the gate. I saw her as a struggling, inexperienced mother and a human who could live with her mistakes better than me. She still pretended to be a connoisseur of the Russian culture and in relationships with men, but her most significant achievement was her grandmotherly ability to mediate between Marigold and me. And she wasn't half bad at it. Of course, many of her solutions involved trips to ice cream or donut shops, but who said those were inefficient solutions? When she retired, Mother fulfilled her dream to visit the Kremlin. It became the main story of any ordinary dinner we had. After the millionth time of hearing the same story, I felt like I was beside her visiting pale-faced Lenin.

During the trip, she met a couple of Russians residing in Seattle for twenty years. They discovered their mutual obsession with all things Russian, so they evidently continued to hang out after the trip. Back in the States, I would see her maybe once a month, in which she only talked about her journey friends. She even learned more words and knew enough details to convince anyone she was a true descendent of a Russian mother. The couple invited her to an authentic Russian sauna, famous for scorching temperatures and ice-cold pools. A place where most Russians would go to better their immunity. Alongside her friends, she felt like one of them and wanted to experience it by the book. First, she downed two shots of vodka, no soda involved. Then, she went into the sauna, where they used leafy oak bath brooms for added effect. After twenty minutes of baking, she jumped into the pool. She was so proud. She even called me right after. Unfortunately, two hours later, she had a stroke. Her friends were too drunk to notice, so she slowly went into oblivion, never to return. Her whole life, Mother pretended to be Russian and failed, but she died like a real Russian. My grief was tinged with a bit of pride for her. Though Marigold took it the hardest. She loved babushka a lot and shared many great experiences with her. When Marigold grew into her teens, she always bragged about her babushka, who could down vodka like a real Russian.

Marigold transformed into a natural beauty, and I am not saying so because she is my daughter. She still possessed a stubbornness beyond what I'd hoped, but I grew to accept it as part of her strive for self-expression. She didn't want to do any of the activities I proposed, she didn't want to dance, didn't want to paint, and, God forbid, I would force her to play the piano. She did, however, love sports. She played softball, lacrosse, soccer, basketball, and any activity which involved kicking, throwing, and winning. She refused to go to college and spend her parents' money. Marigold chose to work when she graduated high school and became a great example of a hard-working woman who could fend for herself. She found her love quite fast, at nineteen, and by the time Marigold reached twenty, she was married and pregnant. You would think my early motherhood experience, which we still talked about, would deter Marigold from having children, but no, she wanted one of her own as soon as possible.

Today was the day when my daughter gave birth. She was sleeping on her hospital bed, tired but glowing with happiness. In my hands, I had a precious ladybug not heavier than six pounds and a half. It had been so long since I held a baby; my forearms trembled with emotions. Marigold gave birth to a girl. From the day we found the gender, I badgered my daughter to name her Jasmine. But as you can imagine, my daughter could not accept any commands, so she said she was "gonna think about it." I, as a future grandmother with experience in Russian manipulations, couldn't let things just happen, so I worked my way to her heart's ladder step by step. I promised to help her for the first year, to cook her meals, share some of the sleepless nights, and many other deals she might invent along the way. I accepted the agreement, secretly, knowing it was precisely what I would do either way.

And now, I look at these puffy cheeks of a ladybug named Jasmine. A baby girl, I will enjoy spending time with, experiencing every moment of her growth. I will witness my daughter become a mother, my son-in-law become a father, my Gavin become a grandfather, and I become a grandmother.

In the end, it was worth it.

ACKNOWLEDGEMENT

I want to thank my husband, kids, parents, family, and friends for the inspiration, support, and patience they have gifted me throughout the entire process. It is because of you that I could gather all my ideas and give them a meaningful home. It takes a village to raise a child, but it also takes a village to produce a novel.

Thank you so much for being my village.

ABOUT THE AUTHOR

Lara Bronson is a former concert violinist and teacher working on transforming music notes into words. Lara pursues new ways to express musicality through her writing to combine her two favorite passions. Before she started writing literary fiction, Lara got a bachelor's degree in Performing Arts, and for more than fifteen years, has taught young souls how to enjoy and perform classical music. After becoming a mother, Lara returned to her passion for storytelling which materialized into "The Shackled Balloon" novel.

Currently, she is working on her next novel and a few short stories. Besides writing, Lara and her husband enjoy parenthood in all its glory with their twin boys.

If you would like to find more about Lara's new writing endeavors, or share your impressions about the novel, you can find Lara on social media @lara_bronson or visit her website: www.larabronson.com

Please do not forget to review the novel on Amazon and other sites.

Thank you!

www.ingramcontent.com/pod-product-compliance
Lightning Source LLC
LaVergne TN
LVHW041909070526
838199LV00051BA/2554